Dedication

In memory of my wonderful friend and fellow
literature devotee, Suzy Fulgham, whose unflagging
support kept me looking forward to hopes realized.
You shall be missed.

INTO THE CLOUDS

Marilyn Leach

This is a work of fiction. Names, characters, places, and incidents either are the product of the author's imagination or are used fictitiously, and any resemblance to actual persons living or dead, business establishments, events, or locales, is entirely coincidental.

INTO THE CLOUDS

COPYRIGHT 2014 by MARILYN LEACH

Contact Information: titleadmin@pelicanbookgroup.com

All scripture quotations, unless otherwise indicated, are taken from the Holy Bible, New International Version(R), NIV(R), Copyright 1973, 1978, 1984, 2011 by Biblica, Inc.™ Used by permission of Zondervan. All rights reserved worldwide. www.zondervan.com

Cover Art by Nicola Martinez

Harbourlight Books, a division of Pelican Ventures, LLC
www.pelicanbookgroup.com PO Box 1738 *Aztec, NM * 87410

Harbourlight Books sail and mast logo is a trademark of Pelican Ventures, LLC

Publishing History
First Harbourlight Edition, 2014
Paperback Edition ISBN 978-1-61116-433-6
Electronic Edition ISBN 978-1-61116-432-9
Published in the United States of America

Praise

[Marilyn's writing] has a wonderfully authentic feel...Move over Agatha Christie. The twenty-first century has Marilyn Leach." ~ Amanda Cabot

Prologue

The moon reflected a lovely gold off the sea.

"You're just lunar light," the woman chided the large orb. "But I've got the real thing." She ran her thumb over the gold band that now decorated her left ring finger and inhaled the salty sea air. The light played itself across the water and onto the polished mahogany boat deck where she stood.

The past three nights, illumination from the Madeira coastline had been in view when they took the boat out. But tonight they went further out to sea.

She turned her gaze upward. "Which one of you is my fortuitous star?" she asked the silvery glowing dots that danced across the dark expanse of night.

Morgan, her husband of five days, was below board making things ready for another evening toast to their love.

After their refreshing paddle in the ocean, and for her it was no more than that, they would come aboard and go below to a bottle of champagne. Two flutes, each with three fresh strawberries, would host the bubbly chilling in a bucket of ice. A piece of rich chocolate would sit next to her flute, just as it had every night of their honeymoon so far.

"And then," the woman said out loud, "and then, well."

"And then what, Livy, my love?" Morgan's

unmistakable voice sounded nearby. "And just who are you talking to?" He came from behind, embraced her around her waist, and placed a peck upon her cheek.

She turned to face the man who had swept into her heart. "Just when I thought life had no more love in it, you came along."

Morgan smiled. "Why don't you go ahead and jump in, darling."

She removed her voile beach cover-up, which revealed a white bathing suit that hugged her slender, middle-aged body. She stepped down the swim ladder on the boat's edge and then thrust herself into the black depths. The cold water covered her completely. For one quick moment, she felt a sense of fear, an overwhelming awareness of being at the mercy of the ocean. The air in her lungs, along with a few solid kicks, brought her to the surface where she took two large gulps of air. Goose pimples popped on her exposed skin, the coolness of night assaulting her. She wiped the water from her face. "The water's cold tonight," her chattering lips warned her spouse, who still stood at the boat's rail.

"Is it? Yes, I thought perhaps it would be." His voice held little surprise.

"In, then."

Morgan's face was just visible, his handsome features chiseled by moonlight. But there was something suddenly very different; emotionless, drained of any warmth. It made the freezing night ocean feel tepid.

"Liv," he said flatly, "you are a lovely woman. Distinct, steady, yet underneath so very vulnerable, but a lovely woman." He retracted the swim ladder. Then he turned away from her, as if it were a eulogy to a corpse.

Liv caught her breath as she paddled. "What?" She called after him. "Morgan? Stop teasing and get in." She blinked, closed her eyes, and tipped her head to one side to drain out the water that must be distorting his words. When she reopened her eyes, he was no longer in sight. "Darling?" As the word escaped her lips, she heard the boat's engine start. She tipped her head again, to empty the wet from her other ear, and shook it.

Water at the boat's stern began to swirl. The sound of a motor became an actual roar, as if it were a lion announcing its ascendancy.

"Morgan?" she yelled.

The word was drowned by the noise of the fully revved engine that thrust the luxurious *Island Flower* forward. Like a torpedo shot from its port, the craft flew into the dark.

The wake created by the departure slammed salty wetness into her eyes and mouth. She choked and tried to move from the surge. A sense of panic charged her entire being, an electrical storm. Her mind churned like the displaced waters. *Where's he going? Why's he doing this? Oh, what's happening?*

"I'm in the middle of a dream." She wheezed. The icy wetness kept her cognizant that this was, indeed, happening in real time.

The boat had vanished.

The man who pledged to be faithful forever had just abandoned her in the depths of a black sea with no hope of survival.

Internal turmoil overwhelmed her like the sea in which she now struggled. The more the reality of it slapped her in the face, the less she was able to maintain herself afloat. "Help," she screamed. Her survival instinct rose above the bitter disbelief. She fought to keep her hands and legs churning, paddling, churning. How long? Five minutes? More?

Her teeth chattered uncontrollably. The salt of her distressed tears now mingled with the briny liquid that held her captive. Her arms flailed as every muscle in her body tensed. The cold bit into her like a feeding shark.

Her stamina sapped by shock, she succumbed to the anguish of emotional destruction and waning body strength. Water laid its cold fingers along the edge of her nostrils.

She reared her head heavenward where one low star shone brighter than the others. "My fortuitous star." Her chin sank. She couldn't feel her legs. She weakly breathed. "He said he loved me," barely eked through her numbed lips as the cloak of darkness embraced her. "He said he loved me."

1

Berdie Elliott could hear it clearly. Despite the beehive-like activity that filled the nave of ancient St. Aidan of the Wood Parish Church, an unmistakable *swoosh* of the video chat's "doorbell" emanated from the computer in the sacristy. "Hugh," Berdie called above the din to her husband, who was vicar of this flock. "It's Nick." Excusing her path through balloon-toting youth, choir members, and strewn banners, she managed her way into the pastoral room.

Depositing herself in the chair at Hugh's desk, where the laptop was opened, she smoothed an errant tress of her dyed, red-brown bob and perused the screen. "How did Hugh say this worked?" Excitement raced through her at the anticipation of seeing and speaking with their son, who was abroad serving as a naval officer. This software almost made it feel as if he was actually in England, in their midst. "I believe I click on this."

The system went down.

"No," Berdie yelled at the computer. She knitted her brows, pulled her tortoiseshell glasses down her nose a bit, and started clicking on whatever presented itself as something clickable. "Silly thing. You appalling, silly thing." Berdie raised her voice. "Nick, love, can you hear me?"

"Berdie?" Hugh was next to her. "Oh, dear," he muttered viewing the empty screen. "We've lost him."

"Well, silly thing." Disappointment and genuine frustration filled her.

"Not a problem, love." Hugh put his hand on her shoulder. "And it's not a silly thing. It's a very handy thing if you know how to operate it properly."

"Yes, well." Berdie sighed.

"Bunch up, then." Hugh gave Berdie's shoulder a little nudge.

She rose from the chair.and Hugh planted himself in it.

"We'll have him back in no time." Hugh's fingers began to dance on the touchpad.

Even now, Berdie felt a light flutter as she watched him work. This handsome man with his silver hair and blue eyes had asked her to marry him nearly thirty years ago, and she had never regretted saying yes. She rested her hand on his capable shoulder. "You need to go through with me how this works, Hugh."

"Again."

"I wasn't paying proper attention the first time. All the preparations for Ascension Sunday took my concentration."

And hadn't they just? Had the specially ordered eco balloons arrived? Were enough ingredients purchased for the lemonade? Had the altar guild finish the banners? Was the village band well-rehearsed?

"Indeed. Well, it's only hours away, now." Hugh spoke as he watched the screen. "Our Ascension Sunday procession will be an uplifting time for our entire community. All the planning and work will have been worth every minute." He made a final tap on the touchpad. "Here we are."

Nothing happened.

Berdie hoped to see something that resembled her

fair-haired Nick with his lovely blue eyes, like his father, and that admirable smile. But there was no Nick in sight.

"He must have left his computer," Hugh offered in explanation. He took Berdie's hand. "We'll try again later."

Berdie nodded. And she vowed she would pay proper attention to operational procedures. In her former career as an investigative journalist, she was quite technologically savvy. But having followed her husband into the church upon his distinguished retirement from the Royal Navy, she hadn't the time or opportunity to sharpen her skills. It seemed as you learned to master one program or gadget, another new one came along.

"We'd best re-enter the fray." Hugh's tone conveyed a slight disappointment that their son's call was missed. He ran a finger round his clerical collar and exited the room.

Berdie pondered how precious was the time when they were all under the same roof: she, Hugh, Nick, and Clare. Both children were abroad.

But now, there was another family of sorts. And they were in the adjoining room going about the business of getting all in order for the great Ascension Sunday procession and concert that would take place tomorrow immediately following the morning service.

As Berdie re-entered the nave, she spied Lillie Foxworth, her best friend, who was St. Aidan's accomplished choirmaster.

"No, like this, Linden." Lillie directed the somewhat gangly Mr. Linden Davies, who was bent over the sheet music on a music stand.

While the choir chatted, he rubbed his forehead as

if trying to decipher secret code. "Yes, I think I see," the man said with little confidence. Though not yet thirty years old, his light blond hairline was ebbing to high tide, giving him more and more forehead to rub.

When Saint Matthew Church in Mistcome Green called Lillie for a recommendation to fill their choirmaster position, she proposed Linden Davies, her voice student of the past eight months. He was the only one with any amount of willingness to take on the task.

While slender Lillie tapped a rhythmic finger along the sheet music, her short brunette hair in soft curls, danced with the tempo.

Mr. Davies metrically nodded—in complete counterpoint to Lillie's pace. Quite a grand leap from student to director. Tomorrow's fete featured a combined choir that included the little group from St. Matthew. It seemed Linden's success was inextricably entangled with Lillie's own. And Lillie was investing herself as if it were a royal performance.

An earsplitting *screech* shot across the nave.

Berdie smacked her hands to her ears and scrunched her nose.

Hugh and Edsel Butz were by the audio system. Edsel twisted knobs on the mobile unit. The second generation owner of Butz and Sons Electrics was proud to be named after his grandfather, an American who served in England during WWII. At last Edsel unplugged something that halted the unholy wail.

Hugh lifted his masculine hand and grinned. "Sorry about that. I shouldn't wonder if some lovelorn poultry may be racing to our door."

Ripples of laughter danced across the nave.

There had not been an Ascension procession at St.

Aidan's in fifty years, and her husband wanted everything just right, especially the aging sound system. When Hugh originally suggested reviving the celebration, the parish council thought it a wonderful idea. Without hesitation, they gave themselves to the work of bringing it about.

Cherry Lawler swished by Berdie, pin cushion in hand. "We're just putting the final stitches on the last banner. Come look when you can." She smiled. "It is lovely."

"Yes, indeed, I will." Berdie knew very little about needlework, but as the vicar's wife, she was expected to approve. Although in the two and a half years that Hugh had shepherded this parish, Berdie had learned a great deal about what was expected of her by the small community, there seemed much more to learn.

"A penny for them."

She turned to find Lillie's love interest at her side. "Some might say my thoughts are worth far more than pence." Berdie smiled. "So they let you escape from the morgue, then."

Dr. Loren Meredith, a staff pathologist with Timsley Hospital, cleared his throat. He lifted a corner of his mouth into a diplomatic grin, as his warm brown eyes narrowed. "I see Lillie's told you how unavailable I've been of late."

"Of late?" Berdie questioned.

"Oh, dear. Am I going to get a fair hearing on this?"

Berdie nodded.

"I needn't tell you that Timsley, as modest and relaxed as it is, is burgeoning and frenzied."

"Yes, that's a given." From market town ho-hum to explosive is what the *Kirkwood Gazette* said about growth in Timsley—the whole area, really.

"And?"

"And our pathology department hasn't grown with it. I don't suppose Lillie has told you that due to cuts, we've lost two staff members at the lab?"

"Have you?"

"I thought perhaps she hadn't. I don't mind telling you I'm dancing faster than a cat on a hot grill."

"I say. That's terribly cruel. Cats shouldn't be anywhere near heat appliances." The well-dressed woman, here to see the vicar, wrinkled her aging forehead. "I should hope neither of you are involved."

"What?" Berdie tried to stay cordial. "Oh, my, no. It's just an expression." This was exactly how rumors buzzed into life in a small village. "Rest assured, no one is harming cats, are they, Dr. Meredith?"

Loren nodded. "Nothing remotely like that happening here, madam." His dark, shoulder-length hair, fastened at the nape of his neck, wafted with his movement.

"I should think there are expressions far more suitable that do not involve cats and hot cookware." She straightened. "One of great wisdom has said, 'If man and cat were to combine, man would elevate and the cat would descend'."

The white-haired gentleman with the woman put his hand on her arm. "Come along, my love. I'm sure these kind people have no ill wishes toward felines." He offered Loren a polite smile. "Please excuse us." The couple moved in Hugh's direction.

"That was a bit odd." Berdie murmured.

"That edged on lunacy," Loren corrected. "Who are they?"

"No idea."

"That old fellow would appear to be someone of rank."

"Is he?"

"His tie colors, old school. Stobbworth Hall, if I'm not mistaken?"

The couple cornered Hugh.

"Moneyed, I shouldn't wonder." The doctor ran a finger over his own non-school tie.

"What do you suppose they want with Hugh?"

"A cat blessing?"

Berdie put a hand on her hip and eyed the smiling doctor. "I think there's someone here who awaits your inspiring company."

Loren chuckled. "A tiger stripe?" He laid his gaze squarely on Lillie. "I'm off, then." He moved along to his lovely woman.

Loren was not the only one to observe Lillie. The old school gentleman watched as Loren grasped Lillie's hand and placed a quick peck on her cheek. The fellow lifted an arched brow, frowned, and turned quickly back to the conversation with Hugh.

Curious though she was, Berdie directed her attention to the balloon brigade. "Don't overfill that balloon," she called across the lively church nave to thirteen-year-old Milton Butz.

He haphazardly filled the red swollen sphere with helium gas and placed it on his lips. The barrel-chested teen grinned. "Yes, Mrs. Elliott. Overfill remedied," Milton squeaked in that annoying high-pitched tone that comes from a helium gas inhalation.

Kevin McDermott, his ever-present school chum, howled with laughter, which only goaded Milton into a full rendition of "Rule Britannia."

"That's enough," Ivy Butz, Milton's mom, said.

"Out with the pair of you. Go on now."

The boys made for the door, the ample Ivy behind them.

Martha Butz, Milton's twin, tied a string to a full balloon. "I apologize for my brother," she said in a rather aggravated tone. "He's such a child."

Berdie smiled, stepped to the helium gas tank, and took up a balloon.

"Mrs. Elliott, there's someone wants to see you," Ivy trumpeted from the door where the boys had just exited.

Of course, someone wanted to see her. How many times in a day didn't someone in a small English village want to see the vicar's wife? How many times in the course of parish life did someone come knocking at an inopportune time? Berdie worked at knotting the end of the red, biodegradable balloon she had just filled. "Who is it?" she called against the laughter of several church youths who tied ribbons to the festive balloons.

Ivy shrugged her shoulders.

"Tell them to come back after the Ascension Fete," Berdie directed.

Ivy nodded and ducked out the door.

Berdie passed her balloon to Martha, placed another empty balloon over the nozzle, and turned the handle that instantly shaped the red droop into a vibrant orb.

Then, Ivy backed into the church from the door and nearly stumbled.

A wiry young woman with ginger hair burst in. It appeared that whomever this woman was who had asked to see Berdie would not be denied. "Mrs. Berdie Elliott," the anxious woman spoke loudly and examined the church inhabitants one after another. A flushed face, eyes large with anxiety, and gasps for breath indicated that this was not a casual call.

At that same moment, the balloon Berdie absently filled exploded. The blast bounced round the stone nave sending shrieks skyward and bodies downward.

The choir, who had been practicing, came to an abrupt halt.

"Mrs. Elliott, you've *got* to help me." Above the complete silence came the terrified scream of the stranger. The woman's untamed bristly hair was a stark contrast against her milky skin and wild pale eyes.

"Of course. I'm glad to be of help." Berdie pushed the breathless words out. Her fifty-something-year-old heart beat like hummingbird wings, more from the balloon burst than anything else. Still, being called out in the midst of the congregation was a bit discomforting. "Let's find a quiet corner." Berdie approached the woman.

Hugh was already at the stranger's side. "Can I offer some assistance?" he asked in a calming voice.

"It's Mrs. Elliott I want."

"Sacristy," Hugh said. He gently took the young woman by the elbow, and with Berdie on her other side, they proceeded to the solace of the tranquil room.

Hugh seated the stranger in a comfortable overstuffed chair near the hearth where a bouquet of fresh garden flowers occupied the space normally reserved for fires in the colder months. Berdie eased her more-pudgy-than-lean body into a chair near the woman while Hugh remained on his feet.

"No disrespect to you, Vicar, but it's your wife I want to see," the somewhat calmed woman explained.

"I want her to work for hire."

"Hire?" Berdie asked with a sharp tone.

"What do you mean, Mrs.?" Hugh questioned.

"It's *Miss* Norman, Harriett Norman. And what I mean is, I want her"—she jabbed her finger toward Berdie "—to find my sister."

"Where is your sister?" Hugh questioned.

"For heaven's sake." Harriett flared. "If I knew that I wouldn't be here, would I?"

Hugh fumbled for words.

"Miss Norman, your sister is missing and you want to hire me," Berdie reiterated.

The woman looked from Hugh to Berdie, her brow knit. "Isn't that what I've just said?"

"Hire me for what, exactly?"

The woman scowled. "What do you think? To boil my morning egg? To *find* my sister, of course. Word's about that you're a dead good detective, and I want to hire you."

Berdie nearly laughed when she saw the shock that registered on Hugh's face. If the woman hadn't been so edgy, Berdie would have broken into a hearty chuckle.

"My wife is not for hire, especially for investigative work," Hugh said firmly.

The woman turned her gaze to Berdie. "Don't you want to help me?"

"Of course," Berdie assured, "but am I the best person for the job?"

Hugh's shoulders tightened. "This sounds like a police matter to me." He pulled a mobile from his pocket.

There was a light rap at the nearly-closed door, and Lillie Foxworth unapologetically burst into the room. "Hugh, Edsel needs…" Lillie stopped abruptly. Inquisitive delight shone in her face. "Sorry for interrupting," Lillie said with only a mild hint of apology. Her hazel-green eyes burrowed into Berdie's. *What's going on?* she mouthed.

"She's not for hire," Harriett responded.

"Sorry?" Lillie's inquisitiveness turned to amusement.

"Constable Goodnight? Vicar here," Hugh spoke into the mobile phone.

"The police were no help," Harriett nearly screamed.

Berdie placed her hand on the woman's arm. "You've spoken to them, then?" she asked in a calm voice.

The woman stomped a foot. "And what little good it did."

Lillie put her hand over her mouth and sat. The choir-director robe that draped over her slim body made her appear almost angelic. There was a twinkle in Lillie's eyes, and her hand covered a grin.

"Miss Harriett Norman is with me." Hugh paused. "I'll ask." Hugh put his hand over the mouthpiece. "Do you live in Mistcome Green, Miss Norman?"

"And what if I do?" The woman frowned and eyed Hugh as if trying to decide if this vicar could be trusted.

Hugh went to a corner of the sacristy and continued the phone conversation.

"My husband wants only what's best for you, Miss Norman." Berdie looked reassuringly into the large, pale eyes.

"What about what's best for my sister?" Harriett pushed her hand into her skirt pocket and retrieved a postcard. "You see?" She shoved the picture of a sunny marina dotted with palm trees into Berdie's hand.

Lillie stood, positioning herself to peek over Berdie's shoulder.

Berdie flipped the postcard over. It had a Portuguese postmark. *Harriett,* it read in what appeared to be hastily scrawled words; *I'll be back in Timsley at the end of the week with a rather wonderful surprise.*

"This is your sister, I assume?"

The woman nodded her head. "I got it nearly six weeks ago."

Lillie gave a quiet gasp.

Harriett leaned forward and gripped the arms of the chair. "Now, can you help my sister?"

"Berdie," Hugh beckoned.

Lillie took the postcard from Berdie, who arose.

"I want you to hear this for yourself." Hugh handed the phone to her. "Mind you, heed these words. And this is the last of the matter."

She brought the mobile to her ear as Hugh made a quiet exit. "Yes," Berdie spoke into the mobile.

"Mrs. Elliott," The unmistakable voice of Aidan Kirkwood's Constable came over the phone. Albert Goodnight growled his words. "Vicar says you got that nutter there."

"What?" Berdie frowned.

"Harriett Norman. They call her 'the Mad Hatty' of Mistcome Green." The constable laughed heartily with an edge of mockery.

"What do you mean?"

"She's in Wonderland, that one."

Berdie understood that Goodnight was the law in Aidan Kirkwood, but she had little patience with his uncouth manner and brash incompetence to do his job. "She's trying to find a missing relative. Harriett just showed me the postcard from her missing sister," she said in as even a tone as she could muster.

Goodnight's howl of laughter caused her to pull the mobile from her ear. She took a deep inhale and returned it to listening position again.

"Hatty Norman does not, never has, and never will have a sister," Goodnight bawled.

Berdie blinked. "No?"

"Send that nutter back to Mistcome Green, and let her bother the law somewhere else."

Silence as he rang off told Berdie that Albert Goodnight was done with the matter.

She pursed her lips and nearly throttled the mobile.

Harriett Norman clung so tightly to the arms of the chair her fingers were white.

"Are you going to find my sister?" she asked with wide eyes.

Berdie searched for the right words. Should she ask about the sister, a description, something that would make sense of things without creating turmoil? There was definitely a postcard addressed to Harriett from someone. The need and concern the young woman displayed appeared very real.

"Of course, she will find your sister."

Berdie's delay in responding made room for Lillie to fill the momentary silence.

"She's wonderful. She'll get to the bottom of this in no time."

Harriett released her grip on the chair. Her eyes grew more serene, and her shoulders relaxed. A huge grin spread across her face that had now dismissed the furrowed forehead. She jumped to her feet with what seemed a sense of fresh wellbeing. "I'm ever so grateful."

"Now, Miss Norman..." Berdie began.

"I'll just see Harriett to the door," Lillie interrupted Berdie's train of thought once more.

"Lillie, I'm not at all sure..."

Harriett acquiesced to Lillie's guiding hand on her elbow.

"We'll be getting in touch with you soon, Miss Norman," Lillie pattered as she and Harriett walked out the sacristy door.

No sister? Really? How often had Goodnight gotten his so-called information from sitting around a late night table with the lads at the local pub, the Upland Arms? The pub certainly was not the most reliable source.

Harriett seemed so relieved that someone was willing to help. Still, at this moment, Berdie couldn't possibly commit to Harriett's task, even sorting out the real from the fantasy. She must get on with the events at hand. She returned to the church nave.

Lillie deposited Miss Norman at the church door and sent her on her way. Despite her entrance, few noticed the woman's departure.

"Lillie." Berdie grabbed Lillie's hand as the choirmaster raced toward the choir.

Lillie abruptly stopped.

Berdie took hold of the angel-wing like sleeve of the choral robe and gently shook it.

"What are you doing?" Lillie scoffed.

"Just looking for your little mouse."

"What?"

"*We* will be getting in touch with you, Miss

Norman. Of course *we* can help."

Lillie leaned close to Berdie. She made her voice barely audible but the spark in her eyes spoke thunderously. "Don't tell me, my dear friend, that you aren't keen as mustard to find Miss Norman's sister."

"There's more to it, Lillie."

Lillie's eyes widened. "When is there not?" She almost giggled.

"Miss Foxworth." The bright, but tentative tenor voice of Linden Davies pierced the clandestine conversation as he called from the choir. "I need your assistance, please."

Lillie nodded to Linden as Loren, who stood near him, eyed the needy fellow.

"We'll talk later," Berdie said.

"Oh, indeed we shall." Lillie beamed. "An adventure is in the making, I shouldn't wonder." With that, Lillie scurried to the aid of her protégé.

"Adventure." Berdie loved the opportunity of it, but rarely found it came without misfortune for some poor soul.

"That's it for the balloons, then." Ivy's full moon cheeks decorated the edges of her cheerful smile.

Berdie took in the balloons that were cellotaped to the back of some pews. "I hope we have more balloons than children tomorrow and not the other way round."

"I shouldn't worry." Ivy's optimistic sparkle danced. "I'm sure everything tomorrow will be tickety-boo."

"Tickety-boo," Berdie repeated as she reviewed in her mind the colorful people she had met today. She took a deep inhale. "From your mouth to God's ear, Ivy."

2

"It's a perfect day for the procession," the sturdy Mrs. Braunhoff sputtered as she raced past Berdie in the front church garden, red ribbons in hand.

"Just so," Berdie returned.

Indeed, the mid-morning Sunday sun beamed its lovely spring rays as if to bless the ancient church and all who gathered for the Ascension Sunday procession.

Berdie let the welcoming warmth caress her face. Pushed aside momentarily, were thoughts concerning Harriett Norman.

"Berdie," Hugh called as he exited the church. Coming into the bright light made his fine church vestments almost dazzle. "I need to go position myself." He nodded toward the procession participants while clinging to the large altar Bible. "Will you please go through the queue to make sure everything is set to begin?"

"As you know, my darling husband, putting things in order suits me."

"Precisely." Hugh's smile was almost as dazzling as his vestments.

Grayson Webb, the parish council chairman, appeared cheerful as he found his way to Hugh's side. "Wonderful this." His gaze scanned the assembly on Church Road. Wearing his mayoral chain of office about his neck, and holding his ornamental staff, he appeared positively commanding. His styled hair was sprayed into obedience. And judging by the assault on Berdie's nose, Mr. Webb announced his presence in applied gentleman's fragrance. "*The Timsley Times* ran a full article yesterday on our planned activities, you know. Front page."

"Now that's a rare occurrence." Hugh nodded. "Constructive church events considered front page news."

"Both our names appeared in print." Mr. Webb ran a finger down his lapel.

"Well then, you two newsworthy men need to place yourselves in the procession." Berdie prompted.

"My wife will signal when it's time to begin the march."

"Your wife?" Mr. Webb spoke in a less-than-gentle manner.

"That is to say," Berdie amended, "I will signal *you* when everything is set so you may raise your staff to start the procession."

"Oh, yes. Important that," He gave the staff a gentle wiggle. "Well then, let's get on with it."

While Hugh and Mr. Webb found their way into the crowd, Berdie went to the front of the assembly where Jeffrey Lawler, a winsome young man with his spiked hair and well-trimmed goatee, held the lead banner skyward on its long pole.

"The Ladies' Guild has done a fine job hand-stitching the banner." Berdie inspected the rich red background awash with white clouds and large golden letters that read, *He Lives and Reigns Forever.*

"Cherry stitched the *Lives*," he said, obviously proud of his wife's handiwork.

"Now Jeffrey, the moment you hear the band

begin, start forward," Berdie reminded him.

"Yeah, ready." This lively fellow, who captained the village football team, would have no trouble carrying the banner the full distance through the High Street to the village green.

"It's not a game on the green this time, hey Jeffrey?" Milton Butz stood behind Jeffrey, accompanied by Martha and several other pre-adolescent church youths, including the ginger-haired Kevin McDermott. All held bundles of floating red balloons to be passed out amongst the children at the village green for the great release.

Kevin tried to swat an offending fly near his eye, sending one of the balloons skyward, adrift with the light breeze.

"You great loaf," Milton barked at his friend.

"Sorry, Mrs. Elliott."

Berdie flipped her hands about the air near Kevin's head knocking the insect on its way. "Just try to hold on tightly, Kevin."

Lillie's student cum choir director, Linden Davies, race toward Berdie from the church car park. The small St. Matthew's choir that followed him continued down the queue, but Linden and an attractive older woman stopped when they reached Berdie. "Hello Mrs. Elliott," he greeted somewhat breathlessly.

"Mr. Davies, good morning." Berdie glanced at the woman.

"Oh. This is my mother-in-law, Mrs. Olivia Mikalos." He waved his hand toward Berdie. "Olivia, this is Mrs. Elliott, the vicar's wife of St. Aidan."

The slender woman nodded her tastefully graying head toward Berdie, emerald earrings sparkling. The woman's face, though mature, held all the fine features of beauty: high cheek bones, almond eyes, nicely shaped nose, contoured lips. The celery green linen top she wore, with matching trousers, was a lovely accompaniment to the light colored espadrilles that adorned her feet. Fashionable, while at the same time, practical.

"It's a lovely morning for an event like this." Mrs. Mikalos said. Though her blue eyes were bright, her words had a must-be-polite tone.

"Indeed," Berdie replied. "Lovely."

Mr. Davies took a deep breath. "May I ask that Olivia, Mrs. Mikalos, accompany you? My wife and children came in a separate car and they haven't arrived yet, you see." Mr. Davies and the woman exchanged furtive glances.

"Well, I was just..." Berdie began.

The man turned on his heel and took flight toward the High Street.

"But Mr. Davies," Berdie called, "we begin the procession any moment."

Linden simply waved a hand.

Mrs. Mikalos lifted her chin. "What would we do without our families?"

"Indeed." Berdie worked at a gentle smile. "I'm marshalling the troops, so to speak, if you care to join me." Berdie gestured forward.

"How very generous, thank you."

This was all rather difficult, but then, when did things go perfectly? Besides, what else was she to do with her unexpected guest?

Hugh and his accompanying acolytes had fallen in behind the balloon squad.

"What's going on?" Hugh half whispered to Berdie.

"Darling." Berdie lifted her brows. "This is Mrs. Mikalos, Linden Davies's mother-in-law. She's joining me."

"Only momentarily," Olivia Mikalos assured.

"Welcome to St. Aidan of the Woods." Hugh was generous, but Berdie heard a hint of hurry up in his voice.

"We'll be underway soon." Berdie gave Hugh that glance he alone understood as her commitment to forge on in her task, accompanied or not.

The acolytes with Hugh fidgeted about and the one bearing the ornate, carved cross nearly dropped it.

"Pay attention," Berdie warned the youngsters. "Children always bring an air of adventure to a gathering like this, don't they?" Berdie directed to Mrs. Mikalos.

"Adventure. Is that what you call it?" The woman's smile was genuine as she drew her hand across her linen top, and glanced in the direction Linden had taken.

Just a quick step and they were upon Lillie, who anxiously looked about. "I can't seem to locate Linden Davies. His choir is here, but..."

"Linden is a dear. He works desperately to try and manage things," Olivia broke in. "He's sure to be here in a flash. Ah." She pointed, and Linden, with robe aflutter, jogged toward them.

Lillie looked to Linden and then stared at the woman.

"I'm Linden's mother-in-law," she explained.

"Oh, good morning," Lillie bounced. "Well, all's well, then, as they say."

Linden arrived gulping the warm spring air. "Not there," he panted to Olivia.

"I'll go find them myself." The woman's shoulders tightened.

Linden's eyes widened. "Are you sure that's a good idea?"

Mrs. Mikalos cocked her head. "I said I'll find them." She turned to Berdie. "Thank you, Mrs. Elliott. As I said before, what would we do without our families?" With that, the woman turned on her heel and marched down Church Road with no little determination.

Linden shook his head. "Mercies upon us, dear God."

"Something wrong?" Berdie asked.

Linden gave a weak smile. "No, no, nothing."

This turn of events gave Berdie the freedom to put her entire concentration on things at hand. However, she perceived a large, imaginary elephant sitting right on Church Road between Linden and his mother-in-law.

"Come on, Linden. We must start." Lillie grabbed his elbow to guide him the few steps where three other choirmasters waited in front of the massive choir.

Berdie gave Lillie's hand a light squeeze, and then soldiered on through the eighty plus choral members. Vocalists from surrounding churches and villages joined together to form The Ascension collective choir. Everyone wore red robes borrowed from the W.H. Monk School of Music in Timsley.

"Very smart." Berdie addressed Dr. Avery, a mezzo soprano with St. Aidan's choir, who simply nodded while conducting her breathing exercises.

Grayson Webb had edged between the choir and the band, staff in hand. He cleared his throat and thrust his chin forward, a sign, Berdie surmised, that meant, he was ready.

The gathered musicians, also from various outlying areas, were poised to begin, with the exception of Lucy Butz, who wiped lip gloss from her clarinet reed.

"Ready are we, Lucy?" Berdie called to the seventeen-year-old.

The teenager shot an I'll-be-ready-when-I'm-ready glance at Berdie.

Berdie took a deep breath. *Teenagers*.

Berdie called to Jamie Donovan who stood behind the band holding the final banner. "Standing sure, Jamie?"

"Easy-peasy," the best striker on the village football team proclaimed. His strapping arms showed no strain at all.

"Now be sure all who are on the streets and join the procession do not tag after you, but are in front of you."

"I'm the closer, Mrs. Elliott," he said with joviality in his Irish accent.

Berdie eyed the banner and paused. She looked for the positive. "It's quite colorful."

Jamie wasn't quite so kind, although he kept his voice low. "I think the slain dragon looks like a lizard sunning itself. You know?"

"But what it represents, that's what's important."

"Death to evil," Jamie declared in full voice. "And that's why I'm proud to carry it."

By now, Lucy was once again in the process of reapplying fresh lip gloss.

"Really," Berdie muttered and decided the music would have to commence without the primping teen. "Well, Lord, here goes, then," she whispered. She caught Mr. Webb's eye and gave him the nod that put the full brigade in motion.

He raised his staff high above his head, held it steady for three counts, pulled it down, and the band commenced playing.

Berdie took her place beside them.

Her husband thrust the Bible with both hands upward as the front banner began to move forward.

The musicians played the joyful introduction to the exuberant "Hymn for Ascension Day." A wrinkle of movement became an expansive wave of humanity that edged forward. At just the right moment, the eighty-voice choir began and lifted their many voices as one.

> *Hail the day that sees Him rise,*
> *Ravished from our wishful eyes!*
> *Christ, awhile to mortals given,*
> *Reascends his native heaven.*

A ripple of excitement coursed through Berdie's body. Music swirled with grandeur. The choristers and band sounded as if they performed from the very portals of heaven itself. "Magnificent," Berdie breathed. Her body stepped with the river of praise that proceeded the few yards down Church Road. Berdie caught the scent of a nearby magnolia tree in full bloom. She inhaled, her nose bathed in the fragrance of spring.

The troupe began their turn to enter the High Street, where shops, offices, and a few residences comprised the village center. The green, at the bottom of the lengthy street, was the parade's destination.

Once round the corner, Berdie could scarcely take

it in. The pavements in front of shops and offices brimmed with people. Exhilaration ricocheted up and down the paved street. An explosion of applause began to swell through the onlookers.

Then the great engagement began. People observing stepped to and fell in behind the band. Berdie even heard some singing the familiar hymn as they walked.

> *Conqueror over death and sin:*
> *'Take the King of glory in!'*

Children eagerly clung to their parents' fingers, enraptured by being a part of the procession.

Berdie watched Batty Natty, along with her caring niece, Sandra, join other elderly congregants who found their stamina and stepped lively alongside the others.

"Lucy," a lad called and waved from a crowd of young men who tried to appear casual. But they, too, were unable to resist the tide and fell in to the procession. Buoyant with laughter, adolescent girls followed after. Waves of people merged with the gladsome crowd.

Parishioners and villagers were joined by a whole host of new faces, never-before-seen guests. Though the village green lay just ahead, it suddenly felt miles away. It seemed the whole of Christendom had come to Aidan Kirkwood. And a few others, as well.

By the time Jeffrey Lawler and the high banner reached the far end of the village green, High Street still teemed with marching people.

Berdie surged forward and arrived just in time to see Jeffrey plant his pole near Edsel Butz, who fiddled with the sound system.

"It seems the world and his wife has come to our fete," she announced.

"Where'd that lot come from?" Jeffrey inspected the crowd.

"They followed you," Edsel joked. "Or had you not noticed?"

Constable Albert Goodnight raced, or as close as he could come to it, across the green. "More illegally parked cars than you've had hot muffins," spouted the red faced constable. His uniform barely fit his rotund stomach. He pointed to an empty button hole. "Lost a button tryin' to squeeze my way through the Upland Arms car park." He pointed to Berdie. "And I'm holding you responsible."

Berdie reared back. "Me?"

"Well, the church, then." Albert's untidy mustache bounced with every word.

"Not that we're at fault," Berdie replied, "but we'll be glad to access church funds to replace your button."

Jeffrey and Edsel put hands to their mouths to hide their smiles.

"Think positive, Goodnight," Jeffrey said. "You lost a button, but imagine all the dosh you can take in today on parking tickets."

Edsel's chuckle became a laugh.

"You could get a proper police vehicle and all," Jeffrey finished.

Goodnight's eyes brightened beneath his bushy brows.

"Jeffrey." Berdie looked at Albert Goodnight. "We need you here." She couldn't believe she was saying the words. Usually she tried to dismiss him as rapidly as possible.

Goodnight lifted his chin. "Would you please repeat that, Mrs. Elliott? You need what?" Goodnight was enjoying this.

What she wanted to say was that she recognized any port in the storm would help, particularly one who wore an insignia of the law. But she chose kinder words. "In a crowd this size the badge could be helpful."

Goodnight took a deep inhale and stabbed a finger toward Jeffrey. "I need you to help me with crowd control. Now," he barked. "I'll send the missus to see to the parking tickets." His wife. How like him to do something so unprofessional and probably illegal.

Berdie turned her attention to the crowd that filled the small green and then some. "Lord have mercy." She had not anticipated this kind of attendance at their first-ever-in-fifty-years Ascension Sunday procession.

In what seemed eons of time, the choir made its way to the stands set up especially for the concert, the band came to rest in front of them, and Hugh stood near the microphone stand.

The balloon-toting youths arranged themselves on the outer edges of the square, and Jamie finally arrived, planting the final banner on the far side.

The air reminded Berdie of a gymkhana, even though there was no carousel or Coconut Shy for those with good aim.

Some people were already besieging the refreshment table where Ivy and Lila Butz, plus Cherry Lawler, struggled to cope with the demand.

Hugh clicked on the microphone and tapped it lightly. No sound. He turned it off. His lips formed a simple, *Dear Lord*. He flicked the switch again. *Tap, tap, tap.* "Our Father in heaven." This time, Hugh could be heard all across the green. He raised his hand. "The Lord be with you," his voice boomed, "and welcome to our Ascension Sunday procession and concert."

An attentive few responded and clapped.

"Let's bunch up, so everyone can be accommodated on the green. We have a wonderfully large crowd." His voice steady and demeanor calm, he was not in the least ruffled.

Berdie relaxed. Still, in a throng this size it was vital to stay alert.

"Please make your way toward the choir. They will begin their concert in three minutes. Then we'll distribute balloons and have an Ascension blessing after which we'll all simultaneously release the balloons. I know you little ones are excited for that."

Bubbles of cheers sprang from young lips.

"Light refreshments will then be offered."

Few paid heed to the reminder that refreshments were after as both children and adults crowded the tables of lemonade and frosted biscuits and buns.

However, as Hugh said, the concert began three minutes later.

Many were attentive as the musical swell filled the green and beyond. All but a few were engrossed as it progressed.

"Lovely." Berdie let the waves of song sweep her into the sea of their beauty.

Dr. Avery's solo was spine tingling, beguiling all who attended. Well, almost all.

Berdie's delight was disturbed when she felt a tug on her skirt.

"How long 'til we get the balloons, Mrs. Elliott?" Five-year-old Duncan Butz held a paper cup and was accompanied by another little lad.

"After the concert," Berdie replied. "But we won't let go of them until Reverend Elliott gives the blessing."

"Mine's going to go way, way high." Duncan's eyes lighted as he pointed upward.

"Mine higher," the little lad next him added, sticky icing covering his chin.

"This is my third cup of lemonade." Duncan took a drink of the liquid.

"Save some for your friend here," Berdie teased.

His chum made a face. "I don't like it. Ugh."

Duncan thrust his index finger toward a cat winding its way through the crowd. "Can Razor have a balloon?"

"Only children get balloons." Berdie eyed the tatty old feline that looked as if he'd stood his ground in more than one tangle. "Is he your cat?"

"I found him. He likes me." Duncan smiled. "I gave him some of my bun, and now he follows me everywhere."

"Does he?"

"Just like Arthur." Duncan nodded toward his little pal, who simply displayed a gapped-tooth grin.

Berdie laughed.

The two little ones ran off toward the refreshment table, the cat in hot pursuit.

The moment the concert ended, an electric verve sizzled amongst the crowd. The refreshment table went suddenly empty. Youngsters thronged the youth who handed out the balloons.

Berdie counted three skyward escapees when she approached the struggling Kevin McDermott.

"Hang about," he shouted to the youngsters. Strings were tangling and young hands tried to grab.

His pleading eyes turned to Berdie. "They're vultures." He raised his clutching fist to hold the orbs out of the little ones' reach.

"As can be seen," Berdie agreed as she caught a wayward balloon. "Form a queue, children," Berdie ordered. In a flash, she had the disorderly swarm in three straight columns.

Each young one, and a few adults, took their prize in turn. The other teens who handed out the inflated treasures managed well. Red spheres all dispersed Berdie signaled Hugh, who tapped the microphone. No sound. *Not again.*

Edsel twisted knobs and dials on the sound gear.

Jeffrey approached Hugh and said something. The young man turned and sped toward the Kirkwood Green Bed and Breakfast, his home and business, across the road.

Hugh continued tapping the dead microphone with his finger.

"Come on, Vicar," someone yelled.

People began to fuss and there was a sense of restless anticipation. Children milled about and adults chatted aimlessly.

All the while, Edsel and Hugh wrestled with the sound equipment. Soon others joined them; gawking, twisting, unscrewing, testing.

Finally, Berdie could just make out Hugh's voice.

"Our Father in heaven." On the barely audible sound system, his words were scarcely heard above the milling crowd. "There it is. Much thanks to Edsel Butz, our electronic specialist."

One person clapped.

"And now may we commence our blessing."

Some came to attention, many appeared to be

woolgathering.

Hugh raised his free hand, palm facing the throng. His voice became instantly thunderous. "May the king of glory fill you with…"

Boom. A deafening blast ripped across the green.

A roar went up from the crowd along with one hundred sixteen helium balloons.

The choir hurriedly burst into a chorus of "Gloria," while oohs and ahhs, applause and gasps, cheers and giggles, emanated from all gathered.

Berdie, despite the agitation of the disrupted blessing, was taken with pleasant surprise at the glorious sight. The mass of scarlet balloons spiraled against the bright blue of the sky. Sunlight dazzled off the circles that danced their way to heaven. It was as if the faith of those present lifted with the red ascent much in the same fashion of the One they celebrated today. *What a fitting commemoration.*

Everyone watched the red dots journey on toward the drifting white wisps that decorated the high azure canopy.

But when the spots had diminished, Berdie's thoughts catapulted back to the loud boom. Where had it come from?

By the look of the long queue at the table, Refreshments were at the top of the crowd's mind, at least for those who had not availed themselves already.

Berdie approached the men.

Hugh spoke with the returned Jeffrey.

"Here's the starter pistol we planned to use." Jeffrey showed Hugh a small black imitation pistol and lifted his brows. "Not that it's of any use now."

"But there was a shot fired, a definite shot," Hugh said with military starch. "I assumed it was yours."

Jeffrey shook his head.

"Why the pistol?" Berdie questioned.

Jeffrey took a deep breath. "When the microphone didn't work…"

"It would get everyone's attention for the blessing," Berdie finished and nodded.

"So who fired a shot?" Hugh knit his brow.

Constable Goodnight's laughter interrupted their conversation. Though a few steps away, it was obvious he was showing a handgun to a nearby gentleman.

A van could've driven through Hugh's open mouth, while Jeffrey shook his head.

"Goodnight," Hugh summoned, "did you fire that?"

Albert Goodnight wore a large grin. "Always wanted to do that," he bellowed.

"A live round?"

The constable's grin widened.

Hugh's grip on the altar Bible turned his knuckles frosty white. "In this crowd?"

"Did the job, didn't it?" Goodnight cradled the piece and radiated an *I-showed-them* satisfaction. "Now, if you please, I have to go relieve my wife." Without apology he strode off.

"Whatever you do, put that thing away," Hugh snapped with volume. It was a rare moment when Hugh became molten.

Berdie couldn't help herself. "And how many times have I said that fellow shouldn't be in law enforcement? And where did he get a gun in the first place?"

Hugh took a deep breath. "God help us." His words were a prayer.

"Well, since it appears no one took a bullet, I'd say

He already has," Berdie quipped.

Hugh's eyes encompassed the square. "Yes."

"His timing was shoddy as well, cutting off the blessing like that."

"Albert was certainly not circumspect in his behavior. Let's leave it at that," Hugh advised.

"As my cousin from York would say, he's a barn pot." Jeffrey spoke up. "But then, everyone knows that."

"Yes, well, no need to disparage the man. Let's just be grateful that the lion's share of today's activities went well." Hugh's knuckles were getting their color back.

"Right enough, Vicar," Jeffrey agreed.

The gathered crowd began to disperse.

"Right enough," Berdie echoed. But something inside began to gnaw at her, and it did not feel *right enough*.

3

The savory aroma of salmon emanating from Lillie's kitchen promised what would be an evening meal fit for a foodie's delight.

The flutter of Ascension Sunday activity was, Berdie reckoned, melting into memory.

"I understand there was a large crowd for the procession and concert today." Loren leaned back in the dining chair.

"I wonder if Lillie used thyme. Can you taste thyme mixed in with the goat cheese?" Berdie hoped, between bites of seasoned cheese on squares of toast, to steer the conversation away from work, for both the men. The evening was full of promise after such an active day. A welcomed rest and well-deserved repast with Hugh, Lillie, and Loren lay before her, the candlelight reflecting from glassware like summer evening stars. And Hugh had promised to silence his mobile. A time to converse about leisurely things.

"Our green barely held everyone," Hugh said with a ring of contentment.

"Apparently, many came from Timsley." Loren took a sip of aperitif. "I should have thought it would appeal to the surrounding villages and hamlets, but why Timsley?"

"Yes," Berdie interjected with a bit higher volume, "she used thyme. And very good, too."

"Urban dwellers sometimes yearn for that small village sense of community." Hugh ignored Berdie's redirect. "I'm assisting the new vicar at St. Mark's in Timsley to prepare his Whitsun celebration for Sunday next, a fete of sorts. He feels it's a good way for his parishioners to interact. There's an ever growing need today to connect with others, and I'm not speaking of just social media. I mean real face-to-face interaction." Hugh took a sip from his fluted glass.

"I hadn't thought of it that way, but you have a point." Loren's eyes looked soulful in the candlelight.

Berdie's attempt to steer conversation away from work was thwarted, and so she pushed into the conversation. "Or it could have nothing to do with community or belonging. It may have simply been a jolly fun thing to do on a Sunday afternoon."

"Berdie." Hugh paused. "You can go to a film, the pub, or have a sing-song on a ramble in the woods for fun. No, though people enjoyed themselves, it's far more significant than that."

"No one wants to be alone." Loren stated.

Lillie swept into the room laden with the tray that held a beautifully presented whole cucumber-dressed salmon, parsley sprinkled couscous, and lemon-buttered asparagus. "Dinner is served."

"Bravo," Hugh cheered. Hugh never complained about Berdie's simple meals, but his eyes were alight at the exquisite food Lillie presented.

"And there's afters. Pavlova with cherries."

Berdie adored Lillie's baked meringue with scoops of fruit, one of her favorites.

After Lillie placed the food on the table, Loren took her hand and gently tugged. "Now join us."

Lillie deposited the tray and sat next to him. "And

what have we been chatting about?"

"Connecting. Belonging to someone." Loren popped Lillie's napkin open and laid it on her lap.

Lillie's gaze clung to the doctor like leaves to a stalk. Her smile was amorous. "Indeed."

"Grace?" Hugh asked.

Lillie turned her gaze to Berdie. "Would you like Hugh to bless the food?" It was as if Lillie had forgotten there were others at the table.

"Oh, yes, of course."

"Dear Lord," Hugh began, "for these Your gifts…"

A soft buzz spilt into the reverent words.

Dr. Meredith felt the coat pocket where he kept his mobile. A gentle smile let them know the vibrating noise did not belong to him.

"These Your gifts we are about to receive…"

Buzz.

Well, it certainly wasn't her or Lillie.

Hugh put his hand on his trouser pocket. His left eyebrow rose. "We give you thanks. Amen," tumbled from his mouth "Vicar," Hugh said into the phone already at his ear.

"Hugh." Berdie put fire in her voice.

Lillie looked relieved that it wasn't her man in the hot seat this time.

And Hugh was avoiding eye contact all together. "Oh, dear," Hugh said sternly. "Yes, of course, right away." Hugh rang off and looked at Lillie. "I do apologize."

Berdie crossed her arms. "That's the second interrupted blessing today." She wanted to bawl out a protest, but she summoned poise. "You promised to turn that wretched thing off," she said under her breath.

"To be fair, love, I said I would silence it, which I did."

Berdie looked at the ceiling.

"You know a parish priest has no real hours of his own."

How very well acquainted she was with that fact.

"Natty Bell has been taken to hospital. Sandra has asked that I come to look in on her. Apparently Natty's in a state," Hugh announced.

"Poor, sweet Natty. Of course you must go." Lillie's gaze reflected the sympathy of her words. "She's at sixes and sevens in the best of times."

Berdie felt a flash of guilt. She uncrossed her arms. "Is it serious?"

"I'll find out when I get there." Hugh gave Berdie's hand a squeeze. "I'm sorry, love." Hugh's military exploits had taken him to ports all round the world and now his pastoral duties demanded she share him with an entire village.

"When you're finished eating will you see Berdie home, Loren?"

"Of course."

"I'll have hot tea and a sandwich waiting for you when you get in," Berdie promised.

"Well, that's me, off, then," Hugh stood. His gaze scanned the food. This time they held much less sparkle. "I'll see myself out."

"Give Natty our best," Lillie offered.

"Well, that's that, then," Berdie announced, glum hanging on every word.

"Now, I could take offense that the two remaining people with you at this table are mere chaff," Loren teased.

Berdie grinned. She appreciated his attempt to

lighten the mood. "I suppose I could dine with cats and be sublimely elevated," she countered.

Both Loren and Berdie had a chuckle.

"Cats?" Lillie knit her thin shaped brows.

"They'd love the salmon." Loren nodded toward the beautifully presented fish.

"What are you two going on about?" Lillie picked up her fork.

"Too silly to explain right now," Loren answered. "I'm famished."

"Shall we tuck in?" Lillie was already putting some buttered asparagus on her plate.

Generous portions were heaped on all three plates, and Berdie couldn't help but *m-m-m*.

"This salmon is superb." Loren pushed another large forkful into his mouth.

In the midst of the contented silence that descended, a knock at the door cut in.

"Who do you suppose that is? Did Hugh forget something?" Lillie sprang from the table and made way to the hall.

Berdie formed a mental checklist. *Keys? Yes he had them. Mobile? Unfortunately, yes. Wallet? I should think so.*

Lillie re-entered the dining room, a flushed Linden Davies behind her. His sweat-beaded forehead broadcasted his angst. "I'm interrupting," he observed.

"Would you like to join us?" Lillie pointed to the empty plate that once was reserved for Hugh.

"No." He shook his head. "No, thank you," his voice cracked. Linden looked at Berdie. "I'm glad you're here. Actually, I was hoping to locate you."

"Me? Really?"

"It's just that you were with her." He wiped moisture from his upper lip. "And I hoped you may have some idea."

Berdie put her couscous-laden fork down. "I was with whom?"

"Oh, yes, sorry. My mother-in-law. It's just that she's gone missing." He heaved, hand on his chest.

"Gone missing?"

"But she was at the procession today," Lillie countered.

"That's just it." Linden raised an open hand and bounced it along with each word. "We've not seen or heard from her since that moment. I was hoping perhaps you'd have seen her or spoken with her."

Berdie gently nudged the imaginary elephant she remembered from Linden's interaction with his mother-in-law earlier today. "As I recall, she seemed somewhat agitated, and then went to look for someone."

"Yes, my wife and children." He lifted his chin. "But Elise, my wife, said Olivia never found her. My wife was to take her home."

Loren cleared his throat. "If I may, I can understand your concern. But your mother-in-law is an adult, and fully responsible, I assume."

"That's it. She's very responsible. This is not like her, not at all." Moisture glistened in Linden's eye. "The police said they can only get involved straight away if it's a child or a vulnerable person, like someone with dementia, or if a suspected crime's involved. Otherwise, they have to wait forty-eight hours, anyway." He paused. "I told them that she's a widow and lives alone. But they didn't see any urgency. We've called Olivia's mobile numerous times today. I've been by the house. I'm concerned, but I don't know what to do next."

"Have you been inside the house?" Berdie questioned.

"No, there was no answer to my knock, I didn't attempt to go inside." His eyes grew wide. "Inside. Oh my, you don't think she could be..."

"Now you're dishing the soup before it boils," Lillie cautioned.

Linden grabbed the top of the empty chair to steady himself. "I don't know what I'd do if..." He obviously couldn't finish the sentence.

"That's it, then," Lillie announced. "Berdie and I will go back to the house with you."

Linden's deep sigh signaled his relief. "Yes, would you, please?"

Loren scowled.

"We'd be glad to help, wouldn't we Berdie?"

"Right now?" Berdie hesitated, then plunged the fork full of couscous into her mouth.

"I say," Loren rumbled.

"We'll meet you at your car in a moment," Lillie assured.

The moment Linden was out of hearing, Loren spoke. "Lillie, what are you doing?"

"I'm taking care of a distraught colleague."

"Colleague? He's your music student."

Berdie gobbled several asparagus spears.

"Are you saying my living, breathing student is less important than one of your corpses down at the morgue?" Lillie put her hands on her slim hips.

"Oh, so that's what this is about."

"Not at all," Lillie all but shouted.

Berdie spooned another chunk of salmon from the platter to her plate and made short work of it.

"Linden's welfare is important to me. He's in

distress."

"His mother-in-law probably took the coach home, and then fancied a country drive."

"You don't know that."

"So every time he's stressed he'll run to you?"

Lillie lifted her chin. "I will not dignify that ridiculous suggestion with a response." She fixed her stare on Berdie. "Right, then. Let's go."

Berdie popped one more bite of couscous in her mouth, nodded, and got to her feet.

"Enjoy the rest of your meal," Lillie directed toward Loren. "Make sure the door's latched. Lock up when you leave." She turned and was already halfway down the hall to the door.

Berdie recognized a hint of jealousy in Loren's eyes. "I'd say you may be sailing a bit close to the wind," Berdie offered the disgruntled doctor, tease in her voice. "Maybe you should get a cat."

"Oh, thank you very much, Berdie." Loren smacked his fork onto his plate.

Then Berdie, too, exited. Whether Linden's mother-in-law was truly missing or just not replying, she heard the imaginary trumpeting elephant urge her forward. And the big game hunt was on.

****

Though the structure was completely dark, it was clear that the home of Olivia Mikalos was no small bungalow. The outer edges of Timsley held some grand, new homes with large gardens and this was one of many in this area.

"Has Olivia appeared depressed, not quite herself of late?" Berdie asked.

"She hasn't been dancing about, but nothing more than slightly anxious, I'd say."

"Do you have access to the garage door?"

"Yes."

"Let's do that now, if you please."

He eyed the front door, and then the garage. "Yes. All right. Quickly. But I haven't the key to enter the house from the garage."

"Your mother-in-law has a separate key for the entry door from the garage?"

"Yes." Linden punched the security numbers on the entry pad, and the garage door opened. No exhaust fumes, no engine idled. The unoccupied, expensive silver vehicle gleamed its presence.

"What a lovely car," Lillie observed.

"New. Latest model. My mother-in-law has impeccable taste."

And a fair amount of money.

"Now can we carry on? Why check the garage, anyway?" Mr. Davies was brisk.

"Precaution," Berdie said.

Linden frowned and swallowed. "Olivia wouldn't do anything daft."

He closed the garage and took the stone path that ran from the drive to the front garden, walking ahead of Berdie and Lillie. The borders were awash with purple bearded iris and frothy cranesbill. The welcoming front door sported a wreath of sage, dried lavender, flowering mint, dabs of rosemary, sweet pea, and peach colored tea roses.

"Your mother-in-law shops at the White Window Box in Aidan Kirkwood." Lillie fingered the wreath and then put her fingertips to her nose and sniffed. "Heavenly. This mix of herbs and flowers is their specialty."

"It was a gift, actually," Linden curtly responded. "Mother," he called out as he rang the doorbell several times. He tried to open the door but found it locked. "I'm using my key to come in."

A front light flickered on at another home across the road.

Linden unlocked the door and pushed it open.

A distinct odor hit Berdie's nose like a kick to the shin. "Smoke."

"Oh, my dear Lord," toppled from Lillie's lips.

"Mother?" Linden pushed through the doorway.

Berdie caught him by his sleeve. "Protect your mouth and nose."

Linden, hand over his face, swept into the ample hallway. He switched on the hall light.

Berdie, right behind him, glanced about. There were no flames apparent. She didn't feel heat. But there was a lazy gray haze drifting throughout. She was almost certain of its source. "Kitchen," Berdie directed Mr. Davies.

"Remind you of anything?" Lillie's muffled words came from behind.

"My oven thermostat's delicate," Berdie barked through her covered mouth.

Linden advanced to the open plan kitchen clicking lights on as he went. In the heart of the room, the smoke was thick. Linden looked about.

"Oven," Berdie yelled and charged forward. She grabbed a precautionary tea towel from a countertop. Her shoe hit an object that clattered across the floor. She turned the oven off.

A swish of clean air whooshed in when Linden opened double glass doors onto a veranda.

"Berdie?" Lillie began to cough.

Berdie grabbed her friend's arm and towed her along as she raced behind Linden and out of the smoke-filled kitchen onto the expansive tiled veranda.

Berdie drank the fresh air into her lungs.

Lillie plopped into a substantial wicker chair and took giant refreshing gulps.

Linden, after several deep inhalations, re-entered the kitchen.

Visible through the glass and haze, he donned protective kitchen gloves. Thick smoke escaped when he opened the oven door and pulled the darkened offender from the gaping chamber. He raced to the veranda and flung the blackened roasting pan and its contents past the stone flooring and into the back garden. "Hot," was all he offered, but his grimace said it all. He pulled the scorched pads from his hands and blew on his palms.

A shriveled black morsel was riveted to the pan. A once generous cut of meat, lamb by the shape of it, now launched spirals of gray smoke into the night.

"Well, dinner's off, then," Lillie said.

But Berdie sensed far more was off than dinner.

"I'm going back in," Linden announced.

"Use a wet towel," Berdie called after him.

"Why is he going back?" Lillie leaned forward in her chair.

"He's looking for Olivia, of course."

"Surely she's not home. Wouldn't you notice something like smoke?"

"You would if you're conscious."

"You don't think she's here?"

Berdie took another inhale of fresh air. "Let's have a go at opening some windows."

"I don't fancy going back in." Lillie tipped her head. "And you haven't answered my question. Do you think she's in there somewhere?"

"I would say no, and I certainly hope not," Berdie answered matter-of-factly.

"And you think she's not there because..." Lillie urged, "...go on."

"There are the obvious facts we already know."

"Linden took Mrs. Mikalos to the procession, but didn't take her home."

"Yes." Berdie nodded. "And Olivia never found her daughter and grandchildren in the crowd today. She was clearly agitated about something. But the *ins* are the most convincing."

"Ins?"

"Her car's *in* the garage and the roast was *in* the oven."

"That's it? How does that say she's not in there right now? In fact, a car in the garage means someone is home."

A loud *we-wa* broke the quiet of the outer road. It was accompanied by the night sky dancing with swirls of blue light.

"Here comes the cavalry," Berdie announced.

"The fire brigade?" Lillie stood. "Did Linden call them?"

"If he did, this lot flew aboard the Concorde to get here."

A winded Linden rushed onto the veranda. "She's not there."

"Good news, too." Lillie flashed an *aren't-you-clever* look at Berdie.

Linden Davies bent over and placed his hands on his knees. "I suppose," he said between inhalations, "we really did need the fire brigade. Thank you."

Lillie eyed Berdie, who raised her brows but said nothing about not being responsible for the call.

"They have large extractor fans that can air the place in minutes."

"Yes." Lillie didn't try to hide a grin. "Berdie has had personal experience with them."

Berdie scrunched her nose and glared at Lillie.

****

True to form, the fire brigade had the home aired out in short time.

Linden shared his concerns about his mother-in-law with the fellow in charge.

"If we had a pound for each time an old dear has forgotten about their leg of lamb in the oven, we'd each own a Rolls Royce." The broad shouldered man wore a smile. "Your mother-in-law will have a memory flash and be home soon, I shouldn't wonder."

Berdie was not convinced, but it seemed to relieve Linden for the moment. "May I have a quick look-see about the place?" Berdie asked him after the brigade departed.

"It's a splendid idea," Lillie coerced. "Berdie is so clever about these things."

"Yes, I suppose, but I wouldn't want Mother to find a stranger rooting about in her home when she arrives."

"Five minutes. Just for a safety measure," Lillie endorsed.

Berdie looked toward the stairway. "Her bedroom, if you please, and we won't be terribly invasive."

Linden directed Berdie and Lillie to Olivia's

bedroom with en suite bathroom. The size of the rooms fit with the rest of what they had seen of the home. The bedroom was lighted by a floral-shaped designer chandelier. The interior had a light ivory and sea grass color scheme. A grand bed with a brocade silk duvet made the white painted wardrobe and side tables stand out. The whole of it could have been an advert for distinctive country elegance.

"I must go down and clean up the veranda." Linden left.

"Good," Berdie said when he exited, "that will keep him busy for a bit." Berdie pointed Lillie to the bathroom. "Look for everyday grooming items."

"Aye, aye, captain." Lillie stepped into the small adjoining room.

Berdie eyed a decorated box on an antique dressing table. She opened it to find very fine jewelry, real stones, nestled in an orderly fashion. "So the earrings were real." She stepped toward the neatly made bed. "Oh, and medications, any kind of tablets," she called to Lillie.

Berdie pulled back the duvet and delicately picked up a pillow. A black silk nightdress lay folded beneath it. Putting all neatly back into place, she moved to the expansive wardrobe and opened it to see enough clothing to dress a small village. And enough shoes, all neatly placed, to shod them as well. "All going well?" Berdie could hear Lillie rummaging.

"Fine," she returned.

There was one empty hanger among the goods and a black silk robe hung on a golden hook attached to the interior of the wardrobe door.

"I can't say all is fine here," she whispered.

Two pairs of shoes were on the thick carpet near

the wardrobe, gray clogs and brown leather dress shoes. "And she decided on the tan espadrilles." Berdie heard a rather loud *Oh, dear* come from the bathroom. When she entered, for all it held, it could have been a spa: slipper bath, glassed-in shower, lounge chair, and a spacious sink.

"I would say Mrs. Mikalos will be returning soon." Lillie pointed to a container of tablets. "Two times daily for blood sugar regulation."

Berdie was not pleased with this discovery. "Deodorant, toothbrush?"

"All here," Lillie answered. "Actually, there're two bottles of the tablets. All daily makeup items are here, quite expensive, too." She swept her finger across the items. "Toothpaste, hair brush, and a lovely matching comb in their proper place."

"Though Olivia Mikalos is not here, she's spoken volumes," Berdie declared.

Suddenly something erupted from the slipper bath.

Lillie shrieked and grabbed Berdie with such aggression it nearly knocked her over.

"My good heavens," sprang from Berdie's lips as she regained her balance.

Lillie had recovered a modicum of composure and was shaking her head.

Berdie felt something fuzzy on the calf of her leg. She shot a glare down to discover a cat rubbing itself against her appendage.

"Silly thing gave me a fright," Lillie muttered, hand on her heart.

"I'd have never guessed." Berdie straightened her rumpled blouse.

"Why would it be in the bath?"

"It missed its morning shower?"

"Or thirsty," Lillie noted.

"Or thirsty," Berdie repeated. "The clattering bowl in the kitchen."

Lillie bent down to stroke the creature. She put out her hand. "Hello, sweet kitty." Without warning she jerked straight up with a gasp.

"What?"

Lillie pulled back. "Look at it."

Berdie bent down to behold the feline. The animal had a white face surrounded by black, including a V shape between its eyes, making it appear to have a widow's peak. But the most noticeable and horrifying feature were the incisors. Fangs protruded from the mouth and just overlapped the bottom lip. "Have mercy," Berdie breathed.

The cat's front legs were black with white paws. Black fur encircled the body nearly to the end where a white back end was accompanied by white legs and tail. For the look of it, the cat could be wearing a tiny tailored cape.

Berdie stood up.

"It's Dracula," Lillie uttered with a sound of horror edged with pity.

Linden entered the bathroom. "Oh, I see you found Tiddles."

"Tiddles?" Berdie eyed the fangs.

"I wondered where he may be. Quite shocking, isn't he?" Linden lifted the animal and held it close to his chest. "Actually, Tiddles is a very sweet cat." He stroked it gently. "My son wanted a pet, so for his birthday we let him choose one. Of course, he loved the look of this fellow. However, the moment we got Tiddles home, my daughter broke out in itchy red bumps."

"Hard for your son, I can imagine." Berdie empathized.

"He was devastated. Our home is quite small for a child who's allergic." Linden released the animal, and the cat scampered off. "So my mother-in-law graciously took the creature into her home and offered to let Phillip visit as often as he wishes."

"Good for Grandmum," Lillie cheered.

"Yes. Grandmum." Linden hesitated. "Well, we must be off." Linden smiled for the first time this evening. "As the fire brigade said, she'll probably be home any time."

"You will ring when she gets in," Lillie prompted.

"Of course."

The ride home in Linden's car was a non-stop, good natured barrage between him and Lillie about the qualities necessary for a choral director and how to select suitable sacred music for a performance.

Though Berdie considered it a good distraction for Linden, she mulled over what she had just seen at the home of Mrs. Mikalos. She was convinced the woman had planned to return home that afternoon. Would Olivia cross the threshold of her beautiful home any time soon, or ever at all? *Lord, whatever the case, watch over and keep all concerned in Your care.*

This big game hunt was becoming less sporting and moving into the realm of something much more serious.

What would they come upon next?

4

Berdie stared at the cheese and pickle sandwiches she had just prepared as if her scrutinizing eye might change them into something a bit more gastronomic.

Poor Hugh. He left a lovely meal to attend his parishioner, and now he would come home to a cheese sandwich.

What a way to end Ascension Sunday, but her search in the pantry had yielded nothing more edible. "Lord, a miracle wouldn't go amiss here. You did some amazing things with loaves and fishes." She tapped her finger on the edge of the plate. "Somehow, a seaside feast would certainly suit him better than cheddar and pickle on brown bread."

The unmistakable sound of the front door opening was followed by Hugh's voice in conversation.

"Who on earth?" Berdie glanced at the clock. "And at this time of night." She scooted to the front hall.

"Hello, love." Hugh had a lively tone. "Look who I met on the doorstep."

Loren and Lillie stood behind Hugh. Loren carried a large food hamper, and Lillie wore an enormous grin.

"Surprise, and special delivery." Lillie swirled the words. "I hope you're hungry."

Loren lifted the basket. "Evening meal round two: salmon fish cakes, asparagus mousse, and chilled couscous."

Berdie was gobsmacked. Her jaw nearly touched

the floor. "Now I know how the five thousand felt."

"What?" Hugh's face was aglow. "This comes as a real treat." He rubbed his hands together with delight.

Lillie leaned toward Berdie. "Saying good evening wouldn't go amiss."

"Sorry? Oh yes." Berdie worked at getting the words out. "What an unexpected blessing."

"That's us, a late night blessing."

"Won't you come in?"

"I've got early duty tomorrow at the lab," Loren said. "Must push on. But, I can take this through to the kitchen for you."

"Oh yes." Hugh moved inside. "I'll go with you."

Berdie stepped out to stand next to Lillie. "Aren't we in high spirits?" She tipped her head. "And what happened to 'be sure you lock up when you leave'?"

"Loren's done the sweetest thing." Lillie's eyes could have lit the front door light. "First of all, when I got in, he had finished *all* the washing up."

"A modern man." Berdie wrapped her arms over her chest against the cool spring night.

"He made delicious fish cakes from the uneaten salmon." Lillie nearly gurgled. "He made the asparagus into a mousse, just from what I had in my pantry. And fit for a king."

"The couscous?" Berdie's mouth began to water.

"Oh, that's just the leftover from the dish I made originally."

Berdie smiled. "A reasonable cook, your Loren."

"Reasonable? Brilliant, more like." Lillie leaned against Berdie's shoulder. "Then, as if all that wasn't enough, he not only laid me a table, but he also created a hamper to bring to you and Hugh."

"So Loren is generous to a fault, as well."

"Yes." Lillie put her voice low. "He's agreed to go with me day after tomorrow to visit Aunt Margaret."

"Aunt Margaret in Cornwall?"

Lillie nodded.

Berdie became pensive. "So, why don't you ask him to marry you?"

Lillie pulled back. Her eyes grew large, and her face went crimson. "Loren may need my assistance in there." She tried to dash through the doorway, but Berdie blocked it and dipped her chin with a coy smile. "After all, he sounds the perfect man, Lillie."

"Now, Berdie, you know better than that." Lillie shifted her handbag to the other shoulder. "Besides, that's rather his responsibility. Proposals and all."

"Is it?"

Lillie glanced through the open doorway. "Oh, look. Hugh's coming. Now stop this silly conversation."

Berdie took her friend by the arm. "Would you say yes if Loren asked?"

Lillie pursed her lips. "Perhaps."

"Perhaps?"

"Love the man, intensely dislike his career and its demands."

"Smells good in the kitchen." Hugh arrived at the door. Again, he rubbed his hands together like a child preparing for a dip in the paddling pool. "Loren's just coming."

"I'll go lay the table," Berdie pronounced, but not without giving a smile and a quick squeeze of the hand to the flustered Lillie.

Just as Berdie was ready to go through the kitchen door, Loren exited, nearly bumping her, car keys in hand. "Must be off," he said.

"Yes. Well, thank you so much for sharing your cooking skills with us. We'll thoroughly enjoy our meal."

"Good." Loren fumbled the keys.

Berdie tipped her head. "Can I see you to the door?"

"Actually, may I have a quick word?"

"Of course." Berdie wasn't sure what to expect.

"This evening, when you and Lillie left on your errand of mercy," Loren shifted his weight. "I realized what it feels like for the first time."

"What it feels like?"

"To be left behind." Loren ran a finger over his key. "I'm the one who usually does the departing in the midst of a meal or when Lillie and I are to have time together."

"Yes. I see."

"I realized, I mean, really realized, for the first time how my lovely Lillie has the patience of a saint." He hesitated. "But it's my work, Berdie. And I do love my career. And for all that, when they call, I've got to go."

Berdie took a deep breath. "Yes, she knows that."

"But she doesn't like it."

"Did you like being alone at the table this evening?"

The doctor swallowed. "Be honest with me, Berdie." He gripped the keys as if they opened a grand secret. "If I asked Lillie to," he paused, "to marry me, would she?"

Berdie read the hope in Loren's eyes while beholding the grit of his jaw. This was a moment a vicar's wife was expected to be wise, encouraging, and insightful, despite the fact she was peckish and longed for her first bite of salmon fish cake. Her response could set a course of action. Berdie wanted her words to be just right. Loren wanted honesty. And she hoped to encourage. What to say? "Perhaps."

"Perhaps?" Loren wrinkled his brow.

"Loren." Hugh shot down the hallway. "Lillie is anxious to get on."

Loren shook his keys. He leaned toward Berdie and whispered. "I trust your complete discretion."

"What happens in the vicarage, stays in the vicarage."

Loren gave an easy laugh and strode to the door.

"God go with you," Berdie called.

Hugh entered the kitchen after seeing Loren and Lillie off.

Berdie was still smiling. "Hope springs eternal."

"What?" Hugh yawned. "Nothing springs at this hour. Food, my love. Let's tuck in." Hugh gathered plates as Berdie grabbed some silverware.

"How's Natty?"

"Exhausted and confused. She overdid at the procession today and twisted her ankle. She'll be released to go home in the next forty-eight hours or so."

"Poor dear."

"Yes, speaking of a poor dear, Loren told me you've had a bit of an adventure this evening, helping that fellow, Linden Davies, is it? It was a bit of a ramble, but he said something of the fire brigade, a vampire cat, and someone gone missing. So, will you tell me what's going on?"

"That is a conversation for another time." Berdie didn't want to launch into the whole story. Being tired could easily take things in a negative direction. "I'm knackered, and I dare say, you are, as well."

And a genuinely amazing thing happened. Hugh didn't raise his left eyebrow nor did he insist they discuss it here and now. "Knackered, indeed," he agreed. "Let's eat."

"Two miracles in a ten minute time span," Berdie said under her breath. "Thank you," poured from her grateful lips.

****

Berdie expected it.

At six forty-five A.M. in the morning a panicked Linden called Lillie, and Lillie called Berdie.

"He's absolutely beside himself," Lillie informed. "He decided to clean the people carrier at St. Matthews before going to work this morning and found Olivia's handbag in the backseat, her credit card, driver's license, money, all there."

"Oh, dear. Not good."

"He fully believed she would be there in her home, but when he found the bag he rang her up and she didn't answer. So, he called the Timsley police again and they told him the same thing they said yesterday: at this point the absentee has to be vulnerable, and they don't consider Mrs. Mikalos vulnerable."

"That is their policy, for better or worse."

"We've got to help him Berdie."

"Yes. We can work out what's going on, but it will take some time, and I need to inform Hugh." Berdie took a deep breath.

"But surely he won't object. After all, it does seem she disappeared from a St. Aidan event."

"True," Berdie agreed, "that does rather put it at our door. I'll speak to him."

"You can fetch me at half nine," Lillie said with confidence. "See you then."

Hugh did not fight her on the issue. To the contrary, he encouraged her, which was a delight. "Yes, it is down to us. It appears to have happened at our church event. I understand the law's hesitation, there's no real evidence of foul play as yet. But circumstances do call for some kind of look-see." He set his amazing blue eyes on her. "No church commitments today, and if there's anyone within a hundred miles who can investigate well, it's you."

"Make that two hundred miles, and I'll prepare a fry up for your breakfast."

Hugh placed a soft kiss on her cheek. "Two hundred, it is." He took her hand. "Remember, the first whiff of personal danger, you're no longer involved."

"Of course." But mentally she wasn't so sure. After all, every inquiry had an element of risk. She worked at staying focused as she did her morning prayers from the Northumbrian Community's Celtic Daily Prayer. Even the reading of the scripture portion required her full attention. The anticipation of putting to work her God-given abilities to smell out undiscovered truth gave rise to a certain excitement. Still, she did her morning exercise routine with resolve, then groomed and dressed in her most comfortable skirt and a salmon-colored blouse.

Quickly, she gulped down tea and toast while cooking a fry up for Hugh: eggs, black pudding, sausage, and bacon rashers from the Carlisle Cathcart Farm mobile butchers, mushrooms, tomatoes, and buttered toast.

With a quick peck on Hugh's cheek, she left him heartily enjoying his breakfast and the beginning of his day off, if, indeed, vicars ever really had one.

When she arrived at Swallow Gate, Lillie's three-story Georgian home, the woman herself was standing at the door. And she looked quite smart in her sky-blue frock with sparkling embroidery at the neckline.

A late model car was parked in the gracious drive. "You've company?" Berdie greeted Lillie when she got into the car, and nodded toward the BMW.

"No. I have a new three month let for the garret flat."

Lillie had designed the third floor into a comfortable and attractive living space complete with its own entrance at the back of the house. The flat contained a galley kitchen, cozy sitting room, and a bedroom with *en suite* bathroom that looked out onto the spacious back garden. Though it was not a problem to let, it had been recently empty.

"So you found someone?"

"They found me. Mr. Broadhouse. Very courteous, very quiet when he's in."

"The best sort for a let."

"He said the garret suited him. His wife and family are in Leeds, and he'll be visiting them often. He has extended business in Timsley."

"By the look of it," Berdie nodded toward the car again, "a rather prosperous business."

"Not short a bob or two." Lillie grinned and fastened her seatbelt. "Consulting, I believe he said, in engineering, if my memory serves me." Lillie paused a moment. "Still, it must be difficult to be away from family, all you hold dear."

"Yes, indeed." Berdie knew much about that as a

former military wife, and now with her children abroad.

"Speaking of all you hold dear, any sparkling conversation with Loren last night?" Berdie shot a glance at Lillie.

"We said good night at my door. Is that sparkling enough?" Lillie was not having this conversation. "I should think concern for Mrs. Mikalos is first priority." Lillie's words had snap.

But Lillie was right. Move on. Quickly, they were on the road.

"This is exhilarating." Lillie's voice danced. "There's such a sense of adventure in doing investigation work."

"It certainly can be when things are askew and you're the one who gets to set them in order, but it's primarily grinding and sometimes boring work."

"All I do is instruct music." The dance in Lillie's voice sat down.

"You're a fine teacher."

"And you are a marvelous crime solver as well as a positive role model for the church."

"By God's grace, on good days I'm a positive one," Berdie corrected.

"Hugh cares for an entire parish. Even Loren's job is crucial to the well-being of an entire city."

Berdie tipped her head. "OK, Lillie. Where are you going with this?"

"Well, no one can say life won't go on if there's no voice instruction, can they?"

Berdie glanced at her dearest friend who now looked out the car window. It was Monday, after all.

"Lillie, music is woven into the very fabric of our culture, our lives. Where would we be without Albert

Hall?"

Lillie sighed.

"And your work at the church, the choir is an incredibly vital part of worship and community life. How could we survive without it? There's just no one on earth who can do it as well as you." Berdie peeked again at Lillie, who had a slight smirk.

"OK, Berdie. Now you've over-egged the pudding."

"Look. It's the day after a very grand event into which you poured your heart. I should expect some let down."

"I suppose you're right."

"I find it rare when I'm not."

Now Lillie started to laugh. "So is today a positive role model day?"

Berdie chuckled. "We've work to do."

Lillie stared out the window then turned to Berdie. "What about Harriett Norman?"

"Oh, my word, I almost forgot about her." Berdie's mind quickly reviewed the woman's plea for help in locating her sister, if indeed, she had one. "No, Lillie, we can only pick fruit from one tree at a time, and we are in Mrs. Mikalos' orchard, which happens to be adjoined to our own back garden, so to speak. I'm afraid Harriet, whatever her situation, will have to wait."

"So what fruit will we pick today?" Lillie's perk was back.

"We'll interview neighbors, starting with the twitchy curtains opposite Mrs. Mikalos's home."

"Every road has a nosy citizen."

"Indeed, my dear Watson. Who called the fire brigade? Nosy neighbors can often times be an actual treasure trove of useless information that turns out to play a vital role."

"Well Sherlock, let's hope we discover a gem or two this morning."

"Can you ring Linden and ask if he knows Miss Curtain's number? And if so, could he ring her to make her aware we're coming?"

It seemed only a skip and jump in time before they arrived at the lovely home across the road from the Mikalos residence.

"Mrs. Billie Finch," Lillie said as they moved along the flagstone walk flanked with delicate pink cow parsley. The verdant garden was well kept and invited an extended look around.

As Berdie took it all in, the front door opened.

"My husband's the gardener," the smiling Mrs. Billie Finch said. "The back garden is even prettier. Please come in. I have a pot of tea brewing."

"Thank you, Mrs. Finch. I'm Berdie Elliott, and this is Lillie Foxworth."

"Please, call me Billie."

Mrs. Finch had hair that was more blonde than brown and it curled under just above her shoulders. It haloed her pleasant face which was graced with the lightest brown eyes and highlighted with blushed cheeks and rosy lipstick. She quickly led the way to the drawing room just off the hall. "My husband spends most of the week in London. But when he's home, he's pottering in his garden."

"It's lovely," Lillie offered.

The room was a bit stuffy for Berdie's tastes, but Mrs. Finch brought warmth to it nonetheless. The hostess waved her hand toward the white sofa. "Please, sit down." She indicated the chairs on either side of a gleaming tea service on the coffee table.

"Milk and sugar?"

"Yes, please." Berdie responded.

"Just milk." Lillie nodded courteously.

"It's nice to have guests for tea." Mrs. Finch sat in an overstuffed chair that matched the sofa and poured dark liquid into cups sitting properly on saucers wearing painted spring blooms. "Our Caroline's gone off to St. Monica's this year. The house used to bustle with her friends."

"Yes, I understand. My Clare and Nick both live abroad now."

"They grow up, more's the pity." Mrs. Finch handed full cups to Berdie and Lillie.

"Did Linden tell you why we're here?" Berdie was even toned.

"Not entirely." Billie took a sip of tea.

Berdie shot a glance at Lillie who raised her brows.

"How well do you know Mrs. Mikalos?"

"Mrs. Mikalos? She keeps to herself for the most part. We sometimes chat in passing as neighbors do. It's not much more than that." She stirred the liquid in her cup. "I invite her every year to my holiday lunch the week of Christmas, but it hasn't been but the last two years, since her husband died, that she has come."

"When was the last time you saw her?" Berdie brought the tea cup to her lips.

"Yesterday morning. Her son-in-law came in a rather scruffy people carrier to fetch her. She seemed, I don't know, irritated."

"Did you speak to her?"

"No."

"But you have a good view from your sitting room window."

The woman pulled back a bit. She paused and looked at the floor. "I keep my windows quite clean, yes."

Lillie was mid-sip of her tea but Berdie could see the grin that played the edges of her mouth.

"We think Mrs. Mikalos may have gone missing," Berdie said with gentle firmness.

Billie's eyes enlarged and tea caught in her throat sending her into a coughing frenzy. She bent forward and brought her hand to her mouth, plopping her tea cup on the tray. "I knew it," she croaked, "and I should think so, too." Her face flushed. "I should have called the police."

Berdie sat her tea down. "What are you talking about, Mrs…Billie?"

"Saturday night." She jumped to her feet. "Sir Percival-wretched-Barlow, indeed."

Lillie just gazed at the woman, taken aback. But Berdie stood and came to Mrs. Finch's side.

Billie pointed her finger in the direction of the front road. "Didn't I see him threaten Olivia?"

"Threaten, how?"

Billie shook her head. "It was dusk, and I was reading in the sitting room. My husband had to stay in London this weekend." She swallowed and a light mist formed in her eyes.

"Go on," Berdie urged.

"Well, it was a lovely night, and I had my window open. I heard this horrible shouting out in the road, something about property, accusations of stealing ancestral rights." She sniffed. "I went to the window and saw Olivia and our neighbor, Sir Percival Barlow. I don't know what it was all about, but it was a horrible dust up."

"Billie, why don't you sit?"

Mrs. Finch nodded and returned to the chair.

Berdie bent next to her and placed her hand on her arm. "I realize this may be difficult, but please try to recall as much as possible."

"Sir Percival grabbed Olivia by the arm."

Lillie pulled a tissue from her bag and gave it to Mrs. Finch.

"Thank you," she acknowledged and put it to her nose. "He called her horrible names and shouted that one way or another, he would get what he wanted and she would regret the day she didn't listen to him."

"And then?"

"Well, then a car turned onto the road and he pulled away and let go of her arm. He marched back to his property and she to hers."

"You're sure that's all that happened?"

"That's all I saw. And I've not seen Sir Percival since." Droplets spilled from Billie's eyes. "I was alone and frightened. I had no idea it could lead to...poor Olivia."

Berdie stood and put her hand on Billie's shoulder. "We don't yet know for certain that she's in harm's way, and there's no hard evidence that Sir Percival has anything to do with it."

Billie just nodded her head.

"What you've given us is extremely helpful, and we know you wish the best for Mrs. Mikalos. At this point it would seem prayer on her behalf is something we can all do to help." Berdie nodded toward Lillie, who rose.

"We need to make more enquiries, Billie. And please call the vicarage at St. Aidan of the Woods Church if you see anything at all out of the ordinary around Mrs. Mikalos's home or if something else comes to mind that you think may be helpful. Now, are you going to be all right?"

"Yes, yes." Billie stood. "I'm sorry for carrying on. It's just such a shock that Olivia could be in danger."

"Thank you for your concern. Oh, yes, Billie, did you by chance call the fire brigade last night?"

The woman wiped her nose again. "No, why would I do that?"

"Just wondered," Berdie said. "We can see ourselves out."

"I won't hear of it. It's the least I can do."

Billie led Berdie and Lillie to her door and outside.

Two loud booms, gunshots, broke the morning breeze.

Lillie fired a glance at Berdie. "Is that what I think it is?"

"He's at it again." Mrs. Finch took a quick breath.

"He?" Berdie asked.

"Sir Percival. He's an avid sportsman, a bit too attached to his guns for my liking."

"What's he shooting?" Lillie was approaching breathlessness.

As if Sir Percival heard her question, a large black creature smacked the ground just inside Olivia Mikalos's garden.

"Oh, my heavens." Berdie eyed the fallen prey.

Black feathers floated down in a divine eulogy.

"We've been having problems with kytes," Mrs. Finch informed, "and it seems he's waging war with them."

"They can be bullies when it comes to the avian world, but I see no need for this." Berdie scanned the horizon.

A man emerged from the adjoining garden to Mrs. Mikalos's. The areas were separated by a tall fence that ran the length of the two neighboring properties.

"There he is," Billie uttered and stepped back inside the door. "Perhaps you should come in the house."

"I need to speak to him." Berdie thrust her chin forward.

"Did I get it?" Sir Percival Barlow yelled when he saw the women. His voice was much larger than his slender frame. His dark hair outlined a face that would have been rather handsome if he hadn't such a scowl. A disengaged shotgun hung in the crook of his arm. This, along with forceful footsteps, announced he was not one to be fooled with.

"You did, sir." Berdie nodded to the spot where the bird dropped.

"Blasted creatures."

"Are we really going to talk to him?" Lillie squeaked as they started cross the road. "I mean is it really our place?"

"Lillie, go to the car if you like."

"In for a penny, in for a pound."

"Shoulders back. Walk with confidence." Berdie took fearsome strides.

Lillie was just slightly behind as they approached the man.

"Quite a shot, I should think," Berdie offered the fellow.

"Some say." He ran his gaze over Berdie and Lillie. "You're not from round here."

"Aidan Kirkwood," Berdie delivered with punch.

"And you're certainly not interested in my sporting skills. So what do you want?"

"We're friends of Olivia Mikalos." Berdie could feel Lillie grab her coat from behind. "Have you seen her recently?"

Sir Percival cocked his chin. "It takes a stupid cow to know a stupid cow."

Lillie's slender fingers went into a fist.

Berdie felt a flush rise along with her resolve. "No need to be rude, Sir Percival."

"I'll be the judge of that, and I'll be as rude as I please."

Berdie took a step backward, but went forward with another question. "Were you in Aidan Kirkwood yesterday?"

"No," he railed, "for what business it is of yours." His anger was in full throttle as he waved the disengaged barrel of the shotgun toward the road. "Now, clear off."

Berdie held back the verbal barrage she wanted to unleash on the boorish fellow, armed or not. Instead, she lifted her chin, and carefully backed up an additional few steps. She turned toward the car and walked in military strides of which she knew Hugh would have been proud.

Lillie was now beside her. "Horrible man," she whispered to Berdie.

When they reached the car, Berdie tried to calm herself. She got in the car but didn't shut the door. She noticed an insignia on the man's coat, *Seabrook Marina*.

When Lillie was safely seated inside, Berdie called to Sir Percival. "Next time, I suggest you shoot something that's not illegal." She slammed the door cutting off the sound of verbal abuse being heaped upon her.

"Really." Lillie's tone could have scorched wood.

Berdie glanced toward Billie's home and noticed the door was shut, and no doubt, locked tightly.

In seconds, Berdie was clear of the area.

"I'd say we deserve a good, strong cuppa and some of Villette's fresh scones," Lillie piped. "It feels as if we've put in a day's work and it's only elevensies."

Berdie nodded. "Copper Kettle, here we come. We've done only a bit of digging and look at what's already come up with the shovel."

5

Berdie crossed her arms as she and Lillie squeezed in with others standing outside awaiting a table at the Copper Kettle.

"It never used to be like this," Lillie huffed. "Even when she only had four tables it wasn't like this and on a week day, as well."

Two people entered, and Berdie advanced in the queue.

Lillie leaned near Berdie's ear. "Aidan Kirkwood grew by bounds when they put in the new-builds four years ago. The blow-ins arrived, and we've yet to be the same."

"To be fair, Lillie, it has brought an economic boost to the place. How many of your voice students are *blow-ins*?"

Lillie parted her lips as if to give a sharp response, but then stopped. "Point taken." Lillie's tone was much less pretentious.

"Hello, Mrs. Elliott, Lillie." Cara Donovan was in mid-stride in the road. The young woman's long, blonde hair fell across her shoulder in a single braid. Though Jamie's wife, and the mother of toddling Katy, her lovely figure and gracious facial features hadn't faded.

"Join us for tea?" Berdie invited.

"Should do if I weren't finding myself coming in the going."

Since Cara and Rosalie Preswood went into partnership and bought The White Window Box Garden and Gifts, the business had gone from a sleepy little backwater to a busy High Street shop.

Cara held up three wreaths looped through her arm. "It's our spring design. These are deliveries."

"I should take someone on to do your fetch and carry," Lillie blurted.

"They certainly wouldn't go spare." Cara offered a light laugh. "It's our bestseller ever, a mix of herbs and flowers." Cara gave a quick nod and a wave as she continued on her journey.

Lillie craned her neck. "That's the same style wreath we saw on Olivia Mikalos's front door."

"A gift, I remember Linden saying last evening." Berdie made note that she must find out just who the gift-giver may be.

"Step in," Villette interrupted Berdie's thoughts as she opened the shop door. She pointed to an emptied table for two.

The table was positioned between a larger table that seated six, one that seated four, and a cupboard, all of which were recent additions to the four tables originally in the shop. Villette had done a wee extension to the tiny space.

Still, Berdie had to squeeze past the open-fronted cupboard lined with tea tins and stacked china to get to her chair. "Trying to get a quart in a pint pot." Berdie inhaled as she squeezed through.

When she and Lillie sat, Villette was upon them.

"Tea for two," she stated, rather than asked. "Your usual." The words galloped from the lips of her horseshoe shaped face. "Fresh scones?" Villette pointed to the kitchen. "Out of the oven not more than five minutes."

"Yes, please. And some of your delicious clotted cream."

"And some handmade strawberry jam from Mr. Raheem's shop, as well." Berdie relaxed back into her chair.

Villette wrote the request on her pad and spun away to her duties.

"This will be a nice relief." Lillie leaned Berdie's direction and lowered her voice. "Considering all that's happened this morning concerning the vanished Mrs. Mikalos, do you think Sir Percival is tied up in her absence?"

"Early days, Lillie. We've got to establish that she's really missing before that question can possibly be answered."

"Do you think she is, missing, I mean?"

Berdie considered the question. "Yes, most likely."

"If she is, Sir Percival must be considered as a possible link." She glanced side to side as if their conversation was clandestine.

"It would seem a possibility."

"How do you establish that someone's missing, anyway? I mean, how do you find them?"

"Here we are, then." Villette transferred the goods on the laden tray to the table so quickly, the scones nearly took flight. "Hot this," she warned, splashing steaming drops from the teapot on the table. "Go on. Don't let me interrupt your conversation."

"These scones look delicious, Mrs. Horn," Berdie was wiser than to *go on* with her conversation. "I can imagine they don't stay about long."

The woman stood stick straight. "Not long, no."

"We will enjoy them, and thank you," Berdie said.

Lillie leaned as Villette whisked off to another table. "Not often she walks away from the table without some kind of tidbit to disperse." Lillie splashed milk in her tea. "So, tell me what you do."

"What?" Berdie eyed an especially large chunk of strawberry in the jam.

"How do you find someone who's missing?"

"Just briefly," Berdie said as she split her scone and ladled fresh cream onto her knife, "usually you have a picture to show about and jog peoples' minds, the more the better." She plopped the creamy delight atop the steaming scone and spread it until little rivulets dripped down the edge. The aroma sent Berdie's taste buds reeling. "You find the person or people who last saw the absentee, you look for an on-line footprint, and you check hospitals." Berdie thrust her knife into the rich red jam and came up with a substantial amount of glistening fruit that she piled on the cream covered scone. She raised the prepared masterpiece to her mouth.

"Yes, go on," Lillie demanded.

Berdie lowered the scone. "Well, you can interview family, and nose round: their homes and workplace, address books, personal gear, and find out if they are involved in any disputes, especially domestic." She again raised her treat upward.

"Like Sir Percival and Mrs. Mikalos," Lillie cut in before munching her own well-loaded scone.

"If you like." Berdie opened her mouth.

"And what if they've money?" Lillie wiped jam from her lip.

Berdie took a deep breath, holding the scone just above her plate. "In the case of money, find out who inherits." She could feel warm cream ooze around her fingers.

"My, Villette has outdone herself with these scones. But you haven't even tried them, yet."

Berdie bit into the waiting treasure. The mixture of the sweet fruit, velvety cream, and hot baked scone sent her into soaring delight. "M-m-m." She felt a touch of cream drip from her finger.

Villette was at the table again. "See here," Villette snapped. "You know about these things."

"What things?" Berdie wiped her mouth with the ironed pink napkin.

Villette pulled her head back and dangled a paper before Berdie's nose. "These things."

It was a photo of Olivia Mikalos.

Lillie gaped.

Villette whipped the paper back. "'Have you seen this person?' it says here." She squinted. "Olivia M-M."

"Have you seen her?" Berdie tried not to show her amazement at what was in Villette's hands.

"Should I have?"

"Where did you get this?" Berdie asked.

"Taped to my door when I arrived this morning."

"Are you going to display it?" Lillie pressed.

"Well, no. Look." Villette pointed to the word Mikalos. "She's Greek."

Berdie cleared her throat. "Mrs. Horn, need I remind you that the Duke of Edinburgh is of Greek origin. Surely, if he's good enough for the Queen, it's good enough for the likes of us."

Villette jutted her lower lip. "You know this woman, then?"

"We know her son-in-law." Lillie took another bite of scone.

"It's not an unusual practice to show photos of

missing persons," Berdie said.

"Well, it wasn't Goodnight gave this to me."

"He wouldn't," Lillie explained. "Mrs. Mikalos lives near Timsley."

"Timsley?" Villette shook her head.

"It appears our village is where she was last seen. At the fete, yesterday," Berdie clarified for the disgruntled woman.

Villette slammed the paper on the table, the picture of Olivia now sporting a jam smudge on her forehead. "You see what comes of having big to-dos in our village? Better to keep ourselves to ourselves."

The bell sounded and Hardeep Raheem, sporting his white work apron, entered. "Good morning, Mrs. Horn," he greeted, and then addressed all those in the shop. "Good morning, ladies and gentleman." Apart from wearing the most vibrant smile in the whole of the village, he held a box. Red-filled jam jars could be seen poking their heads just above the opening. Mr. Raheem stepped to the table. "Your order."

Villette unloaded the box from his hands and beat a hasty retreat.

He watched the withdrawing figure for a moment, but seemed to shrug off the abrupt behavior. "How nice to see you, Mrs. Elliott, Miss Foxworth."

"Would you like to join us, Mr. Raheem?" Berdie invited.

"The smell of fresh scones." He sniffed, making his infectious grin even larger. "And kind company. It is a tempting offer, but I have much work," he apologized in his slight Punjabi accent.

"More's the pity," Lillie sighed.

Mr. Raheem spied the photo on the table and picked it up. He studied the picture. "I've seen this woman."

Berdie felt a tingle. "When, where?"

"At the fete, on the green, yesterday." He nodded his head. "Yes, it was definitely her. A very striking woman."

"Mr. Raheem, this is important." Berdie had to calm her words. "Please tell us exactly what you saw."

"Is she your friend?"

"I know a family member."

He shrugged, still looking at the photo. "I was delivering the last of my sugar to the refreshment table. Did you know we ran out of the sugar?"

"Mr. Raheem," Lillie interrupted, "what did you see?"

"It happened so quickly. She and two other people talked together over cups of lemonade. I should say the two with her looked to be man and wife?"

"The two people weren't familiar to you?" Berdie asked.

Mr. Raheem placed the paper on the table. "No. They're not at my store, I've never seen them."

Berdie took a breath to ask her next question.

But Lillie beat her to the punch.

"What did they look like?"

"Older, kind looking." He paused. "The man had a very distinct tie." He furrowed his brow as if to stimulate his memory. "It was blue? Yes, with white and gold diagonal lines."

Villette stepped into the conversation with cash in hand. "Here you are, Mr. Raheem. Paid in full."

Mr. Raheem bobbed his head. "Thank you, Mrs. Horn."

"I'm sure you've much to do." Villette's tone seemed to be all but pushing the fellow out the door.

"Mrs. Elliott, Miss Foxworth. I pray all is well for your friend."

"Thank you, Mr. Raheem." Berdie watched the good man retreat.

"Comes in here wearing his work apron." Villette crossed her arms. "Mr. Raheem knows her, then, that Greek woman."

"Simply saw her. Does not know her," Berdie corrected as she picked up the photo copy. "May we take this?"

"Put it in the rubbish bin if you like," was her curt response before moving on to another table.

Berdie began to place tiny fragments together in her mind that formed a very blurry and incomplete picture. Of what she wasn't sure, but something was beginning to take shape. "Burnt roast, Dracula, Barlow, old couple." She wrinkled her brow. "And Christmastide lunch with Billie Finch."

"What are you on about?" Lillie took another bite of scone.

"We need to talk to Linden about this." Berdie thrust the paper forward. "Did he put this on the Copper Kettle door?"

****

"Can't you go faster?" Lillie seemed keen as mustard.

Usually her best friend asked her to slow down. "I'm doing ten miles an hour over the limit now. Why the rush?"

Lillie tossed a loose curl back with a quick jerk of her head. "Speed suits me."

"Does it?" Berdie hid an interior grin. Perhaps the

encounter with Sir Percival emboldened her dear friend to fresh daring.

The lovely rural road that led to Mistcome Green through open meadows and occasional hedgerows invited quick travel. "We're almost there."

In minutes, they arrived at the road lined with small terraced houses, the third one being home to the Linden Davies family. A single clematis with only a few blooms struggled upward on the wall by the front window, joined by overgrown shrubs that wandered carelessly across the path. Quite unlike the Finch landscape, an occasional foxglove labored to bloom.

After a quick *hello* and a *please sit down*, from Linden they got right to it.

"I've got to go back to work in a few minutes." Linden rubbed his hands as he sat.

Lillie and Berdie were seated on a sofa that all but swallowed them.

"They were kind enough to give me the morning off."

Unlike Mrs. Finch, Linden didn't offer any cordial refreshments. The jam smears on the furniture announced that there were children in the home, and the front window showed water stains on the top corners.

"Right, no need to go around the houses." Berdie pulled his mother-in-law's picture from her purse and held it up. "Did you put this on the door of the Copper Kettle in Aidan Kirkwood?"

"It's Mother." Linden looked shocked. "No, no, I didn't."

"In truth, it's a fine first step for locating someone. But you've nothing to do with it?"

"No." Linden still wore amazement. "Who did?"

"I was hoping you might tell us."

Linden shook his head.

"Actually, quite by accident, we have gotten a small bit of information from the photo already."

"Have you?"

"Mr. Raheem, the green grocer in Aidan Kirkwood, saw your mother at the fete speaking with an older couple."

Linden's brows rose.

"The gentleman had a distinctive tie, blue with gold and white stripes." Lillie ran her finger up and down the bodice of her dress.

"Any idea who the older couple may be, friends?" Berdie waited.

Linden rubbed his forehead. "Not really. Mother certainly had friends her age and older, but none I really know."

"Surely you've met some," Lillie stated.

"Has she spoken of any activities with friends?" Berdie watched the man rub his forehead again as if it were a magic lamp that would produce some genie of memory.

"Mrs. Finch, perhaps. And there's that boorish neighbor of Mother's, although he could hardly be considered a friend."

Berdie and Lillie exchanged glances.

"There was that fellow she was seeing when we moved here. Mr. Long-something, was it?"

"Longmont?" Lillie suggested.

"Longhurst. That was it. Not that it matters. The whole thing seemed to be over before it started. We met him once. Nice chap, I 'spose."

Berdie's sense of loose ends danced. "Was it an amicable split?"

"I don't know that there was really anything to split. Just saw him the once." Linden's brows elevated as if a light had turned on. "I remember she spoke of visiting a sports club with someone."

"And?"

He shook his head. "That's it, really."

"What about relatives?"

"She had a brother who died in childhood. There's a few far flung overseas in-laws. Apart from that, her son, Myles, Elise's brother, lives in Reading."

"Have you contacted him?"

"Oh, yes. He's not seen nor heard from her."

"Did your mother-in-law have any active on-line interests?" Berdie asked.

"I'm not sure she even knows where her computer is. Her husband used it."

"Excuse me, Linden." Lillie tipped her head. "Is that the sum total of what you know of your mother-in-law's dealings?"

Linden stood. He stepped to the window, hands behind his back, and looked onto the narrow road.

"Linden?" Berdie urged as much as questioned.

He turned back to Berdie, and then glanced at Lillie. "Please treat the information I'm giving you as strictly confidential."

"Of course," Berdie assured as Lillie nodded.

"My mother-in-law is a very private person. And it's really not for me to say, so much as my wife's." He stepped closer. "It's just that Olivia and Elise, my wife, have not had what one might consider an especially close relationship for some time now."

"I see." Berdie laid the photocopy on the arm of the couch.

"About a year ago, things seemed to improve

between them, and I thought it could be an opportunity to mend fences, especially for our children's sake. So, at my urging, we moved here to be closer to Olivia. I found a job in Timsley, at only half my former wage. Still, we decided to up sticks, and here we are."

"A rather large adjustment." Berdie wondered how much of a mend would be worth the financial sacrifice.

"The choirmaster position at St. Matthew," Lillie leaned forward. "Feeble pay as it is, you took it for the money?"

"I appreciate the stipend," Linden nodded. "It's enjoyable work. And pennies become pounds."

"Of course." Lillie looked at the worn carpet in front of her.

"And I imagine restoring the relationship of your wife and mother has had its own rewards." Berdie mined more than stated.

"Ah." Linden tapped his fingers on his knee. "Not so much."

"Yes?"

"Not long after we arrived here, Olivia and Elise had a rather large disagreement that made a real mess of things. My wife wanted to move back to Manchester, but I had hoped they could work it out." Linden sat in the chair again.

"All mothers and daughters go through periods of difficulty." Berdie spoke from experience.

"It being only a period of difficulty has about as much chance as a mid-Atlantic rowboat."

The considerable noise of the front door opening was followed by clattering and a child's laughter in the hall.

A fair-haired girl who looked to be about five years old rushed into the sitting room and climbed onto Linden's lap. "Daddy," she squealed with obvious delight as he wrapped his arms around her.

"Daddy?" Elise Davies entered the room, her dark brows knit, carrier bags in hand. "Why aren't you at work?"

Linden put his daughter on the floor as he stood. "Elise, this is Berdie Elliott and Lillie Foxworth."

The woman didn't smile.

Linden put his hand on his daughter's shoulder. "And this is Madeline."

The small girl, unlike her mother, wore a shy grin. She leaned against her father's leg.

"Hello Madeline," Berdie addressed and turned to the sullen wife. "Mrs. Davies."

Elise lifted her brows and gave a terse tip of the head to Berdie. The small-framed woman had her mother's cheek bones. The golden brown hair, straight and parted down the middle, stopped just above her fine chin line, also a motherly inheritance. But the rest of her facial features were apparently contributed by Mr. Mikalos: small eyes, razor thin nose, and considerable lips. "You're *Miss* Foxworth?"

Lillie gave a cautious nod. "Hello, Mrs. Davies."

She threw a sharp glance toward her husband. "What's all this in aid of?"

Linden pressed his lips together tightly at the same moment Elise spied the photocopy of Mrs. Mikalos on the arm of the couch.

"Mother." Elise spit the word out. "Madeline, there's a little raspberry tart in the kitchen just waiting to be eaten. Please take Mummy's bags, as well."

The little girl released her father's leg, took the

carrier bags, and romped out of the room.

Elise tipped her head, put her hands on her hips, and eyed Berdie. "Well, I can tell you where she is."

Berdie was curious, but not overwhelmed. "Yes?"

"I shouldn't waste time worrying about her. She's closeted herself away in some grand hotel, probably in a coastal area, to sulk and make my husband fret over her." She cast an eye on Linden and back to Berdie. "Create as much fuss as possible, that's her game. She'll do anything for attention."

"Elise!" Linden snapped.

Berdie worked to take in this brassy suggestion. "Has she done this before?"

Elise cocked her head. "It doesn't mean she wouldn't now."

"Elise, please." Linden was stern.

"Mrs. Davies, I don't know your mother well, but I do know she intended to return home after the fete." Berdie was steady. "I believe something or someone may have prevented her."

Linden sunk back into the chair. "Oh, no, I feared this was the case."

Elise almost smirked. "Pull the other one."

"Your mother intended to return because," Berdie raised an index finger, "she was looking forward to a Sunday lunch roast. Would she be willing to burn down her house for a good sulk?" She raised her next finger alongside. "Knowing how your son feels about his cat, would she leave it to starve and die?" She raised the next finger. "Your mother obviously takes pride in her appearance. Would she leave makeup, clothing, sleepwear, behind? Her handbag with all the essentials: money, credit card, and so on, was in the people carrier from yesterday morning." Berdie counted off the points on her fingers and raised her brows. "And I certainly wouldn't think she would disregard her medication. Although going into a coma would certainly, as you say, get someone's attention."

Elise lifted her chin. "What do you know about my mother's sleepwear or medication?"

Berdie put her hand down. "Are any of the facts I've just given you concerning your mother not true?"

The woman swallowed hard and rubbed her hand. "Phillip will be home any minute. I need to get his lunch on." She turned and left the room.

"I'm sorry about this. Elise is a bit out of sorts," Linden apologized. "Listen, I really must push off."

"Things most often turn out well in these cases when action is taken quickly." Berdie hoped to induce Linden into more action, as well as giving a sense that someone was in his corner. His wife didn't appear to be. "I don't see the police being in any rush, so we'll need to be the boots on the ground, ourselves."

"I so appreciate your help."

"We'll check local doctors, hospitals, surgeries, and such."

Linden dropped his head and nodded.

"I presume your mother has a mobile. Was it in her bag?"

"Yes."

"Your job is to contact all her listed numbers; mobile and address book. Telephone the lot to see if anyone has heard from her or has any information."

"Yes, I'll do that."

Berdie and Lillie both stood.

"At some point," Berdie discreetly took the photocopy, "perhaps I could contact Myles, as well. And I must speak to your wife in more detail. I should think the sooner the better."

"You can see at this point she's not having it, but I'll try to talk with her." Linden glanced at his watch.

"We'll see our way out." Lillie was already in motion and Berdie fell in beside her.

"Thank you," Linden called to the departing women. "I'll ring if I find anything."

"Anything at all, Linden, ring me," Berdie said.

She and Lillie waded through the overgrowth to get to the car.

"Harriett Norman lives here in Mistcome. Let's go see her," Lillie had a twinkle in her eye.

"Lillie, I've already told you we need to focus on Mrs. Mikalos."

"Seems a shame, since we're both here."

"In the car, if you please."

When she and Lillie were seated and belted in, Berdie turned the key. The engine was not the only thing whirling. "Tell me, Lillie, what do you think of all that in there?"

"You were marvelous. All your deductions."

"That's not what I'm talking about." Berdie pulled onto the road. "What did you think of Mrs. Davies?"

"Well, the few moments I saw Mrs. Mikalos she did not strike me as being attention seeking."

"Nor I. In fact quite the opposite. She came across as one who was reserved, an air of confident purpose."

Lillie tipped her head. "Do you think, for some reason, Elise Davies is jealous of her mother?"

"Olivia's an attractive woman. And she certainly has Linden's attention." Berdie turned onto the main road to Aidan Kirkwood. "But, is it about what her mother *is*?" She tapped her finger on the steering wheel. "Or perhaps what Olivia *has* that's a problem."

"Has?"

"Money, my dear Lillie." Berdie answered without hesitation. "Who stands to inherit? I should say Elise and her brother."

Lillie's hazel-green eyes grew wide. "A child wouldn't do such a thing to a parent. Never."

"I should hope not, but the Davies family seems to be financially down, and it wouldn't be the first time a member of the family has been poisoned by greed."

Music sounded from Berdie's handbag.

Lillie stared at it.

"Oh, bother. Could you please get it, Lillie?"

"What is it?" She continued to stare.

"It's my mobile, of course. I downloaded a musical ringtone. On my own, I might add." Berdie felt rather proud of her technological stretch as she directed a hand to fumble with her bag. The car veered as she reached.

"Yes, I'll get it." Lillie opened the bag, and a heavy blues guitar accompanied a rough voice blasted. "You selected 'The Thrill is Gone' for your ringtone?" .

"I didn't exactly get the song I was going for."

Lillie burst into laughter. "I should say."

"It's by a Mr. King or something."

Lillie's laughter went up a decible. "You better hope Hugh doesn't hear it. He'll think the worst."

"Yes, all right, Lillie, just answer it, please."

Lillie worked to somewhat compose herself. "Mrs. Elliott's house of blues, this is Lillie," she answered with a chuckle. Lillie lost the laughter and her eyes went into a squint. "Who is this?" She fell silent and moved the mobile from her ear, turning it off.

"Who is it?"

"Someone with a very deep, breathy voice." Lillie

pressed some numbers.

"Oh, yes?"

"No Berdie, that was weird." Lillie made a hoarse inhale and graveled out, "Mrs. Elliott?" and waited. She put the mobile to her ear. "Number withheld," she informed Berdie. She sat the phone in her lap.

"Some bored child playing sick at home on a spring Monday afternoon."

"A child who knows it's your mobile phone number."

The phone began its blues guitar once again.

Berdie scooped up the instrument and answered. "Now see here, you little gremlin," Berdie began with a firm voice.

"Berdie?" It was Hugh. "What are you going on about?"

"Oh, hello, love." Berdie did a sideward glance toward Lillie, who smothered a giggle. "I thought you were a wayward lad."

"Yes? Well, since I'm vicar, wayward lad would never do."

"No." Berdie chortled.

"That aside, where are you?"

"Perhaps ten minutes outside Aidan."

"Good. We've been invited by Mr. Webb to join him this afternoon at his sports club, kind of a job-well-done for yesterday's events. I told him we'd love to."

"What?" Berdie grimaced. "Hugh." Her grip on the steering wheel tightened. "I'm driving. I really must go."

"Berdie," Hugh clipped. "This is an extremely gracious offer. We're doing this and I expect you at home in ten minutes."

"Yes, goodbye." Berdie squashed the mobile into

her handbag as if to bury it. "Hugh and I have been invited to Mr. Webb's club this afternoon." She sighed. "Or should I say, we're going to Mr. Webb's club this afternoon."

"I can think of worse things to do." Lillie pointed a finger toward Berdie. "You keep protesting that you get so little time with Hugh. Here's a chance. Why so up in the air?"

Berdie looked at Lillie. "Olivia Mikalos, of course, so much to get done."

"I can do the donkey work. I know I'm not a technical wizard of your standing, but I can ring up the hospitals." Lillie grinned. "Besides, who knows, a club visit could be great fun, especially since the thrill is gone."

"Oh Lillie, let it go." Berdie half barked, half laughed, and sped on to the village.

6

"Where are we exactly?" Hugh sounded impatient.

"I thought we were on Seabrook Gardens. However, seeing that we're not entering the club grounds," she pointed toward a dead end in front of them, "that's wrong." Berdie slightly angled the opened map of Timsley and pulled her glasses down her nose.

Hugh slowed the car. "We're not familiar with this part of Timsley."

"Mr. Webb said it was a labyrinth of streets to get to the club when he offered to lead the way," Berdie huffed. "Who was it that said, 'You go on, Grayson, we'll find our way there just fine, no problem'?"

Hugh pulled the car to the side of the road. "You're in a mood." Hugh's left eyebrow elevated as he took the map from Berdie.

"Well." Berdie scooted closer to the passenger door. She had worked at making this a pleasant outing even though she wasn't particularly keen on going, but when she discovered that this club was noted for its swimming pool, it put her off the idea even more. She didn't relish exposing her aging, dimpled thighs in her faded swimming costume. It was Hugh who loved water sports, not she. Swimming was his exercise regime. He had rowed on a team, and served as a naval officer. He was part fish. For herself, a few random scales, perhaps, were the extent of her marine likeness.

"We're very close to the club, we must be." Hugh popped the opened map as if ironing out the wrinkles would make their misdirection manifest.

Expansive, white semi-detached homes with lovely gardens, built in the thirties by the look of it, shone bright in the late afternoon sun, much unlike her cloudy manner.

A Land Rover pulled to the side of the road just in front of them.

"Perhaps he's lost, too," Berdie quipped and crossed her arms.

Hugh eyed the map. "What street are we on?"

"One that's a dead end."

"I can see that. What's the name?" Hugh ran a finger down the guide.

Berdie made a quick glance about. "I haven't a clue."

"Well, what's the house number?"

A well-manicured house across from them boasted a beautiful tree whose graceful topiary begged her admire it longer, but intent on her task, she inspected the house carefully and saw no numbers. "The numbers must have fallen off," she said flatly.

"What, all of them?" Hugh's voice was much louder than it needed to be.

"Oh, for heaven's sake." Berdie's acerbic tone was not for heaven's sake at all. She opened the car door.

Hugh glanced from the map. "What are you doing?"

Berdie didn't answer. She slammed the door, and walked briskly to the Land Rover. She tapped on the window.

The driver studied her. It was obvious, despite his

sunglasses, that he possessed an unusually confident air. His square chin, well-trimmed goatee, and attractive build had a certain appeal.

Berdie pushed a strand of misbehaving hair from near her eye and became extremely aware of the over-sized gently used athletic gear from St. Mark's Bring and Buy that draped her body.

The closed window opened just a slit. "Yes?" His tone sounded like dark melting chocolate.

Had she seen him on television? "Such a lovely tree," she stammered and pointed to the garden where it stood.

"Yes, it is. Decorative olive tree." He nodded with a half grin.

"Oh, yes?" Berdie felt pink rise to her cheeks.

The man tapped a rapid finger on his steering wheel. "Is there something...?"

"Oh yes, my husband and I are lost." Berdie pointed toward Hugh and the car. "Do you know what road we're on?"

The fellow smiled, nodded, and pointed to the road sign at the top of the street.

Berdie gave it a rapid glance and immediately felt quite silly. "Oh, yes." She could feel the pink of her cheeks go vivid red and blanket her entire face. "Thank you." She had never in her life moved so quickly to get away from a vehicle. "Such a lovely tree? Where on earth did that come from?" she chastised under her breath. She shook her head. She had been imprudent and rather impetuous, plus, she allowed the fellow's charm to put her off balance. She climbed back into the passenger seat.

The map was on the floor, and Hugh held his new phone, a gift from Nick. "Well?" he asked without malice.

Berdie simply nodded toward the not-easily-seen-from-the-passenger-seat road sign.

"Yes, well spotted." Hugh smothered a chuckle.

There was no real need to be sharp. Not really. Hugh simply wanted her to be a part of his afternoon, aging thighs and all. Rather generous, all things considered. And, really, getting lost was just an adventure. She leaned back into the seat and admired the exotic tree designed in an Oriental style that sat in the front garden of the numberless house.

A well-dressed woman approached the home. She shoved something through the door's letterbox, turned immediately, and left. It tickled Berdie's curiosity. Why didn't she knock? What did she slip into the slot? Money? An invitation? A ransom note?

"I should have thought of this straight away." Hugh's finger danced on the phone screen.

"Yes, love."

The door of the house opened and a man burst forward. Though he carried himself well in his suit and tie, he had a face like thunder. What had that woman introduced into that mail slot? Berdie almost expected steam to rise from the man's dogged steps as he made way to a rather fancy-looking car.

"Ah, I think I may have it sorted," Hugh said with great pleasure.

The agitated fellow entered his vehicle, started and revved the engine, made a sharp, illegal U-turn, and raced up the road like a fox with hounds on his tail. The moment he turned the top corner the other car in the lane rocketed off and followed as if in pursuit.

"That's a bit odd."

"Not at all," Hugh grinned and lifted his phone.

"I'm learning how to navigate this quite well."

"That's not what..." Berdie paused. It wasn't worth pursuing. "Jolly good."

The door to the intriguing home swung open once again. A couple stepped just outside.

Berdie puzzled, and then familiarity struck. "Hugh, aren't they the cat people?" She pointed.

He took a quick glance at the doorway. "Cat people? Oh, the Stanfords. Yes, they mentioned being in Timsley. You've met them, then."

"Not exactly."

Hugh nodded as he returned to his exploration. "They're developing another feline shelter, quite comprehensive, by the sounds of it. Came calling for a parish donation to their cause. Very dedicated to the rescue and keeping of cats."

Berdie furrowed her forehead. "Odd."

"I shouldn't think so, especially if you're the cat."

It would be no good trying to tell Hugh all that had been going on while he continued to master his technological toy.

The couple craned their necks to look up and down the street. As quickly as they appeared, they disappeared behind the closed door of their house.

Hugh stretched out his hand and set it on Berdie's knee. "I realize we should probably make ourselves known to them, but we're already quite late. We need to push on."

Berdie pulled her thoughts away from the house goings-on and put her full attention onto her husband. "Yes, push on. I'm sure they didn't even notice."

He took her hand. "I should have followed Grayson. I'm sorry for all this mess."

Berdie gave a squeeze. "And I should be less ratty

as well."

Hugh leaned over and placed a peck on her cheek. "Now, look straight on." He nodded forward. "Past the end of this road and the little fence, to the bowling green, the cricket pavilion, and the large building just beyond."

Berdie strained forward. "Very tidy, pretty grounds."

Hugh wore a smile. "Right."

"Snap! It's the sports club." Berdie looked over her shoulder and back at the sight. "I had us back to front."

Hugh held up his phone. "And in approximately four to five minutes, we'll be right way around."

"So, technically speaking, I did get us to the club."

"If you give *technically* a massive stretch, yes."

"Well, there you are. I do have a certain technical prowess."

Hugh chuckled and shook his head. "Whatever you say, love." With that, he pulled the car into the road.

****

The swim was enjoyable and had left her a bit languid, but happy to be with Hugh.

They had no problem getting home. And now, dinner done, Berdie snuggled next to Hugh while watching an old black and white film.

It was nice to spend these rare moments relaxing together. As they watched the story of a courageous mother and wife who braved the storms of the home front in World War II, Berdie could not dismiss the odd happenings she witnessed that afternoon on the street that was *not* Seabrook Gardens. They tumbled about her mind and dug into corners of her brain.

She wondered at the possibility that she and Hugh, in being lost, may not have been squarely in the middle of where they were supposed to be at that moment. She had a sense of that, and yet it seemed silly, not a reasoned idea.

A home in Timsley, nicely dressed people, a something slipped into the letterbox, an angry gentleman, an impressive car, a handsome man who put her spinning, who raced after the other car, and the cat couple: hardly a congruent line of logic. Yet, an idea had come into her thinking. Could the Stanfords be the last people to have seen Olivia? They were an older couple, and he had worn a distinctive tie. Many people from Timsley had come to the event and they had been at the church during preparations.

"I must seek the matter out," she muttered.

"You say something, love?" Hugh asked.

With the ferocity of a sudden clap of thunder in a spring storm, the vicarage doorbell invaded the treasured moment.

Hugh sighed.

"I'll get it." Berdie pulled away and made way to the front door, deciding not to grumble, but cherish the past uninterrupted hours shared with Hugh. "Lillie," Berdie greeted her unexpected guest at the opened door. "Come in."

"Must get on, but just wanted to tell you that Mrs. Mikalos was not seen by any local doctors nor admitted to any of the area hospitals, including their morgues."

"Well done, Lillie." Berdie looked past Lillie's shoulder to see Granville Morrison and his idling black car with the word *Transport* painted on the side. He and his brother were the newest entrepreneurs in Aidan Kirkwood's village services. "Having dinner with Loren in Timsley? Setting out plans for the Aunt Margaret visit, are we?"

A blues guitar reverberated from Berdie's bag in the hallway at the same moment Granville sounded his horn.

Lillie turned in a flash. "I'll tell you all about it later," she called while walking briskly to the taxi.

"Good, I'll look forward to it." Berdie closed the door and lunged toward her bag just in time to hear Hugh's voice.

"What is that?" he called.

Berdie grabbed her mobile and put it to her ear.

"Mrs. Elliott." A hoarse gasp of air. "She's in danger," the graveled voice caller was no playful lad.

"Who's in danger?" Berdie tried to keep her wits about her.

"She's in danger," the wheezing caller repeated. "No police."

"Who is this?" Berdie hoped she didn't sound alarmed.

A coarse wheeze and a click were the only response.

"Who was at the door?" Hugh asked as he bounced into the hallway.

Berdie shoved her mobile in her bag. "Lillie," she worked at appearing nonchalant. "She's already gone."

"Are you all right?"

Hugh's question bored into Berdie's veneer, but she held her own. "I just hope Lillie and Loren get on well at Aunt Margaret's."

"Someone on the mobile?" He pointed to her bag.

Berdie was not about to tell him the whole of it. "I

have no clue who the person was." She laughed hoping Hugh would not catch the nervous edge of it.

He smiled. "Oh, I had one of those the other day."

"You did?"

"Some bank, I think it was a survey. Those computer generated calls, so garbled and impersonal. Invasive, as well."

"Yes, invasive," she improvised.

"Care for a cuppa?"

"Splendid." She could use one.

"I'll put the kettle on." Hugh advanced toward the kitchen.

Berdie sank to the bottom step of the hall stairway. She pulled her mobile out and tried to retrieve the call but it showed as *number withheld*. "She's in danger, no police," she repeated the words to herself. "Dear Lord, have mercy."

****

Despite the warm morning sun, Berdie pulled up the collar of her short spring coat as a light gust of wind wrapped its cool fingers round her neck. She took a sip of the tea that filled the cup of her flask. "Anytime now, Linden, I've got a church committee meeting in just under an hour," she said to keep her senses awake.

His call earlier this morning was brief, but his voice held a sense of urgency when he asked her to meet him here at Olivia's house. And now he was late.

She hoped the brown liquid would give her a jolt of energy. She hadn't slept especially well last night. "She's in danger. Lord, protect her," Berdie had prayed in the night. "No police means it's up to me." Then a gentle reminder floated through her semi-consciousness. "That is, rather, You and me."

Another wisp of wind urged her to take a larger gulp of warm tea. She considered getting inside the car, but decided the coolness was keeping her attentive. Pulling her mobile from her coat pocket, she telephoned Lillie, only to get her voice mail. "Probably packing, or already off." Berdie pushed the mobile back in her pocket.

She felt as if someone watched her. She turned toward the Finch house. Ah, yes. Berdie waved at the inquisitive Billie Finch, who stood at her large sitting room window still in her dressing gown. The woman hastily returned the wave and scurried off.

"Linden's late, but Mrs. Finch is dead on time." Berdie leaned against the car and scanned the street where wheely bins sat on the garden edges, waiting for the dustcart to grind its way up the road and collect a week's waste.

An especially forceful gust of wind lifted the lid atop the wheely bin at the edge of Sir Percival's garden and scattered rubbish everywhere.

"Oh, bother." Placing her tea on the bonnet of the car, still warm from engine heat beneath it, Berdie chased after the loose papers that fluttered near her. She gathered the newspaper sheets, a take away menu, numerous carrier bags, and stuffed them back in the bin. In doing so, something caught her eye. In bright red letters *Joe's DIY* was printed on one of the carrier bags.

Berdie pulled it back out. The bag was clean despite being in the rubbish. "That's Joe Lawler's tiny do-it-yourself home repair shop in Aidan Kirkwood. Why is it in Barlow's rubbish?"

A car turned onto the road and stopped just behind hers.

Berdie quickly stuffed the plastic in her coat pocket and tightly closed the lid of the bin.

Linden emerged from the car followed by a small lad. "Sorry I'm late," he apologized. "This is my nine-year-old son, Phillip. Phillip, this is Mrs. Elliott."

The lad's brown-blond hair did a little salute as the wind whipped past. "Good morning," he said with no luster.

"Hello, Phillip." Berdie smiled.

The fellow looked a bit peaky.

"Phillip stayed home from school today with tummy ache," Linden explained, "but he felt well enough to come with me." He winked.

"I'm helping Daddy find Tiddles," the boy amended in a somewhat somber tone.

"Find Tiddles?"

Linden handed a key to Phillip. "Go on inside and have a good look round, Mrs. Elliott and I will be there straightaway."

As the lad sauntered to the door, Linden rubbed his forehead and spoke in a quiet voice. "I think Tiddles has gone missing. Just what we don't need."

"Missing?"

"Oh, it seems unlikely. Hopefully he's just hiding in the house somewhere, at least that's what I've told Phillip."

"What makes you think Tiddles could be gone?" Berdie sipped the tea.

"Yesterday afternoon, Elise came here. She couldn't find the cat so she just put the opened tin of cat food on the floor. I stopped on the way home from working late and I couldn't find him, nor was the food touched." He took a deep breath. "I called him several times, did a cursory whip round, but no Tiddles to be seen."

"So you're saying he may have gotten out?"

"That's it, I'm not sure. We've been in and out. I suppose he could have slipped through. I mean if he's truly missing he would have had to."

"Yes, well. It's a large house. His caretaker is gone, perhaps he's off somewhere having a good sulk." Berdie was being generous.

Even sulking cats get hungry. But if he had gotten out, it seemed likely that he would have returned by now looking for breakfast.

Linden took steps up the drive, Berdie with him.

"Are neighbors familiar with Tiddles?" Berdie was now working a missing cat investigation, as well.

"Sir Percival certainly was. He complained that the silly thing pursued his doves and he threatened to do in Tiddles if he touched foot on his grounds." He pointed to Sir Percival's back garden. "Look at his large dovecote. Him and his precious birds. What cat wouldn't be curious?"

Berdie could clearly see the dovecote sitting atop a high pole. "And kytes are deadly to doves."

Linden squinted. "For any number of species."

The mortally wounded black kyte tumbling from the sky dropped vividly into Berdie's memory. It didn't bode well for the cat. "Poor Phillip."

The boy's father nodded. "Oh, and by the way. We've told the children their grandmother has gone on holiday."

"Of course."

Berdie and Linden reached the front door.

"Anything   gathered   from   Olivia's   mobile

telephone numbers?"

"If I needed Elise's number, or my own, I'd know where to look," he offered with sarcasm. "And her bank. That's about it."

"Nothing gained from the address book?" Berdie took the last sip of tea.

"No. It was primarily businesses, tradesmen, that kind of thing. Would you like to look at it?" Linden opened the door.

"Yes, please." Berdie stepped inside, Linden behind her.

A child's faint voice could be heard. "Tiddles, where are you?"

"I'm going to help Phillip." Linden pointed to a hall table. "There's the address book."

"When I'm done with this I'll help as well," Berdie assured. She didn't leaf through the pages. She went straight to letter Z in the alphabet, and then X. "Ah." Berdie eyed the page closely. A telephone number was scribbled on it with no name or identification of any kind. "Thank you, Mrs. Mikalos, for being rather predictable." Berdie pulled the carrier bag from her coat pocket. Using a nearby pen, she wrote the telephone number down. In a blink, she pushed her flask lid into her pocket, pulled her mobile from the other, and dialed the number.

"Thank you for your call," a kind recording said. "Please leave your message."

Even more predictable. "Yes," Bertie rattled off her mobile number. "I look forward to your discreet response to my call." She shoved the mobile and bag back in her pocket.

Assisting Phillip and Linden gave Berdie a reasonable enough excuse to nose around Olivia's bedroom again. Everything was just as it was on Sunday. In the en suite bathroom she opened the medicine chest. There was an empty spot where a bottle of tablets had stood when Lillie and she scrutinized the cabinet on Sunday. "Missing."

She went back to the kitchen. "It seems both Tiddles and some tablets have gone missing," Berdie reported to Linden quietly as she spied the still full dish of cat food and inspected a kitchen window. "You didn't move any medication, by chance?"

"Why would I do that?" Linden frowned.

"And neither you nor your wife saw the cat scurry out."

"No, I've told you that."

"Linden, I think you need to consider that there may have been an intruder."

"No, nothing shows signs of being disturbed. They would have taken the telly, computer, any number of things."

"It's not that kind of intruder."

"What other kind is there?"

"Did anyone other than you and your wife have a key to the house?"

"No." Linden was sharpish. "Not that I'm aware of," he said in a more civil manner. The man sat on a near-by chair. He seemed overwhelmed with this new development.

"Why don't you and Phillip go look for Tiddles in the back garden and I'll just poke about the windows and doors?"

He shook his balding head. "Why won't the police get involved?"

The air caught in Berdie's throat and she swallowed. "Police? As they said, they're not willing at this point. But Linden, think of me as your private investigator right now. And Lillie, as well. In time, the police will get involved."

"You're right. I don't mean to be ungrateful."

Berdie smiled. "Out you go, then. Fetch Phillip and search the back garden."

The large front sitting room window was her next candidate for an intruder's place of entry. And, it would seem, this particular intruder was keen that Mrs. Mikalos stay in good health, thus alive. And yet, one who would hold her against her will? No ransom note. It didn't make a great deal of sense.

"Mrs. Elliott," Linden interrupted as he entered the room. "Come see this. I don't believe my eyes."

"What is it?"

Linden didn't respond. He briskly stepped to the back garden.

Berdie followed.

"Look." He pointed to the back of the property. "What do you make of that?"

Berdie scanned the scene. Tidy flower beds, a fence, neatly mowed green lawn. There was nothing exceptional. "Yes?"

"The fence!"

"Yes?"

Linden gestured with both hands toward the tall wooden fence that stood guard between the back gardens of Olivia and Sir Percival. "There. That's my mother-in-law's tree."

All Berdie could see were stubs of tree branches sticking up beyond the fence. The arbor looked like some giant's razor had made a clean even stroke straight cross.

"Not really much of a tree," Berdie said.

"It was tall and majestic, very old, very grand."

Then Berdie understood. The pillaged tree of Linden's mother-in-law was *beyond* the fence.

Linden's forehead furrowed. "He's gone and moved the fence, taking a piece of Mother's garden for his own and done the tree. He said kytes were nesting there."

"Who?"

"Blasted Barlow." He blinked. "Sorry, Mrs. Elliott."

"Mr. Barlow seems to stimulate all sorts of murky vocabulary."

"And well he should."

"Why do you think Sir Percival is responsible for this?"

"He's gone round after round with my in-laws about that tree. But more importantly, he's carried on accusing them of stealing his land. Since Mr. Mikalos passed, he's been relentless toward Olivia. He claims the property lines are wrong and part of Mother's garden belongs to him."

"And does it?"

"No." Linden threw the word like a dart going for its target. "Well, I'll have words with that brute." He turned on his heel.

"Linden," Berdie caught his arm, "even though you have a right to be upset, a dust up with Sir Percival really isn't going to help find your mother-in-law at this moment, is it?"

Linden blew out a large huff.

"I'll deal with him." She had no idea how, where, or when and hoped Linden wouldn't ask her. "Leave the matter to me."

"Daddy," Phillip called out woefully from near the

house, "I don't think Tiddles is here."

Berdie let go of Linden's arm. "It sounds like Phillip needs a kind word."

"Don't we all."

"Linden," Berdie salted her words with reassurance, "we're never without hope."

Linden sighed. He looked none too sure of it. He made his way toward Phillip.

Berdie stared at the fence. What on earth was going on? Was Percival Barlow dove obsessed, land hungry, or even mad? Was there more to it? Could he be tied into Olivia's disappearance? Berdie eyed Sir Percival's home. Could Olivia be in there? No, even if Barlow was involved, he wouldn't hold her in his own home. Too risky. She shook her head.

There was something missing, some thread or threads that hadn't shown themselves yet. And she had some knots to untie concerning Barlow before approaching him. Berdie squeezed the plastic bag in her pocket. "Joe's DIY may be just the fingers needed to untie one of those knots."

However, the church garden committee meeting was soon to take place, and she must fly. A quick adieu to Linden, and then she had to be off. It wouldn't do for the vicar's wife to be late.

****

Berdie fumbled her mobile in her coat pocket that hung on the back of the chair in which she was seated. She glanced at the ancient and faded wall fresco that adorned a tiny section of the south wall of the church's nave. Saint Aidan was presenting the Gospel to hungry souls with large eyes and wearing peasant dress. She wondered if Aidan, even though a saint, would have endured the present meeting at which she was in attendance at Hugh's behest.

"Horrible lemonade," Bridget McDermott, co-chair of the committee announced. "Rather embarrassing, that."

When Mr. Webb had introduced a wedding package scheme to help beef up church funds, the garden committee was appointed to oversee the first event, simply because it was an outdoor wedding to be held in the church back garden. Now, the committee, whilst in the throes of planning it, had spent the lion's share of the last hour discussing the Ascension Sunday activities.

"My young grandson can make better lemonade than the slosh served there," Mrs. McDermott went on.

Berdie remembered little Duncan Butz at the fete asking about balloons and holding his third cup of the "horrible" stuff. "What was wrong with the lemonade?"

"I take it you didn't have any, then." Bridget lifted her chin. "I should think the vicar's wife would have made a point of at least tasting it."

Of all the women in the church, Mrs. McDermott had a real knack of winding Berdie up. "Quite busy, actually," Berdie quipped. "Far more to do than imbibe at the treats table."

Mrs. McDermott crossed her arms.

"Terribly sour," sweet Maggie Fairchild interjected. "It made my eyes water a bit." She gave a slight shudder. "I had one sip and discreetly disposed of it."

"I drank it," Mr. Whipple informed. "It shivered me timbers, but I liked it. Of course, my wife says I have a cast iron stomach and no taste buds to speak of."

"Well, the whole lot should have been put down the sink." Bridget lifted her brows. "I heard Ivy Butz had to ration the sugar because there were far more people than expected. Rather poor planning, I'd say."

"Well, on the other hand, isn't it wonderful that so many visitors came to our celebration?" Berdie worked at a smile. "That is what the church always hopes for, to gather the multitudes." She nodded toward the nave fresco of Aidan and the peasants.

Bridget McDermott frowned, obviously not amused.

Hugh bounced into the nave from the front door. "It's approaching elevensies, ladies and gentlemen, and you're still here? I need my wife for a moment, if you don't mind."

"Of course," Mrs. McDermott sniffed.

"We really must get along ourselves," Maggie piped with the authority of her co-chair position.

Berdie nodded to the committee and walked with her husband, heels clattering over the worn stone floors, to the church's front entrance.

Hugh took Berdie's hand. "Outside," he directed with genuine concern in his voice.

"What is it, Hugh?" Berdie suddenly had the feeling his answer to that question may not be the best of news. She readied herself for whatever was ahead.

7

Once outside the church, Hugh spoke in a hushed manner. "When was the last time you saw or spoke to Lillie?"

"Lillie? I spoke with her last night. She came by the house before meeting Loren. Why?"

"Loren and Lillie did not get together last night. He left for a conference in London late afternoon yesterday."

Berdie knit her brow. "She never said."

"Apparently there's quite a bit she never said." Hugh's left eyebrow rose. "I was just rung up by Dr. Avery who informed me that she would be the choirmaster while Lillie was away on holiday in Portugal."

"Portugal? Oh, come, Hugh, Lillie would have said."

"She called Dr. Avery from Madeira."

Berdie gaped. "What is she doing in Madeira?"

"I was hoping you'd know."

"This is so unlike her. Mind you, recently she has been a bit...well...off."

"I'd say this is more than a bit. Among other things, she's in charge of our special music at the Whitsun service Sunday. You've really got to speak with her."

"Does Loren know?"

"No idea."

"I'll ring her up," Berdie promised. "I'll just go fetch my mobile, it's in my coat pocket in the church."

The words no sooner left her lips than Maggie stepped out the door and into their conversation. "Excuse me," she offered hesitantly. "Mrs. Elliott, I just thought I should let you know that…" She looked at the ground. "Your mobile phone has been, umm." She meekly looked up. "Ringing."

"Ringing," Berdie repeated, and then put a hand to her mouth as she recollected the downloaded music. "Ringing."

"More a kind of loud guitar, really, and…" Maggie flushed.

Hugh opened the door. "Well, you had better see who it is. It could be Lillie."

Berdie raced in and retrieved her coat amongst the giggles and stares of the committee.

Mrs. McDermott was almost indignant.

Berdie felt her face go red. "All a mistake," she nearly bellowed. With great haste, she raced out. "I've got to change that ring tone."

"What?" Hugh was still at the door. "Was it Lillie?"

Berdie looked at the missed call telephone number. She swallowed. It was a number withheld. The raspy voiced caller, possibly? "No, not Lillie."

"Well, reach her and find out what's going on. I need to push off. I'll be home for tea."

Berdie nodded as Hugh left. What on earth was Lillie doing? More specifically, what was she doing in Madeira?

****

Knowing Hugh's appetite would be healthy by tea time, Berdie set off with her pantry shopping list to Mr. Raheem's Greengrocers. As she clipped down the High Street, she tried to call Lillie twice and still got only the voice mail.

A faint memory danced through her mind, Lillie asking if they could call by Harriett Norman's house the previous day when they were in Mistcome Green.

"Oh, no," Berdie breathed as she paused in front of the produce store. "That postcard was from Portugal, but surely she wouldn't be that silly."

The loud blues guitar chords sounded from her coat pocket. "Lillie?"

"You haven't gotten her yet, then?" Hugh sounded rushed.

"Still trying."

"Listen, I have something I need you to do for me, love."

"Oh, yes."

"Dr. Avery is on duty at the surgery but needs some sheet music for tonight's choir rehearsal. Linden Davies has it, well, his wife has it at home. I'm soon to start my hospital visits."

"Yes, I'll go get it," Berdie interrupted.

"That's splendid."

"Mind you, I'm at Mr. Raheem's store at the moment, but I'll go as soon as I'm done here."

"Thank you, Berdie. I know it's a bit of an imposition."

"Not at all." Actually, she wanted to speak with Elise Davies and this gave her a wonderful excuse.

"See you at tea."

"Bye, love."

As she slipped her mobile in her pocket, Berdie

caught sight of Joe Lawler, just down the street, unlocking his shop. Another opportunity. "Mr. Lawler," Berdie called. She waved when he saw her. Her need for vegetables and a teatime ragout was trumped by Joe's returned wave. "May I have a moment?"

"Please, come in," he responded and made his way into the shop.

Berdie stepped lively past several store fronts to reach Joe's DIY. The smell of rubber-handled tools and linseed oil greeted her upon entry.

"I'll be right out," Joe Lawler answered faintly from a back room.

Goods stacked on shelves, in bins, and on the floor conjured images of families plunging into home improvement projects.

"I'm surprised you're open today," Berdie yelled.

"We've had to extend our hours," came from an unobservable space.

The business had started when Joe, who owned and operated Kirkwood Green B and B, decided on early retirement. He passed the guest home business over to his son and daughter-in-law, Jeffery and Cherry Lawler. Joe and retirement, as it turned out, were not compatible. And it wasn't long until what had been a car boot sale consisting of building materials left over from his bed and breakfast maintenance, grew into a real shop, though quite small, on the High Street.

"No more driving into Timsley to get a nail or washer," Berdie called out. She fingered the bag in her pocket. But why would someone in Timsley, with any variety of DIY businesses, come to Joe's little place in Aidan Kirkwood?

"Thanks for your patience, Mrs. Elliott. What can I do for you?" Joe emerged from the back room, his grin complimenting the enthusiasm with which he pursued life. His work apron now in place, the large pockets bulged with pencils, tape measures, and a spanner.

"I have a few questions, actually."

"Ask away." Joe stuck a pencil behind his ear, just grazing the slightly-ginger close cut hair.

"I know the people here appreciate your shop so much."

"Like I said, we've gone from three half days a week, to being open four full days, and half day Sundays, after church, that is."

"Do you get much trade from Timsley?"

Joe scratched his head. "Not that much, but surprisingly, I do have a few." He pulled a package of cinnamon gum from his large pocket, took a stick out, and unwrapped it. He extended it to Berdie. "Like some?"

"Thank you, no."

"I suppose personal service gives those big box fellows in Timsley a run for their money." He popped the gum in his mouth.

"I wondered if a fellow has been in your shop, perhaps recently. Distinctive, pleasant features, a bit gruff: Sir Percival Barlow. He may have been wearing a coat with a Seabrook Marina insignia."

"Oh, that fellow, gruff indeed." He nodded. "Building a fence. A good cash customer."

"Cash you say. When was he here?"

Joe scratched his head again. "Oh, the first time was well over seven, eight weeks ago. Put in a large order for my new, sustainable wood fencing."

Berdie felt the wheels spin in her cognition. "The

first time? He's been here more than once?"

Joe nodded. "He just came in this past Sunday."

"Did he?" Berdie tried to steady her voice.

"Needed galvanized nails."

"Indeed. Well, there you see, Mr. Lawler. Personal service, as you say, brings them back."

"I'd like to think so."

Berdie wasn't at all sure that Sir Percival cared one bean about personal service. So why did he come to Joe's shop?

The sound of the door opening sent Joe's gaze to the entering patron. "Pete, is your central heating still on the blink?" Joe tipped his head toward Berdie and moved to the man's side.

"Thank you," Berdie chirped as she passed the men, who had begun their conversation. Once outside, she took steps toward her original destination. Her thoughts spun.

Sir Percival planned to change that property line, to erect a new fence, weeks ago. And he was in Aidan Kirkwood on the day of Olivia's disappearance.

"Motive perhaps, and opportunity, but the means?"

The now familiar and brashly loud blues guitar broke into her thoughts. The telephone number made her purse her lips, and she brought the mobile to her ear. "Lillie!"

"Now let's not get on our high horse, Berdie."

"Are you really in Madeira?"

"Oh, Berdie, it's wonderful here. No wonder Livana chose to come here."

"Who's Livana? Lillie what are you doing?"

"Can you sit down, Berdie?"

"I don't like the sound of this. Sitting down is not

a choice at the moment. I'm standing in front of Mr. Raheem's shop."

"I'll chat with you on video about seven thirty this evening."

"What?"

"Be at the computer."

"Lillie."

"We'll talk when you're settled and calmed down, Berdie."

"I am calm," Berdie almost yelled into the mouthpiece which suddenly had no one at the other end. She took a deep breath. "Lord, have mercy."

The shop door opened, and Dave Exton, the young *Kirkwood Gazette* editor, zipped out, just catching Berdie's shoulder. An abrupt "Sorry," flew from his lips. His youthful face peeked above the opened Timsley Times he held in his hands. "Just reading about a hit and run. Don't want another, do we?" He chuckled. "You all right, then?"

"Fine."

"Have you seen this news, Mrs. Elliott?" He shook the paper. "Say, you may know."

Berdie tried to adjust to this new conversation as she mulled over her former one with Lillie. "Seen what and what might I know?"

Dave turned the paper around and held it in Berdie's sight line. "There was a hit and run in Timsley last night. A witness says a vehicle went over the verge hit someone walking out of a restaurant, and then took off."

"I certainly wasn't the witness."

"No." Dave half smiled. He folded the paper and tucked it under his arm, took off his trendy glasses, and proceeded to tap them on his chin. "The victim lives here in Aidan Kirkwood, no name given."

"Really?"

"I thought perhaps you, or your husband, may have gotten a call."

"No. What's the condition of the victim?"

"Not critical, overnight stay at the hospital. Bit of a miracle considering it was a Land Rover that hit them."

Berdie felt her eyes grow large. "A rather attractive man, the driver?"

Dave tipped his head, the edges of his mouth turned upward. "I dare say the driver could have been handsome, or possibly quite beautiful, as the case may be. But no one saw them."

"I do have a reason for asking that question," Berdie defended.

"I'm sure you do, Mrs. Elliott. And I'll let you attend to it." The young man gave a quick nod. "Must rush." He replaced his glasses.

"Wait." Berdie took his arm. "I was hoping to talk to you about something, actually. I have a bit of a favor."

"Do you?"

"It's about Olivia Mikalos."

"So it's true." Dave smiled. "I've heard rumors. Gone missing, has she?"

"Could you print her photo in the *Gazette*?"

Dave snapped his fingers. "Special edition." He looked Berdie in the eye. "When all's said and done, I get the scoop first, and in full."

Berdie nodded.

The young man all but danced. "E-mail the snap and any information."

"Download, hit send, good as done," Berdie promised.

The lad rolled up the paper and tapped it on his leg. "I'll do an on-line version, as well." Dave, obviously giddy and appearing lost in his plans, scurried away.

"Pray all turns out well," Berdie reminded.

Already in a dash, the departing figure raised the rolled newspaper into the air as an apparent acknowledgement.

Berdie reached for the door handle to Mr. Raheem's shop. "Pray, and then pray some more," she reminded herself, as well. Her shopping took only a matter of minutes. A quick walk home, vegetables washed and ready for a tasty oven ragout, she set out in the car for Mistcome Green.

Elise Davies was in the front garden wrestling the overgrowth with a pair of large garden shears when Berdie arrived. The woman looked rather sour.

"Not so good," Berdie spoke under her breath as she exited the car. "Hello, Mrs. Davies."

A squint was followed by a terse, "I'll just go inside to get the music."

While Elise fetched the item, Berdie glanced about at the garden. No "good afternoon," no "would you care for tea,"not even a "please come inside." But she couldn't blame the woman for being a bit sharp. There was a great deal of work to be done to get this space in order. For a gardener, it would be an enjoyable challenge. For a person not keen on getting their hands dirty, it would be a drudge.

"Here you are." Elise returned and handed Berdie the materials. The woman ran the back of her work-gloved hand across her forehead. A sunhat shaded her face and a garden apron protected her clothing.

"Actually, I hoped I might take just a quick

moment to ask you something." Berdie used her authoritative tone.

"Yes, well be quick about it." Elise shook her shears at the greenery. "Rotten job, this."

"It concerns your mother."

Elise wacked some growth with her shears and put her hand on her hip. "If I may ask, why is a vicar's wife so flaming concerned about my mother?"

Berdie straightened. "Linden is terribly worried about her disappearance, and may I say, for good reason. I can help."

Elise frowned.

"My previous career was investigative journalism."

"Now we're getting to it." Elise executed another snip with her tool.

"Do you know of anyone who may want to harm Olivia?"

"No," Elise answered without hesitation.

Berdie kept her gaze on Elise steadfast. "If, God forbid, your mother should be found unwell or deceased, who would benefit?"

Elise furrowed her brow and took a tiny step forward. "You're asking who gets Mother's money when she pegs out."

Berdie took a deep breath and stood firmly planted.

"You've got a nerve."

"It's a standard question that helps the investigative process." Berdie heard her volume rise as Elise commenced a hardy chop, and another, and another.

"I'm her daughter. My brother is her son." She stretched her free hand to the side, fingers spread.

"Who would you imagine gets her wealth? If there's anything left, that is."

"Anything left?"

"Myles, my brother, all but begged my mother for some funding to help him with his newest financial scheme. A profitable investment by some accounts. She turned him down with no consideration." Elise Davies put a hand back on her hip. "Little bunny didn't get his way this time. And why?"

"Perhaps there's a good reason," Berdie offered.

"Oh, I can tell you the reason." The woman shook her head. "She's considering buying a boat, something just smaller than a royal yacht by the sounds of it, with hopes of sailing 'round the world with a friend." Elise squeezed the shears handle so tightly, her knuckles nearly ripped through the glove.

"What friend?"

"No idea at all. Didn't think she had any. Then she joins a flash sports club, wants to stay in shape she says."

"The Seabrook Sports Club?"

She shrugged. "But, I can certainly think of other ways to slim without spending the small fortune required for membership." Elise lifted her chin. "She's gone money mad since Daddy died. And he was concerned about Myles and me overdoing." Her face went red and she threw an arm in the air as if to encompass the house, the leaky window, the neglected garden. "Like Linden and I didn't need the money ourselves."

"I can see this is disconcerting for you."

Elise shook her shears in Berdie's direction. "Great legal mind, indeed. Wenn-Patton, that's who's to blame for this mess." She knit her brow and thrust the shears forward. "And as for your concern about my mother being apprehended, she has an average physique. But if she wanted to resist someone, she has grit that makes Attila the Hun look like a ballet dancer." She snapped the shears open and in one swift closure beheaded a struggling foxglove. "I think we're finished here, Mrs. Elliott."

Something sparked in Berdie's mind. "Grit, lemonade," she muttered, and then paused. "So inept."

"What?" Elise strained forward. "Lemonade?"

Berdie leapt upon this display of curiosity to continue her inquiry, albeit in a slightly different direction.

"Something you said brought our Ascension Sunday celebration to mind."

"Did it?"

"Linden told me you were unable to locate your mother there."

Elise glanced at the ground and back at Berdie. "It was the crowd, you see." Her tone went a bit limp.

"Yes, very crowded, indeed." Berdie found her new lode to mine. "Most seemed to enjoy the event, apart from the lemonade, of course."

"Oh, yes, as you said, lemonade."

"At the treats table, you know." Berdie carefully eyed Elise. "Some said it was far too sugary."

"Did they?" She shifted her garden tool to her other hand. "Yes, come to think of it, I 'spose it was." She took a deep breath. "Now, as I said before, we're finished here."

"I appreciate your time, Mrs. Davies. And thank you for the sheet music."

Elise eyed Berdie momentarily, and then nodded.

Berdie got into her vehicle.

Elise turned her back to the car and began whacking away at the helpless vegetation with great force.

Once on the open road, Berdie wished Lillie was beside her to help sort this matter. The whole inheritance issue seemed just the right combination for a multitude of iniquitous motives. Both Elise and her brother were financially needy. Why was Olivia apparently spending money so lavishly? What friend? And who was this advisor, Wenn-Patton, for whom Elise had such sharp words? Just what was the "mess" she mentioned? So many loose ends.

Berdie tapped her finger on the steering wheel. And why would Elise lie about the Ascension gathering? Did she even go? "Oh dear," Berdie spoke aloud. "The more I converse with Elise Davies, the less I really know, except that she's hiding something concerning our fete. Perhaps even more."

****

Laying the table for tea wasn't going as Berdie hoped.

Hugh, helping with the task, was pleasant.

The conversation between them, however, was becoming a bit strained.

"So you did hear about the hit and run in Timsley last night?" Berdie straightened the floral tablecloth that graced the small kitchen table.

"Edsel mentioned it this morning," he clipped. "You put the sheet music in the church?"

"Yes." She ran her hand over a wrinkle to even the cloth. "Did you know the hit and run victim lives in Aidan Kirkwood?"

Hugh looked from the plates he sat on the table. "I'd heard nothing of the sort."

Berdie took silverware from a drawer. "Did you know the perpetrator was in a Rover?"

"Were they?"

"Yes, indeed." Berdie placed the silverware properly by the plates. "Did the cat people mention anything other than cats when they spoke to you at church?"

"The Stanfords?" Hugh retrieved glasses from a cupboard.

"Someone wearing a distinctive tie may have been the last to see Mrs. Mikalos." Berdie paused. "Have you noticed that all the people around them seem to be, I don't know, well groomed or nice looking? But, of course, you wouldn't have noticed all that with your new toy." Berdie waggled a fork in her hand. "I mean the woman, the angry gentleman, even that fellow." She placed the eating utensil on the table. "Elise Davies wouldn't fit that profile. Does money draw handsome people?"

"What are you going on about?" Hugh looked up from his task.

"And the Mikalos cat has gone missing." Berdie sighed. "Of course, Sir Percival has pleasant features, but would rather bump off Tiddles as soon as look at him."

Hugh planted the glasses on the table. "Berdie, how did the Stanfords, and Mrs. Mikalos, and someone who wants to bump off someone..."

"An animal, not a someone."

"Yes, well, how do they all end up in the same conversation?"

"Back to my original question," Berdie calmly redirected. "How did the Stanfords appear to you?"

Hugh's left eyebrow raised and he slowly lifted his chin. "Oh, I see now. It's the car."

Berdie ran a finger across the top of her plate.

"It was a Land Rover in front of their house, and it was a Land Rover involved in that accident."

"Hardly an accident."

Hugh crossed his arms. "In all of Timsley, there must be dozens and dozens of Land Rovers driven by dozens and dozens of different drivers."

"I shouldn't say dozens and dozens."

"Anyway, how would that suggest anything at all to do with the Mikalos affair? I appreciate your talents, Berdie, but what a fetid invention."

Berdie felt heat rise. "Fetid invention?"

Hugh held up his palms. "Wrong choice of words. It's a stretch. That's all I'm saying. That there's any connection in the slightest, well, it's no more than stretching facts like a rubber band." He had a point. "Besides, the Stanfords seemed nice enough. Perhaps a bit eccentric, a bit stuffy in their old school way, but certainly not venomous."

"Yes, well, sometimes that sort can be the most dangerous. Still, I suppose it's more questions than answers, really." Berdie's stomach now competed for her attention. "Anyway, the ragout is ready and tea is on."

With those words, Hugh's smile returned and all eyebrows were in their appropriate place. "By the way," he pronounced, "I'm taking the garden committee into Timsley tomorrow morning, and I'd like you to come, as well."

"Oh, Hugh, must I?"

"Apparently there's an urgent need to ferret out a

suitable cake for the garden wedding. I'm going, but you're much better at that kind of thing."

"Am I?"

Hugh rubbed his hands together. "Now where's that ragout?"

Though Berdie dropped the conversation about both spying out cake and her expanded rubber band discussion, she couldn't let go of the possibility that all the various bits of her 'fetid invention' in some disparate way smelled of the same soup. And she wondered how soon it would come to a boil.

****

The sacristy clock read 7:25 PM.

Berdie sat before the opened laptop computer reading a tutorial on video conferencing operations.

Not until she had her conversation with Hugh did she realize how much she missed Lillie. Her friend was always keen to let Berdie talk about her investigative ideas and even relished her stretches. This elephant hunt had developed into far more, but relating her musings to Hugh was like bouncing balloons onto a needle.

The swoosh of the video doorbell on the computer alerted Berdie to Lillie's arrival. Berdie clicked the correct icon and Lillie appeared on the screen before her. "Right on time," Berdie greeted with a giant smile.

"I see you're settled." Lillie returned the greeting.

"You've got a bit of color." Berdie observed Lillie's flush of pink that crossed her nose and cheeks.

"It's gorgeous here. Why have I never traveled to this island before?"

"Why did you travel there *this* time?"

Lillie squirmed. "You get right to it, don't you?"

Berdie quietly waited for Lillie's response, although she was almost certain now what it would be.

"All right." Lillie didn't blink. "I'm here because I told Harriett Norman I'd try to locate Livana Norman, her cousin."

"Aha. Her cousin, you say?"

"Indeed. You see Harriett, whose parents died, was the ward of an uncle who had a daughter, Livana. The girls grew up together under his care. Harriett thinks of Livy as her big sister, and rightly so. Harriett isn't as scatty as some would paint her."

"Closing in on the far end of normal, I shouldn't wonder."

"She's concerned about her cousin's absence. The post code stamped on the card Livy sent was from Madeira."

"And, have you been able to find anything?"

Lillie looked down. She raised her eyes and sighed. "I'm not adept at speaking Portuguese, but she's not in hospital, or at the morgue, as best as I can decipher."

Berdie leaned back in her chair. "Lillie, why didn't you say?"

"Say?"

"Portugal, Madeira."

"I knew you'd try to stop me."

"That's very true, but for good reason."

Lillie straightened. "I'm here. And that's for good reason, as well."

Berdie could see this conversation going into a circular pattern that would do neither she nor Lillie any real good. Lillie was on a Portuguese island. Heaven help her. "So what have you uncovered besides no *apparent* hospitalization?"

"That's just it." Lillie's voice was suddenly timid. She leaned forward. "I was hoping you might help me."

"Lillie, I can't dash to Portugal."

"No, I mean, you know." Lillie's eyes expanded. "Berdie, I haven't any idea what to do next."

"Of course you don't, lovey. You're not an investigator."

Lillie reared. "You're not going to make a meal out of this?"

"No, Lillie. Do you see me laughing?" Berdie tried to maintain, but the corners of her mouth rose just a bit upward.

Lillie jabbed a finger toward the screen. "I see that, Bernadine Elliott."

In a flash, Berdie and Lillie were laughing, Lillie so heartily that she bumped her head on her laptop screen. When Berdie finally collected herself, Lillie's hilarity subsided as well.

"Lillie, for heaven's sake, go relax by the pool, overeat, and dream under a palm tree like holiday makers do."

"I'll sneak in a bit of that, but truly, Berdie, I want to find this woman."

Berdie shook her head. "It's a great deal of work, and it could be dangerous."

"First sign of danger I'll return."

Berdie acquiesced. "Do you have a photo of Livy?"

Lillie's eyes lit. "I did remember the photo bit." She held it up so Berdie could see it. The woman in the snap had a pleasant smile, kind eyes, but no truly outstanding features.

"Have you shown it to *a Policia*?"

Lillie shook her head in the negative.

"First thing in the morning, then. Not that they'll do anything, but they may know something."

"First thing."

"What I recall from the postcard Harriett showed me, it was a seaside harbor, right?"

"Madeira is an island."

"Check all the seaside hotels, inns, and especially those who cater to tourists, first. Show the photo to reception, maids, concierges, any who will take the time to look. Ask them if they've seen her and when."

"That will take a while."

"You're the one who's in Portugal. Now where are you staying?"

"I'm at a small guest house, O Palms. It has a lovely veranda and a sea view."

"Does Loren know where you are?"

"I'm famished. It's time for me to go overeat."

"Lillie."

"He's at a pathology workshop in London." She ran a finger through one of her curls. "A work colleague had to bow out due to illness. Or that's what he claimed when he called yesterday, just hours before we were to depart for Aunt Margaret's."

Berdie dipped her chin. "Ah, I see." That explained a great deal. And by the look on Lillie's face, the topic was done being discussed.

"I really am quite peckish, Berdie, and I've gotten what's needed for a good start in finding Livy."

"Yes, well. Get in touch tomorrow and let me know how things go. And, Lillie, please do be very careful."

"I won't do anything you wouldn't do."

"Oh, my, you could be in for a peck of trouble."

Lillie laughed. "I'll call tomorrow."

"God go with you." When the screen went dark, Berdie felt a sudden longing. Not only were her children in far flung places, now her best friend was away. "Oh, buck up, old girl. She'll probably be home in two days, tired and ready to give up hunting about altogether." Still, she did miss her Watson.

Then she thought of the longings Olivia Mikalos could be feeling, if she drew breath, wherever she may be. And now, the absent Livana. "Oh Lord, keep them all in Your hand."

8

"Let's see. Access the Net. Yes, here we go." Berdie held her mobile. She had asked Hugh, due to some morning chores, that she be the last to board the church people carrier bound for the Timsley cake safari with the garden committee. Now, delightfully, she had a few minutes going spare as she waited.

She scrolled through the mobile Net offerings. She had decided, for her bell tone, on a lovely and lively song from the fifties. It would be a new delightful ring for the mobile, and she needed to make up ground from the embarrassment created by her former ring amongst the garden committee.

"Yes, very good." The songs popped up, and she browsed them. The loud blues guitar began its howl. "Oh, bother." Berdie hurriedly danced her finger on the OK button and took the call. "Mrs. Elliott," she answered.

A heavy wheeze.

Her whole being went on alert accompanied by a slight chill. "Please, who are you?" she almost begged.

A deep inhale and then a graveled, but sharp gasp followed. "Examine the money."

"What money?"

"Promptly," barely eked out across the connection.

Berdie was suddenly conscious of the vehicle horn blasting outside in the drive.

"No police," the caller reinforced.

"I'm doing my best, but I need more…"

Click.

Berdie pulled the mobile from her ear and stared at it. "I need more blooming information," she yelled.

"You need what?"

Berdie jumped and turned.

"Sorry to startle. I did knock." Maggie Fairchild, topped with a bright pink hat, pointed at the kitchen back door.

"Maggie. Oh. I didn't hear you."

"Vicar said to come straight in. So sorry." She craned forward. "Are you all right, dear?"

"Yes, I'm fine. Rather distracted." Berdie took a deep inhale. "I'll just get my bag."

In no more than a minute, the door was locked firmly, and Berdie and Maggie stepped to the people carrier.

Hugh at the wheel, Bridget was in the other front seat. Conversation spiraled through the vehicle amongst the passengers while they scurried their way to Timsley.

However, Berdie was almost immune to the talk sprinkled about. Her thoughts centered on whose money to "examine". Sir Percival, perhaps Myles Mikalos and his enterprises, or possibly Elise and her great lack of money. There was the cat couple. They apparently had money. On the other hand, rather than some*one's* money, perhaps it was some*thing's* money. The sports club? Olivia was presumably a member, the cat people lived near it. However, her best deductions fell squarely on Olivia Mikalos' fortune. But, where and how could she quarry-out any facts about the wealth of a missing person? Then, when she considered the word *promptly*, the little vehicle in which she sat almost held her captive as it shuttled her to another task entirely. How could hunting for "a superior wedding cake" as Bridget McDermott had put it, be of greater value than finding someone in danger?

"Do we really need to do this?" unconsciously escaped Berdie's lips.

"I agree." Mr. Whipple, sitting next her, whispered. "I'm a gardener, not a baker."

Berdie, realizing what she had prompted, considered her response to the recently retired, easy going gentleman who had a real way with roses. "Why, then, did you come, Mr. Whipple?"

He nodded toward Mrs. McDermott. "She said I was to come, and I've learned not to cross that one."

Berdie nodded her head toward Hugh. "Nor do I cross that one."

A slight chuckle slipped from Mr. Whipple's lips and Berdie joined him.

It was then Berdie became aware that the energetic conversations around her had come to rest.

"And what are you two chuckling about?" Mrs. McDermott queried.

Dear Mr. Whipple's gaze met Berdie's as they exchanged glances.

Hugh peeked in his rearview mirror at Berdie, recognizing the situation at hand. "Mrs. McDermott," he addressed, "just what is it that sets a wedding cake apart so as to be excellent?"

Berdie grinned in gratitude for her husband.

Mr. Whipple offered an all-wise wink.

Poor Hugh. Bridget McDermott's incredibly lengthy diatribe about the praiseworthiness of a well-done celebratory cake lasted the rest the way into Timsley.

By the time they reached their destination and disembarked, most seemed to have lost enthusiasm.

Berdie leaned closely to her husband and whispered, "I owe you one."

"Indeed, you do," he responded discreetly.

The aroma from The House of Helensfield Bakery begged that all should enter. The display windows showcased lovely tiered cakes, beautifully decorated with artistically etched icing. Photos of brides and grooms, birthday children, retirees, and guests of all sorts reveling in the cake-eating experience appeared as translucent clouds suspended above the model cakes.

"All masterpieces fit for a royal table," Bridget beamed before the window.

"Do you 'spose there's any chance of free samples?" Mr. Whipple gazed at the cake-eating photos and looked suddenly interested.

A ripple of zest was renewed amongst the troop as they entered the bakery.

The lion's share of the shop was composed of glass showcases that displayed both easy-to-order and ready-to-go celebratory cakes. But, there was a little area off to the right where a glass case of everyday breads and cakes were accompanied by a few small tables. Several people sat munching buns and other yeasty treats.

Mrs. McDermott adjusted the emerald brooch that was pinned on her floral design dress. "Those at Barlow House always ordered their cakes from this fine bakery."

"I thought they had to sell up years back," Maggie countered.

"Yes, dear, that's why I said *ordered*."

"Barlow House?" The words no sooner left Berdie's mouth when a young woman, smartly dressed down to manicured fingernails, greeted the group.

"Welcome to The House of Helensfield." She looked down at the notebook appointment calendar she held. "You're the garden committee from St. Aidan of the Wood Parish Church in need of a wedding cake?" She raised her head. "I'm sure we have just what you want. Please browse among our offerings. Samples of each flavor will be forthcoming."

Mr. Whipple's eyes sparked.

"I suggest you narrow your options to three choices, and I'll be glad to discuss pricing, delivery, and dates."

The party dispersed amongst the showcases, Hugh accompanying Mr. Whipple.

Berdie glanced at the area that served the everyday pastries only to observe Elise Davies behind the glass case serving patrons their chosen delicacies. All in white, her duties appeared to be done in a perfunctory manor, swift and with little conversation. Berdie glanced at the committee. With as much stealth as she could manage, she made her way to the eatery showcase. "Good morning Mrs. Davies. What a nice surprise to see you here. I had no idea."

Elise stared at Berdie, raised her eyebrows and set to on rearranging several tea cakes on the top shelf. "Well, Mrs. Elliott, you found me out."

"Found you out?"

"Course work at university, the best of four years as an event planner, all to spend two mornings a week doling out cakes and pastries with an occasional foray into deliveries. Not something you bring up in conversation, is it?"

"It seems a pleasant place. Busy. The window display is quite well done."

Miracle of miracles, Elise Davies smiled. "I did it." Elise glanced toward the shop window. She caught her breath as her eyes grew round.

Berdie glanced in the direction Elise scrutinized.

A gentleman, ramrod straight with an arm in a sling, eyed the window display. He looked somehow familiar.

"Excuse me." Elise was off in a flurry, bumping two seated patrons in her flight to the door. As she reached him outside, the fellow turned and now had his back to Berdie.

While Mrs. McDermott and party considered edible works of art, Berdie focused on Elise Davies' visage which she could clearly see through the window. The woman wore a grin that consisted of more paste than Bridget McDermott's 'emerald' brooch. A conversation ensued of which Berdie could make neither heads nor tails.

Mrs. Davies, in Berdie's dealings, was direct to a fault. "So why the pretense with this fellow?" Berdie spoke under her breath and tried to observe without being too obvious.

"Berdie." Hugh tapped her on the shoulder and begged her full attention. "You're distracted, clearly. But could you find it in you to join the rest of us?"

"Hugh, any idea who that man is?" She nodded toward the window.

"What man?"

She returned her gaze to the window only to see the gentleman gone and Elise's lips in a distinct purse.

"Berdie?" Hugh now took her by the elbow. "You owe me one? Remember?"

As much as Berdie wanted to bolt for the door and catch the enigmatic fellow, she considered Hugh's plea. And seeing as Elise was now involved with another customer who eyed the window-displayed cakes, she succumbed. "Yes, all right."

Thirty minutes of lively discussion ensued amongst the committee. Which size was best? What design suited a garden wedding? Mrs. Fairchild was quite keen it should be a floral motif. And, of course, there was the tasting, several times for each flavor. At last, three finalists were chosen. But, following the initial price tag shock, another choice was made altogether. A simple cake, one that Hugh and Mr. Whipple had recommended early on, was chosen from the economy selection whose cost was just less than three figures.

Hugh wore relief like a bright spring morning, and then beckoned the troupe to board the people carrier.

Berdie made her way to Elise at the counter, as the others went for the door. "I'll take one of your crusty bloomers, please," Berdie requested.

Elise set about collecting the bread.

"That chap you spoke with earlier, outside, he looked familiar. What is his name?"

"From where do you know him?" She wrapped the order in a long, narrow sheath of paper.

"I'm not sure."

Elise handed the goods to Berdie. "Broadhouse. Mr. Gavin Broadhouse."

"Gavin Broadhouse," Berdie repeated, and gave Elise the exact amount.

"I need a dozen tea cakes," a rushed customer interrupted. "Quickly, if you please."

"Excuse me, Mrs. Elliott." Elise attended to the

client.

Berdie stepped to the shop window and searched her memory. "Broadhouse." Then she quite remembered the morning she fetched Lillie to go visit Billie Finch. Lillie's lodger. Broadhouse. "But I never met him," she whispered. "Why should he look familiar?" How did Elise know him? Why were Elise's lips pursed? One thing was certain; Berdie certainly knew where to find him.

"Mrs. Elliott?" Maggie stood at the open door.

"Coming," Berdie declared and she quickly made way to the door. Suddenly, cake shopping had taken on a whole new horizon to become another foray into the ever growing stretch of a rubberband.

The return trip to Aidan Kirkwood seemed quicker.

Of course, Mrs. McDermott wasn't rabbiting on about superior cakes, either.

Once Hugh dispersed everyone back to their homes, he turned into the High Street. "I've grown extraordinarily appreciative of your committee participation in this whole wedding package ordeal."

"Ordeal. Yes, that word suits."

"I'm just glad the bride has a cousin, who's a vicar, to actually perform the ceremony."

"That's you off the hook." Berdie grinned.

"Even so, I could do with a hot cuppa."

"Yes," Berdie agreed enthusiastically.

"Let's stop at the Copper Kettle."

"A treat for your longsuffering wife?" Berdie teased.

"Well, that and Villette always has today's editions of the local papers about the place."

"Ah."

Once there, just before stepping into the shop, Berdie spotted Constable Goodnight rapidly making his way down the street, blustering and holding a *Kirkwood Gazette* in his hand. It appeared he was beating his way to the small newspaper office.

Two village women, just leaving the Copper Kettle, emitted a slight giggle.

"Our law man should wear one of those big broad hats. Fancy, Aidan Kirkwood's very own, wild west cowboy."

"Albie get your gun," the other woman quoted a title.

This was not the first time Berdie had heard comments of this nature concerning the constable. Since Sunday's live ammunition debacle, like remarks had circulated throughout the county. And it seemed Albert Goodnight did not take kindly to them.

"Hello Vicar," one of the women offered with regained composure.

Hugh nodded.

Once in the shop, Villette appeared quite pleased to seat Hugh and Berdie even though others waited for a table. Promptly, she took their order: a simple pot of steaming hot tea.

Hugh pulled two newspapers from an empty table, one of which was the *Kirkwood Gazette*. "Special edition," he read aloud.

Berdie spied the front page photo with the word *missing* below it.

"It's official, then." Hugh held the newspaper so Berdie could clearly see the picture of attractive Mrs. Olivia Mikalos.

"Official?"

"Well, surely, this is Goodnight's doing."

Berdie slipped down a bit in her chair.

"Perhaps you can suspend your own investigation now."

"I shouldn't count on it, Hugh. Linden has come to quite rely on me." Berdie poured a splash of milk in Hugh's cup.

And wasn't Villette Horn's timing impeccable as she arrived at the table with a hot teapot?

"Here you are, Vicar." Villette's smile accompanied her graceful pour into Hugh's cup.

"Thank you, Mrs. Horn."

"I've put my best tea cozy on the pot, keeps things toasty warm."

"Very kind." Hugh tipped his head.

"Now let me know if there's anything else I can do for you," Villette gushed.

"I will, indeed." Hugh took a quick sip. With cup in hand, he settled down with the newspaper.

Berdie worked at not gaping. This was not the general treatment served up at Villette's hand when she and Lillie frequented the Copper Kettle. She stared at her empty cup and then cast her gaze on the hostess.

Villette pulled her shoulders back while Berdie poured milk into her cup.

A quick sniff preceded Mrs. Horn's retracting of the tea cozy and an obligatory tea that half-filled Berdie's cup. The hostess placed the teapot back on the table and put the cozy over it again. "Now Vicar, let me know the minute you need topping up."

"Thank you." Hugh smiled at Villette, who left.

"I never," Berdie mumbled.

"What, love?" Hugh's eyes stayed on the newspaper.

Berdie sighed and put her elbow on the table, chin

in her hand.

Dave Exton burst through the door of the Copper Kettle, newspaper in hand, sending the little shop bell into a frenzy. He flew past Villette and came directly to Berdie. "What do you think?" He beamed and held the paper high in the air, displaying the front page photo.

Tongues wagged as the tea drinkers observed.

Berdie sat up straight in her chair.

"Well?" he asked.

"Fine work."

Hugh studied the newspaper editor.

The young man tossed a nod in Hugh's direction. "Vicar."

Berdie read excitement in Dave's eyes as they grew large behind his smart glasses. "And with my nosing round, you'll not believe what came up with the spade."

Berdie stood as quickly as Dave had entered the shop. "My husband's having a quiet read." She raised her brows and nodded toward the door.

The editor squinted and took a quick breath. "Oh, yes, I see."

"No, go right ahead," Hugh encouraged, his nose out of the pages.

"It's quite all right, Hugh. I need a moment with Mr. Exton, anyway. Continue your browse." Berdie stepped to the door, Dave in tow. "We needn't bother my husband with these things," she offered in a low voice.

A smile spread across the editor's youthful face. "Oh, that's right. None too keen on your exploits, is he?"

"There're no flies on you, my dear Mr. Exton."

The newsman's chest seemed to expand. He

leaned forward. "Have you heard of an eco-exploratory firm called Miles to Go?"

Berdie shook her head. "Eco-exploratory?"

"Hydrogen powered cars, solar transport, all the same old ideas but with a fresh spectrum of possibilities. Anyway, Miles to Go is the brainchild of Myles Mikalos, the son of the missing woman."

"Oh yes, his sister spoke of his financial exploits."

"Well, millions of dollars have been sunk into the project, but it seems the whole thing is doomed to go belly-up unless there's a fresh infusion of cash."

"Truly?"

"Oh, that's not all. Word in the city is there's suspected mismanagement of funds, and a court case was mentioned. It could leave Mr. Mikalos absolutely skint."

"This is reliable information?"

"As reliable as you can get in the murky edges of the journalistic world."

Berdie could feel Hugh's gaze observing her interaction with the newspaperman as he switched the *Kirkwood Gazette* for *The Timsley Times*.

Villette peeked out her large open window. "There are those who might be put off with you two gossips standing in front the door, you know."

Berdie looked out the glass door window and saw no one. Still, she didn't want to stir things up. "Perhaps we should move on," Berdie offered. "You've done well."

The fellow smiled.

"Keep that nose active."

"Count on me, Mrs. Elliott."

Villette discharged a very loud clearing of her throat.

Dave tipped his head toward the shop keeper. "She's just jealous that she's not got her nose in."

"Be that as it may."

"I'll keep in touch."

Berdie nodded and the young man exited the shop.

"Well." Villette spoke just loud enough for Berdie to hear as the woman peered out the window. "Comes in with a hue and cry, but purchases nothing."

Berdie quietly returned to her seat and took a sip of her now cool tea.

"That seemed rather cozy," Hugh remarked.

"He's excited to speak with another journalist."

"Former journalist," Hugh corrected.

"Oh, I shouldn't say that if I were you. I still contribute once a week to 'Recipe Corner.'"

Hugh chuckled. He laid *The Timsley Times* aside. "I'd like to sound you out on something." Hugh folded his hands on the table.

"Yes?"

"This package wedding scheme, Mr. Webb hopes to do more of it. But it's not really a job for the garden committee."

"I'd say not a job for any committee. One person, a specialist of sorts, a wedding planner, is much more sensible."

Hugh wore a half grin. "That's what I was thinking. I'm glad you see it that way."

Berdie nodded.

Hugh said no more, he just gazed at her intently.

"What?" She drew back. "Oh, no, Hugh. Not me."

He leaned toward her. "Don't reject it out of hand, Berdie. You'd be very good."

Berdie crossed her arms.

"You're good with details. You like to put things in order. You arranged our wedding almost single-handedly."

"Our wedding was nearly thirty years ago."

"You're unflappable if something should go awry."

"And it always does."

"Well, there you see. And there could be a new hat in it for you."

"Hugh, I've got more hats than Sundays. I'm just not the person to do this." Berdie paused and uncrossed her arms. "Oh, I see what this about. I suppose you've asked absolutely everyone in the church if they would do it."

"Not everyone." Hugh tapped a finger on the table. "There's Mr. Whipple, yet."

Berdie couldn't keep from chuckling, and Hugh, with a gentle shrug, joined in. The chuckles turned to a good laugh.

In the midst of it, Hugh's mobile rang. "We're not done with this discussion," he warned Berdie before he answered. "Vicar."

Hugh's face became somewhat somber. "Yes, Loren." Hugh looked at Berdie. "I see you got my voice message, then. Yes, it's true. She's in Portugal." He paused. "My wife could tell you more about that."

Berdie shook her head no. "I got a text from Lillie. We're video conferencing in an hour or so. Tell him that I'll ring up this evening."

"Lillie's not answering your calls? Yes, difficult, indeed. Loren, can Berdie call you this evening?"

Berdie knew she would feel better conversing with Loren after speaking with Lillie to see if frustration and lack of resolve would mean her imminent return.

"This evening is fine? I'm sure Berdie will look forward to your call." Hugh paused. "You're back in Timsley tomorrow afternoon?" He nodded toward Berdie.

She was pleased to hear this.

"Yes, good, yes, bye." Hugh rang off.

"Home tomorrow, then. That's good," Berdie quipped. It could be just the thing to help motivate the lovely Lillie to come home now. Perhaps Lillie had forgotten and forgiven. At least she hoped so.

****

Berdie was glad Hugh was out of the sacristy as she leaned toward the laptop and saw that Lillie's eyes sparkled. They enhanced her sun-kissed tan. In fact, she almost glowed. Even her tone of voice was alive with sunshine days of a Madeira spring.

"Things have gone quite well." Lillie opened up a personal-sized notebook and scanned a pencil over the page. "I've made some real discoveries."

"Have you?"

Berdie's protégé perched stylish, black-framed glasses on her nose. "Now, I'll start at the beginning."

"That's usually the way it goes."

"I purchased a map of the island and created a grid over it so I could keep track of what hotels I've visited." Lillie raised it so Berdie could see.

"Lillie, when did you get glasses?"

"What?" She put the map down. "I didn't." She stuck her finger through the frame where glass should be, then retrieved the map. "I've marked the places I've visited."

Berdie had not expected empty frames, or this

eagerness from her far-flung friend, nor the obvious sense of adventure that seemed to percolate her whole being. "Why the glasses, or rather, the frames?"

Lillie lifted her chin and ran a finger over the upper edges. "They give me an authoritative air."

Berdie felt an edge of her mouth curve upward as she tipped her head. "Do they?"

"Berdie, do you want to hear what I've discovered or not?"

"Go on."

"Now, when I spoke to Harriet, she said Livy came into money a few years back when her father died, apparently not just a little. So, I targeted the more posh hotels."

"Good." Berdie still worked at trying to find the authoritative air the empty frames gave her Watson.

Lillie grinned. "Well, she was seen dining at two of the hotel restaurants here several weeks ago." Lillie circled her pencil around an area on the map.

"Really?"

"Here's the significant part. In both cases, she wasn't alone, she was with a fellow. I mean, *with* a fellow, according to servers."

"There you go, Lillie. That's it, you've cracked it. She's met someone and decided to stay in Madeira. Well done. Case solved. You can return home."

Lillie puckered her lips. "Will you be patient? There's more." Lillie leaned in closer to the laptop. "She's married."

"Married?" Berdie reared back.

"Exactly." Lillie now wore a certain smugness.

"How did you make that discovery?"

"Well, the evening they dined at the Hotel de Hopedes, they made dinner reservations for Mr. and

Mrs. Thing-a-me and arrived hand in hand." Lillie dipped her chin and raised her brows as if it was astounding that such a thing happened.

"Thing-a-me?"

"The hostess couldn't remember the name, but she remembered the Mr. and Mrs. part. That's certainly significant."

"Is it?"

Lillie frowned.

"It's just that there are still people today, who wish to be discreet. If Livy and her man are having a bit of an affair they may want to keep it private, particularly if he could be married. Sorry to say, but there it is."

Lillie's frown deepened. "Harriett said that near Christmas Livy had disclosed how tired she was of being alone, how she longed for love and enduring companionship."

Berdie leaned forward. "All the more."

Lillie furrowed her brow. "Are you saying needy people are reckless?"

"Not at all, Lillie. I'm just saying consider your options when you're at the top of your game. It makes for better choices."

"Well, Livy's not the kind of woman who would pick forbidden fruit."

"You know that?"

Lillie took a deep breath and frowned even more.

"All right, Lillie. Did the hostess notice wedding rings?"

Lillie simply stared at Berdie.

"Is there a way to check marriage registries in Portugal? What about venues offering wedding packages, particularly for tourists?"

Lillie removed her glasses. Gone was the island

sunshine. "Well, I haven't gotten every detail worked out, yet."

Berdie decided to bring out the bait and put on a broad smile. "Speaking of love, Loren's back tomorrow."

Rain clouds seemed to appear over Lillie's head. She crossed her arms. "Is that significant?"

"Yes. Isn't it?"

Lillie grabbed the laptop screen and leaned her face into it. "I'll get back to you when I've made more noteworthy progress," she said with vinegar and snapped it shut.

"No, Lillie, Lillie, can you hear me?" Berdie tapped on her now blank screen. "Lillie, let's talk about this. I'm sorry, I thought..." It didn't matter what she thought. Lillie had ended the session and that was that. This was not the outcome Berdie had hoped for. "Oh, bother."

Hugh entered the sacristy, and snapped a book into its place among other theological tomes on a bookshelf. "You've spoken to Lillie?"

Berdie still stared at the blank screen. "I have, yes." She closed the laptop and sighed.

"Oh, that didn't sound very enthusiastic."

"Well, it wouldn't."

"Not coming home on the next plane, then?"

"No."

"Did you tell her Loren was...?"

"Yes."

"Oh, dear." He ran his finger over another book. "What's she doing out there, anyway? I mean alone, unplanned."

Berdie didn't want to go into all of it, especially since it involved investigating Harriett Norman's relative. "Seeking adventure and getting sun-kissed."

"She'll come around soon. Hopefully, by Sunday." He tugged a book forward, eyed it, and grasped it in his hand. "Speaking of adventure." He moved next to Berdie and put his free hand on her shoulder. "Grayson has invited us to accompany him to the sports club again."

"That's kind of him." Berdie, still thinking of Lillie, spoke idly.

"Good, then we'll go." Hugh squeezed her shoulder and it brought her fully into the current dialogue. He became energized and started for the door. "Three o'clock, it is."

"Three o'clock? Today? What about tea?"

"Is that a problem?" Hugh's liveliness tapered as he paused at the door.

Berdie was of no mind to go for a paddle with the privileged of Timsley, but she couldn't bear to see her lovely husband's good spirits dashed. How could she deny him? She placed a finger on her lips. And when she actually considered it, this could prove to be an excellent opportunity for a good snoop around if she approached it properly.

"I noticed when last there it had a lovely lounge, just right for snuggling into a great book. And I'm in the middle of a book you'd appreciate, *Computers and Their Functions*. Perhaps I could dig in whilst you and Mr. Webb swim?"

"It's settled." The pep returned to Hugh's voice. "Three o'clock, it is."

Berdie felt a rush of vibrancy as Hugh departed.

Lillie was fiddling about.

But Berdie had a real case that needed all the attention she could give. This morning, her trip to the bakery had yielded some unexpected surprises. Who knew what the afternoon could bring? The Seabrook Sports Club visit could be her own fresh adventure in stretched rubberbands.

9

Berdie snuggled into the comfortable armchair, one of several sprinkled throughout the club drawing room, opened her book, and waved Hugh and Grayson Webb on their way to the men's changing room and a relaxing swim. "Now you must enjoy yourselves for as long as you please," Berdie insisted.

Ten minutes in, Berdie decided it was time.

Hugh and Grayson would now be pacing their strokes through the water.

She wasn't entirely sure just what she was looking for, but she had the sense she would know when she found it. A ripple of enthusiasm surged within and she launched into a walk about.

What first? "Outdoor terrace," she whispered.

Lavish garden furniture held an abundance of lovelies in skimpy attire, both men and women, soaking up the sun. Many didn't even appear to have stuck so much as a toe in the swimming pool. And it would seem a flirty air permeated the gathered bunch. But then it was late spring, after all.

Passing an especially amorous fellow who ogled her, Berdie coughed, bringing her left hand to her mouth where she hoped he could clearly see her wedding band. It didn't seem to detract his stare. Whatever insight she was seeking, she was sure this patio did not hold it, and became suddenly aware she was quite peckish. She'd not had anything to eat since her pot of tea with Hugh at the Copper Kettle. Just a quick bite of something would do, and she could return to her task at hand. "Excuse me," she spoke to a couple strolling past. "Is there a café here?"

The woman took her gaze off her companion just long enough to offer a brief--"Main entrance, next to the indoor pool"--and moved on.

"Sorry to have troubled," Berdie offered. When Berdie found it, the glass door to the café, which read "Healthy spoken here" was held open for her by a gentlemen, who by his gear, was a member of the bowls team. As she made way to the bar where smoothies and other treats were being served up, she felt rather conspicuously overdressed in the trousers and blouse that had suited her morning outing.

Conversations spun from the tables of people enjoying fine fare along a glass wall that overlooked the indoor pool.

Then she spotted a familiar face.

Preston Graystone, Aidan Kirkwood's own solicitor, sat at a table. Leaning back in his chair with legs extended, the widower and father of Cara Graystone Donovan was swathed in what looked to be a very large bath towel, but indeed, was a sort of robe. Its soft texture stood in stark contrast to Mr. Graystone's angular fifty-something features.

With him was a woman who looked to be close to his age, gray-blond hair swept up and fastened. Her long legs were crossed beneath a short rose-colored wrap that only half covered her white bathing costume. Both she and Preston sipped what looked to be some sort of tomato juice cocktails, chatting as if seated seaside on the Costa del Sol.

Berdie's intrigue about Mr. Graystone and friend

pulled her like a giant magnet and she approached their table.

"Mrs. Elliott," Preston called out. "What a surprise seeing you here."

The woman eyed Berdie.

"Hugh and I are guests of Mr. Webb," Berdie informed the man, who was generally just cordial enough not to be considered offensive.

"Oh, I see," Preston offered in an almost enthusiastic tone. He didn't stand.

Berdie glanced at the woman.

"Yes. Mrs. Elliott, this is a colleague of mine, Mrs. Audrey Wenn-Patton."

"Hello Mrs. Wenn-Patton." The moment Berdie said it, she sparked. Wenn-Patton. Preston's colleague. Could this be the advisor of whom Elise Davies spoke of with such displeasure whilst pruning her garden? How many legal Wenn-Pattons could there be?

A broad smile highlighted by lustrous lips greeted Berdie along with a friendly, "Won't you join us?"

Mr. Graystone looked admiringly at the woman. Perhaps this explained his buoyant attitude.

"Do fetch a chair, Preston," Audrey directed.

"I don't mean to interrupt," Berdie prevaricated politely.

"Nonsense." Mrs. Wenn-Patton patted the table and took another sip of her drink.

Preston didn't appear to be especially thrilled with Audrey's invitation to Berdie, but set to dragging an empty chair from a nearby table.

"So, you and Mr. Graystone are colleagues," Berdie reiterated.

"How many years has it been?" The woman looked at the ceiling and released a puff of air. "More years than I care to remember, I dare say."

Mr. Graystone placed the chair at the table and Berdie seated herself with a "Thank you."

"Mrs. Elliott's husband is the vicar in Aidan Kirkwood," Graystone lifted his brows as he spoke.

"Oh, very well done." Audrey's words seemed to frivolously bump into one another.

"You said Mrs. Wenn-Patton is a colleague," Berdie redirected.

"A fine solicitor." Preston raised his glass to the woman, who did likewise. Both took another swallow.

Cocktail glass in hand, the woman continued. "I was a solicitor, well, still am, really, but no longer in private practice."

"Audrey, Mrs. Wenn-Patton, chairs Timsley's Council on Aging." Preston spoke with almost hallowed tones.

Audrey smiled and leaned back. "As I'm joining the ranks of the wrinklies, I jolly well want to have a say in the policies the government develops for us. Right, Preston?"

Mr. Graystone flushed a bit.

Berdie wanted to let go a good laugh, but only allowed a wide grin.

"Audrey's not one to beat about the bushes."

She leaned toward Berdie. "When I became a solicitor, it was a man's game, and I had to learn to wield the bat with the best of them."

"Yes, I should think," Berdie agreed.

"Mrs. Elliott may have a sense of that." Preston whirled the celery stick of his cocktail in lazy circles. "Before her occupation with church affairs, she was an investigative journalist. Quite good, by all accounts."

Berdie worked at not showing her surprise.

Preston was not only conversational, but complimentary.

Mrs. Wenn-Patton lit up like a summer sunrise and raised her glass to Berdie. "All girls together."

Berdie tipped her head to the woman.

Audrey frowned as if she realized all at once. "Preston, Mrs. Elliott is empty handed." She lowered her voice. "I'm afraid a traditional morning cocktail that mixes organic tomato juice with a hint of Russian bite is the closest thing I can abide for a health drink. You have to get them in the dining room of the café where they serve full meals. Angelo fixes us up." She looked at Preston. "We must remedy this, and it's your round, I believe." She lifted her chin with expectation.

It tickled Berdie to see the man who was generally gruff and distant, the legal mind of Aidan Kirkwood, dance to the tune of Audrey Wenn-Patton's commands. He stood. "Of course. Excuse me, ladies." The man ambled off.

Berdie jumped on the opportunity to sound out the slightly mellowed Wenn-Patton. "Actually, Mrs. Wenn-Patton, I'm in the course of an investigation unofficially, as we speak. A missing persons."

"Are you?" The woman closed one eye and peered at Berdie with the other. "You need legal advice."

"Well, not as such. But I am curious if you may have any information on a specific client."

"There's client confidentiality, you know. Still, out with it."

"Have you ever had any official dealings with a Mrs. Olivia Mikalos?"

"Ah, Mikalos."

"You have, then."

"No," the solicitor said baldly. "But, I was once in

the employ of the team that did legal work for Spiro Mikalos, her husband."

Berdie felt her itch for discovery outweighing her sense of propriety on legal ethics. "It's a matter of the will."

Audrey's shaped brows rose. "I'm assuming we're not speaking of will as in inner resolve."

"No."

"Spiro Mikalos was a bit, shall we say, unconventional."

"How unconventional?" flew from Berdie's lips.

Mrs. Wenn-Patton ran a finger down her slender drinks glass.

Berdie replayed the husky words, 'examine the money' in her mind. She hadn't considered the fortunes of Olivia's husband. "It's just that it could be a primary thread in finding Olivia Mikalos. She's in dangerous trouble, I'm sure of it. Can you help? All girls together?"

The woman took a deep breath. "Technically, the man's no longer my client. But you know I cannot disclose that kind of information."

"No, of course not." Berdie wanted to shake the woman into divulging what she knew, but at the same moment understood her legal position.

Audrey's gaze wandered to a nearby table. "To change the subject entirely," she smiled, "that family seems to be enjoying themselves." She nodded her head toward a mother, father, and two children clad in swim wear, all seated at a table.

Berdie looked their direction.

No one seemed especially cheerful.

"I did notice that the father brought a fully laden food tray to the table."

"As fathers often do," Berdie offered in vacant patter wondering why this information was even vocalized.

"Ah, and now he's departing." Audrey nodded again at the family.

Berdie watched the father dash off, towel in hand, probably for a swim.

The solicitor leaned toward Berdie. "He brought a full tray to the table." She dropped her chin.

"You said." Berdie studied Mrs. Wenn-Patton's eyes that had a special sparkle. "He, *the father*, brought a laden tray, yes. I see."

Audrey leaned back in her chair. "He's left mother, for the most part, to dole out the food to the children."

"Yes, he has." Berdie now watched the family closely as the mother took smoothies from the tray and placed them before the two squirming youngsters.

"You know, the father may have wanted his children to wait some period of time before they actually got to eat their food."

Berdie tipped her head. "How long, exactly?"

The woman shrugged. "Perhaps some minutes after he left the table. But children being children, it could seem like five years."

"Yes, well, he wouldn't want them to get tummy ache after swimming. That is, best to calm down, resist gobbling?"

"Calm down, indeed." Audrey took another quick sip of her drink. "He may even appoint a person of trust to keep the smoothies in hand, and then see that each child gets theirs at the appropriately elapsed time."

"Yes. I see." Her thoughts were aligning

information. "But, now, mother still holds the lion's share of the tray of goods." Berdie no longer eyed the table of innocent characters in the unfolding revelation.

Audrey nodded. "It looks like the children will each get a smoothie, but Mummy gets a smoothie plus three sandwiches and three bags of crisps."

Berdie faced the 'advisor' squarely.

"So, the offspring get their smoothie at the appropriate time from a trusted friend, and eventually, when Mum also leaves the table like Daddy, they get whatever she hasn't eaten herself. And that could be a full tray or merely a bag of crisps."

Audrey simply smiled.

"And if Mummy should leave the table prematurely, *before* the proper time has elapsed for the children to begin sipping their smoothies?"

"The little ones will get the lot, the entirety of the edibles Daddy brought to the table."

"Do they, indeed?"

Preston Graystone seemed to arrive from nowhere and sat three lovely tomato juice cocktails on the table. "You seem deep in conversation."

Audrey and Berdie exchanged glances.

"We were just talking about families," Berdie quickly responded.

"Thank you, Preston." Audrey placed her hand on his momentarily, sipped the last of her drink and took up the replacement. "Preston's been such a good friend since my ex-husband decided to hang his hat on another's peg rail."

Preston quickly pointed toward the pool. "Isn't that the vicar?"

Berdie turned her gaze just in time to see Hugh pull himself out of the water, and grab his nearby towel.

"That's your vicar?" Audrey asked with whipped cream on her tongue.

"Yes, that's my husband," Berdie responded quite pointedly.

"Our vicar's with the council chairman." Mr. Graystone nodded toward the pool as Grayson Webb emerged.

"You're familiar with them?" Audrey addressed Preston and took another slow sip of Russian bite.

"Mr. Graystone attends church regularly," Berdie answered.

"Why haven't you taken me to church with you?" Audrey swept her gaze to the pool.

Preston Graystone's eyes widened, while he appeared to collect his words. "But you never said."

"It would be a delight to see you there." Berdie made sure her tone was circumspect. "Perhaps you could bring Audrey this Sunday, Mr. Graystone?"

Preston Graystone tapped a finger on the table. "If Audrey is so inclined."

Audrey just smiled and nodded toward the glass window.

Hugh, by now wrapped in his towel, tipped his head toward Aidan Kirkwood's solicitor, then flashed his wondrous smile at Berdie and nodded toward the exit. "Meet you in reception, love," was barely audible through the glass.

Berdie smiled. "I'll be there." As Hugh and Grayson made way from the pool, she looked at the composed Mrs. Wenn-Patton and stood. "Thank you for your hospitality. I appreciate our discussion about family life." She then eyed Preston, who seemed none too sad that she was departing. "Perhaps I'll see both of you in church Sunday."

The village solicitor tipped his head.

Audrey interrupted her swig of cocktail just long enough to offer a wet, "Lovely chat."

As Berdie made her way to reception, she marveled. The information she had just gleaned from this clever woman and solicitor was far more than she anticipated finding here, and in a completely unexpected vein. But then, it seemed it often went that way in God's economy.

Then she considered the raspy-voiced caller. Who was he? How could he know such intimate details concerning the Mikalos fortunes? She had 'examined the money' and came up with a great deal of information. But as yet, she still didn't know where Olivia Mikalos was, nor who may have secreted her away. But she felt fairly confident she now knew the why. And it was all to do with love of money.

Berdie didn't wait long for Hugh in reception.

"Did you enjoy your paddle?" She gave a brief squeeze to Hugh's hand. He looked refreshed and smart in his clerical collar.

"It was a bit quick, but there's no better way to get the juices flowing."

"Where's Grayson?"

"He's staying on."

Hugh opened the door for Berdie. On the way to the car she had to work to keep step with him. "Where's the fire?" she quipped.

"Oh, sorry, love. Am I moving too quickly? It's just that I have an appointment."

"You didn't say."

"No. As a matter of fact, Grayson just set it up. He met a fellow this week, new to the village, who's interested in a pastoral call, and now's a good time."

"Who is it?"

"A Mr. Broadhouse."

Berdie caught her breath and took a slight wobble.

"All right, love?" Hugh slowed. "We're meeting at Barlow Gardens. I was hoping to go straight away, on our way home, if you don't mind."

"Mind? It's at the top of my list of things to do on a late spring afternoon."

Hugh laughed.

Little did he know that Berdie couldn't be more serious, nor could he see the verbal spade she had at hand to dig into the content of the conversation Mr. Broadhouse shared with Elise Davies this morning at the bakery.

****

Barlow Gardens was situated in an area just a mile or so off the main road that ran from Timsley to Aidan Kirkwood.

Berdie couldn't help but wonder why they were meeting in that spot. This would be her first time visiting the gardens.

They arrived at the small decorative sign that announced Barlow Gardens, parked, exited, and began to walk the garden path. It was a feast for the senses. The striking colors of the flora and fauna were highlighted by their scents.

Berdie was sure she heard the call of a nightingale among the wrens and finches who heralded the warm season amongst trees and shrubbery.

With virtually not another person in sight, there was a kind of peacefulness about the place that invited sweet thoughts and a shedding of cares.

Still, they were here on a mission of sorts.

"Why are we meeting him here?" Berdie asked Hugh.

"Apparently, he was in the area when Grayson called him about a visit. Whatever the reason, it works well schedule-wise."

"Where exactly are we going?" Berdie puffed a bit while keeping pace with Hugh up a slight incline.

"There's a folly," Hugh explained.

On the path before them, Berdie spied a writhing creature. "Ahh." Berdie grimaced. "It's a snake. What's wrong with it?"

Hugh gave a quiet chuckle. "It's just a little garden helper in the midst of one of God's everyday miracles. He's changing his outgrown clothes. Let's not alarm him."

"Shouldn't he be doing that somewhere more private?"

"I don't believe snakes have changing rooms."

Berdie eyed her husband. "Very droll."

Hugh took Berdie's hand and drew her off the path with him to delicately move through a grassy area and avoid the creature. Back on the path, Berdie and Hugh rounded an especially large hawthorn tree, populated with bright pink blooms, and spotted the folly ahead.

Appearing as a Grecian temple of sorts, it had Doric columns shadowing a lovely colonnade with benches, one of which contained a silver-gray-haired man of pleasant features, nicely dressed, and an arm in a sling: Mr. Broadhouse. He rubbed his free hand on his knee while looking across the horizon that stretched before him.

When she and Hugh arrived, the fellow stood with some apparent discomfort. Moisture formed above his brow, and a guarded smile was his greeting. "It's wonderful of you to meet me like this," he welcomed. "Gavin Broadhouse."

"Reverend Hugh Elliott." Hugh gave a responsive nod. "And this is my wife, Berdie."

When Berdie smiled, the gentleman's gaze clung to her. "My absolute delight." He gave a gracious tip of his head whilst still keeping his ogle.

She wasn't about to be taken in by his obvious charm. Something troubled her memory as it had when she saw him at the bakery. She was certain she should know the fellow. And there was something about his tie's colorful design that looked familiar.

Mr. Broadhouse turned his attention to Hugh. "I didn't realize your dear lady would accompany you. A wonderful spot to share together."

Hugh cleared his throat. "This is a lovely area."

Berdie sat down on a bench opposite the fellow.

Mr. Broadhouse returned to his seat.

Hugh wedged next to Berdie on the bijou bench.

"Some of my favorite moments have been in this garden." Broadhouse released a slow exhale.

"We've passed this many times, but didn't realize it was here." Hugh put his arm around Berdie.

"That's one of its most attractive features; it's solitude. It was once part of the Barlow estate."

That was the second time today Berdie heard of the past glories concerning the Barlow estate.

"Have you had opportunity to meet many people in Aidan Kirkwood, apart from Mr. Webb?" Hugh asked.

"No, not as such. Well, my generous and kind

landlady."

"You're living in the garret flat at Swallow Gate," Berdie announced.

"Are you?" Hugh wore surprise. "Miss Foxworth is our choirmaster for the church, although currently on holiday."

"Yes, Cornwall, I believe she said." Gavin nodded.

"Portugal," Hugh corrected.

Mr. Broadhouse tipped his head. "Portugal? Are you sure? She told me she was visiting family in Cornwall for a few days."

"Her plans changed," Hugh quipped.

Gavin Broadhouse simply nodded.

"Elise Davies, you've met her, as well." Berdie could hear a slight edge in her voice. She watched the fellow's jaw make an ever-so-slight jut.

"Yes, but then, she doesn't live in Aidan Kirkwood, Mrs. Elliott."

"You do know where she lives, then."

She felt Hugh's corrective thumb pressing on her back, but she continued.

"I saw you speak with her just outside House of Helensfield Bakery earlier today. Do you know her well?"

Mr. Broadhouse took a shallow breath and shifted in his seat.

"We were there as a part of a church function." Hugh emphasized the word church with a quick glare at Berdie.

Mr. Broadhouse looked at the floor of the picturesque shelter. "Very observant, Mrs. Elliott."

"There's very little that escapes my scrutiny, and, quite frankly, Mrs. Davies didn't appear to especially relish the chat."

Hugh's entire hand now wrapped around and gave Berdie's shoulder a tight, admonishing squeeze. "I'm sure whatever you were doing at the bakery is entirely your own business, Mr. Broadhouse." Hugh said it to the fellow, but Berdie knew it was meant for her as well.

The man ran a stiff thumb cross his chin as his forehead became increasingly moist.

"I can't help but notice your unfortunate circumstances." Hugh glanced at the man's arm in the sling.

Something sparked in Berdie's put-it-together mind. Mr. Broadhouse's attractive features, the tie he wore, that house, not being truly known in the village, could he be *that* fellow? "There was a hit and run accident in Timsley yesterday evening." The words tumbled out her mouth. "May I ask, were you the victim?"

Hugh's thumb dug so deeply into Berdie's back, she almost gave a yip.

Mr. Broadhouse reared his head back. Then a gentle smile appeared. "Yes, I read about that in the paper. If only it were something that dramatic." He rubbed the fingers protruding from his sling. "As embarrassed as I am to speak of it in the hearing of a lovely lady, I'm afraid I came off some stairs at a building site where I'm consulting."

"How long will you wear the sling?" Hugh quickly jumped in.

"Not long. It's the ribs that may take some time to heal."

"Ribs, as well." Hugh studied the fellow. "That must have been quite a nasty tumble."

Mr. Broadhouse glanced back out at the horizon.

Pull the other one. Berdie wanted to resume her needling for more information about his acquaintance with Elsie Davies. "How did you meet Elise Davies?"

He cast an eye toward Berdie.

She thought he had the look of a fish struggling to get out of a net.

"I met Elise Davies when I was seeing her mother, Olivia Mikalos."

"Indeed," Berdie said in a low voice.

"Olivia and I were," he rubbed his hand on his knee, "keeping company together. But not for long, I'm afraid. Seven months ago, after just a short time together, we parted. It had to end." The fellow's voice sounded rather tentative as he turned his head once again to observe the vista of sky and garden. "I'm married, you see."

Lillie's words, "his wife and children live in Leeds," toppled through Berdie's memory. She glanced at his bare left ring finger. Why would Elise greet him with a smile if she had found him out? What prompted her display of discontent when he departed? Berdie had bucket-loads of questions for this randy fellow.

"Yes, I can see that would be problematic." Hugh's voice was clear.

Berdie prepared to launch into several questions, but Hugh cut her off.

"Mr. Broadhouse, I can see this is rather difficult for you." Hugh spoke gently. "Would you consider getting together at church, or perhaps at your home in Swallow Gate, to continue this discussion where we would be unattended?"

Berdie thrust her glare toward Hugh. Unattended? Why not just say 'Woman, go to the car so this ruinous fellow and I can speak without you putting your oar in?' She took a deep breath and bit her tongue. Yes, this was a pastoral call. But this man could be a critical link in finding Mrs. Mikalos.

Hugh's lips pursed. "Berdie?"

Berdie was aware that it was his professional duty to see to the confidential wellbeing of those who earnestly desired it, and Broadhouse presently resided in the parish. Plus, he did have at least the scent of an earnest truth seeker. Why else would he have wanted to meet with Hugh?

She certainly knew where to find the man. "If that suits you Mr. Broadhouse, perhaps it would be best."

Hugh was on his feet before the gentleman could breathe out his, "Very gracious of you, Mrs. Elliott."

Berdie felt Hugh's hand on her elbow, raising her to a standing position more quickly than a disturbed mother hen. "We'll continue our conversation," Hugh assured Mr. Broadhouse. "Are you aware of Mrs. Mikalos' present situation?"

The man rose with a labored breath and nodded. "I saw the Kirkwood paper this morning." A glint of moisture appeared in the corner of his eye.

Berdie wasn't sure if it was grief, or simply pain from his injuries.

His face flushed. "Despite things being as they are, I'm very fond of her."

"Berdie, go on ahead. I'll catch you up." Hugh motioned toward the path.

Berdie had to force herself to step away from the folly. Though she moved forward, she glanced over her shoulder.

Hugh handed a church information card to the man.

Continuing a few steps further, she looked again.

Hugh and Mr. Broadhouse exchanged what appeared to be cordial words.

In less than a minute, Hugh was next to her and put his arm around her waist scooting her along the garden path. "Back to the car as quickly as possible," he commanded. "We'll talk there." Once in the car, Hugh took to the road like a hound on the chase. "Two things of which I want you to be acutely aware, Berdie." Hugh's left eyebrow nearly skyrocketed off his forehead. "First, church affairs, especially a pastoral call, is not a playground for your investigative probing. Why didn't you tell me you were familiar with the man?" Before she could answer, Hugh went on. "I was under the impression that this appointment was to be nothing more than an informational welcome to visit church. But, it was obviously much more."

Berdie summoned her words of defense.

But Hugh didn't stop. "And secondly, I do not want you anywhere near that fellow."

"You felt something was off, as well."

"I *observed* a man in turmoil of whatever making. Off or not, I *felt* pity for the fellow while you recklessly poked away with your verbal intrusions and not-so-cloaked accusations."

Berdie took his reprimand about pastoral calls to heart. Hugh was right. "I'm sorry, Hugh, for anything that disrupted your purposes."

His eyebrow rested at its appointed place. "Let's just pray it hasn't put Mr. Broadhouse off altogether."

Berdie plunged into her justification concerning his second demand. "Broadhouse could have something to do with Mrs. Mikalos' disappearance. I need to see him. He's hiding something, Hugh."

"So it would seem, his behavior gave some

indication of that. But unlike you, I'm not ready to place him in a hangman's noose just yet. He's trying to communicate, and it's *my* job to hear him out and deal with him as is fit for my profession. Is that clear?"

Berdie sighed.

"You are not to go within a mile of him."

"In that case, I'll have to move out of the village, won't I? And who then would prepare your afternoon tea?" Berdie hoped to create some levity.

But, Hugh wasn't having it. "This is non-negotiable."

Berdie took a deep breath. "As you say." She answered without protest, though it pained her to do so. Allow forty eight hours to lapse, let Hugh carry on, and see what comes. That was the closest she could come to a promise of nonintervention concerning this full-of-flannel Mr. Broadhouse fellow. After that, it would be all systems go.

10

Berdie seated herself at the kitchen table, not yet fully awake, cup of steaming tea in hand. Her night's sleep had been restless after the intriguing afternoon she experienced.

Not only did she try to puzzle together the new information, but also, as was planned, she called Loren just before retiring to bed to talk about his non-responsive Lillie. The conversation had not gone especially well. "She's on an adventure, Loren. Feeling a bit underappreciated, and on an adventure." Berdie offered no details about an investigation.

"I had a legitimate work call, short notice, yes. But still..." Loren's frustration-laden words were in high volume.

Berdie perceived Loren's irritation as his own reckoning with a certain amount of guilt for the situation. An attempt to reassure him of Lillie's wellbeing was difficult when she was skeptical herself. She was glad the call hadn't lasted long.

The sound of something similar to a bleating lamb sounded in the vicarage hall.

"Oh, bother," Berdie offered to the morning warmth of the kitchen. Sitting in her robe and slippers, she had a mind to let it ring itself out, but then, it could be someone in real need. She clumped her way down the hall. "Vicarage." Berdie wiped an eye.

"Mrs. Elliott, it's Billie Finch, and I just saw Mrs.

Mikalos' car."

Berdie had to give her brain a mental shake. "Where, Billie?"

"A small distance down the road from her house. I noticed it when I went to get the morning milk delivery, just minutes ago."

"Is the vehicle still there?"

"I'll go look."

Berdie wondered how Mrs. Finch knew that it was Mrs. Mikalos' car. Had she seen anyone in it? Then Berdie remembered the number she watched Linden input on the garage door opener the first time she went to the Mikalos home.

"Not there," a slightly breathy Billie informed.

"Did you see anyone in the car, check the registration number, scrutinize anything?"

"No."

Berdie took a deep breath. "Billie, I need you to do me a rather large favor."

"Oh," came down the line hesitantly.

"You've been right to ring me and this is nothing dangerous. I'm going to give you the number that opens Olivia's garage door. If her car is, indeed, in there, feel the bonnet to see if it's warm. Close everything up when you're done."

"I'm not sure, Mrs. Elliott."

"This is in aid of getting Olivia the help she may need, Mrs. Finch. Please."

"Shouldn't I knock first, I mean, just in case?"

"Whatever makes you feel comfortable, Billie. But please do it as soon as possible."

"I've got to dress."

"Of course. Remember it's for a good cause."

"If you're sure, Mrs. Elliott."

"Very sure, Billie. The garage security number is 7477. Now ring me as soon as you get back." The receiver back in the cradle, Berdie shot a wee prayer upward for Mrs. Finch to overcome her timid apprehension.

Hugh bounded down the stairs, still knotting the belt of his robe. "Who is it?"

"Mrs. Finch, a new friend of sorts."

"She's ringing early."

"Yes, and that's you off the hook." Berdie grinned and moved away from the topic. "Hot tea's on."

Hugh rubbed his hands together. "Very good."

"I'll join you in a tic."

He placed a kiss on Berdie's cheek and navigated down the hall to the kitchen.

Meanwhile, Berdie sat on a stairway step and wondered if it was actually Olivia's car that Billie Finch saw. Whatever, it had its place somewhere in the scheme of things.

Brrnng-Brrnng. "That was fast." Berdie sprang from her momentary chair. She hastily picked up the mouthpiece. "What did you find?" she blurted.

"No, Mrs. Elliott. What did *you* find?" It was the raspy-voiced caller.

Berdie held the phone with both hands. "Spiro Mikalos's fortunes."

"Very good," he graveled, "but I said no police."

"I've not gone to..." Berdie considered what might prompt this remark. "You didn't say anything about journalists."

The caller spewed a long growl.

He's in the area, he's seen the Gazette. Berdie ruminated. "Listen, you're the one who seems to be on the inside of all this. Why aren't you doing..."

"Follow the cat."

Berdie frowned. "What?" Her mind bounced to the Mikalos vampire. "Tiddles?" Now she became edgy. "Please, you must give me more than that."

A click and silence were the responses to her plea.

Berdie let out a long sigh. Must she now mount a campaign to find the missing feline? Perhaps she could fob that off on to Linden. But then, the villian had given her sound information before and it had opened up a clear motive for Olivia's disappearance. Still, spending her valuable time searching for a cat? And she wasn't sure it was Tiddles to be found, but it seemed the most likely. "Lord, does any of this make sense?" Berdie jumped as the vicarage phone once again wailed. "Vicarage," she answered.

"You are so clever, Mrs. Elliott." Billie Finch sounded almost exuberant.

"Truly?" At the moment, Berdie didn't feel especially adroit.

"The car I saw this morning must have just been one that resembled Mrs. Mikalos's vehicle. Hers is dead cold in the garage."

"Well, there you see, Billie. You've been very helpful. Thank you."

"Oh, my pleasure."

"May I ask? Mrs. Mikalos's cat, the one she's caring for, seems to have gone missing. Have you, by chance, seen it about the house, in the area? Hopefully, not near Sir Percival's garden."

"That poor, unsightly creature? No. And I should think it wouldn't be such a bad thing if it found another home elsewhere."

"Yes, I know it's not lovely, but the cat could be somehow important. If you do see it, please call me straight way. If you've a mind, perhaps try to catch it."

There was a laden silence.

"Billie, thank you for keeping an eye. It's invaluable."

"I shall do my best," Billie chirped.

Goodbyes given and phone back in its proper place, Berdie went to the kitchen to find Hugh drinking his tea and perusing the morning edition of the Timsley Times.

"Your friend seems awfully keen," Hugh remarked from behind his paper. "Ringing thrice in a few minutes time."

Berdie took a moment to get his meaning. "Three times." No need to divulge it wasn't just Mrs.Finch. "Oh, yes, Mrs. Finch is helping out a worthy cause."

"Which is?"

Berdie took a sip of tea. "Which is in aid of Mrs. Mikalos."

"Speaking of Mikalos, it says here in the paper that Myles Mikalos's business enterprise, Miles to Go, was set to go belly up. Isn't he her son? It seems a private investor has bailed him out."

"Truly? Does it say who the investor is?"

"No."

"Suspicious."

Hugh looked over the top of the paper. "What? Are you suggesting a son would kidnap his own mother for her money? How sinister."

"Certainly not our son, but one never knows, especially when it involves substantial amounts of capital."

"Where's the ransom note? How would he get the money without proving her dead?"

"Well, I've not got it all sorted, it's just an odd

coincidence."

Hugh stuck his nose back in the paper. "And how is your Mrs. French giving aid in the Mikalos situation?"

"Olivia's cat's gone missing, and *Mrs. Finch* is watching for its possible return." Berdie took the crispy bloomer of bread from the bread box and sliced two large pieces.

"Cats seem the topic of the day," Hugh continued.

"In what sense?" Berdie's ears went on alert.

"Any chance for some toast and jam?"

"I was just setting about to do that." Berdie placed the slices into the toaster. "In what sense are cats the topic of the day?"

Hugh put the paper down and ambled to the fridge where he began to rummage around. "Edsel asked, kindly I may add, if I could see my way clear to take Ivy and Duncan to the cat rescue today."

Berdie could almost feel the sparkle that was surely in her eye as she turned to her husband. "Really?"

"Yes. It seems Duncan came upon a lost cat and has cared for it the past few days, becoming more attached to it by the hour. But, Ivy isn't having it. So, it's off to the rescue." Hugh brought out a laden butter dish. "Edsel has a work project in Bridgeton today, Lucy has classes at the Tech, and Ivy doesn't trust her Uncle Wilkie's driving. So, Edsel asked if I could take them."

"The new rescue's nearly twenty miles, anyway." Berdie recognized an opportunity in the making. "That could take up the better part of your day."

"Perhaps not the better part, but certainly some of it." Hugh added a jar of Mr. Raheem's homemade strawberry jam to accompany the butter dish. "But, Edsel and Ivy do so much for the church, I could hardly refuse."

"Of course. Don't you have an appointment with Reverend Simpson at St. Mark's today?"

"And leading the parish prayers for the nine days of Whitsun, here and at Mistcome. I had planned to do some sermon preparation, as well." Hugh brought the butter and jam to the table and sat. "But there you are."

Berdie put her hand on his shoulder. "Your plate is full. Let me take Ivy and Duncan, and you can get on with your work."

"Just like that?"

"Why not?"

Hugh smiled. "Why not."

The toasted bread sent a gentle aroma through the kitchen as Berdie sat it on the table.

Hugh spread a great swathe of butter across the warm toast. He stopped abruptly and pointed his buttering knife in Berdie's direction. "The Mikalos feline, that's what this goodwill is about, isn't it? You're up to something."

Berdie sat down and tipped her head. "Hugh Elliott, are you saying I haven't any goodwill?"

"Not at all. I'm just saying, in this case, it's to your investigative advantage to be among cats."

"Well, actually, yes it is. But, I certainly don't mind taking Ivy and Duncan to the rescue. And, if at the same time, I can see if Tiddles is there, all the more so."

"Tiddles?"

"Olivia's cat, well, her grandson's cat, really."

"I thought you were looking for the person, not their cat."

"Finding the pet could be important to finding

Olivia."

Hugh heaped jam onto his toast. "How?"

"I'm not sure, yet."

"That's not a very reasoned argument."

"No, it's not." Berdie took the knife Hugh had just used and slipped it into the butter. "But someone has suggested it may be vital, so it's worth a look see."

Hugh appeared contemplative. "Well, it would free up my time if you took Ivy. You and she could have a good chin wag on the journey. But mind you, no trouble."

"It's settled, then. What time do I fetch them?"

"Half nine."

"Half nine, it is."

As Berdie spread butter on the toasted bread, she knew she wasn't just looking for Tiddles. 'No trouble' Hugh said. No trouble for whom? She hoped the cat people may be there, as well. Wouldn't they manage the shop? She had a multitude of questions to ask them. And about time, too, she reasoned.

****

Ivy had a rather beleaguered look about her when she answered Berdie's knock at the door of the Butz home, rather unusual for ever-bubbling Ivy.

"Where's Reverend Elliott?" Ivy cast her gaze to the drive.

"Change of plan. *I'm* taking you and Duncan to the rescue."

"Oh, dear." Ivy shook her head and wrung her hands together. "Dottie's got a tummy. Everything going in one end is coming out the other, if you'll pardon me saying."

"Oh, dear, Ivy."

"So you see, I can't possibly go out. I'm so sorry, Mrs. Elliott." Ivy ran a hand across her forehead.

"Oh, it's no problem." Berdie made sure her voice was very reassuring. "I'd be delighted to take Duncan and his furry pal to the rescue."

Ivy brightened. "I wouldn't want to impose."

"No imposition, none at all."

Ivy displayed her familiar grin. "Gracious, how kind." The woman turned around and yelled in the direction of the stairwell. "Duncan!"

Berdie was surprised the rafters were still in place after Ivy's booming voice.

The lad appeared and struggled to bring the cat carrier that held his treasure within.

"Mrs. Elliott has come to fetch you and your Razor."

Duncan looked like a wet weekend. His usual pizzazz seemed in some distant place where he and his four-pawed pal played together endlessly. He halted at Ivy's side.

"Now, no nonsense, love. You know what we've agreed."

Duncan nodded his five-year-old head.

Ivy ran her hand cross Duncan's brown hair, smoothing it, and bent down. "Be Mummy's big boy, and don't give Mrs. Elliott any grief."

Duncan, chin down, gazed up at Berdie. "Yes, Mummy," he mumbled.

Ivy stood and moisture glistened in her eye as she turned toward Berdie. "Let me know if there's any trouble." She leaned closely to Berdie. "He's taken to this tattered creature. By Dunc's insistence, we took a picture of him holding it. Then I found the feline on his bed in an evening. It just won't do," she whispered.

Berdie nodded. "I quite understand. Don't worry yourself. We'll be fine." She eyed Duncan. "Off we go, Duncan."

Ivy planted a big kiss on Duncan's forehead.

Berdie took the cat carrier. This could be a decidedly long ride. Her attempts to cheer the child on their journey went for naught.

Duncan only nodded occasionally. He held the carrier in his lap.

The cat, a rather calm creature, leaned its scarred body against the side of the cage closest to Duncan. It appeared the affection was mutual, rather unusual for such a battle hardened tom.

Berdie's childhood family cat was not like this one. Someone was forever trying to get it out of some hard to reach area where it disappeared for days at a time.

Duncan's find seemed an entirely different species.

After traveling the lane to a tucked away area, the view upon arrival at the rescue car park was astonishing. An expansive low-lying building, gleaming white and surrounded by well-kept gardens, sported large, lighted letters that read *Queen's Gardens Feline Board and Rescue.*

"Duncan, just look at Razor's new home. It's fit for a king," Berdie encouraged.

"It's big," he breathed.

It was the first verbal response she had gotten from the forlorn lad since getting in the vehicle.

"Let's see what the inside is like," Berdie offered with buoyancy.

Once through the automatic glass doors, Berdie took a deep inhalation of mint scented air as her astonishment only grew.

And by the size of his widened eyes, Duncan's, as well.

A well turned-out woman sat at a long counter marked *Reception*. Holographic photos of cats playing, resting on satin pillows, eating from personalized bowls, and sitting in a vet's lap apparently pleased they had just received a healthful jab, filled the walls. A video about feline care played on a giant flat screen television in a lowly lit area that held several pillowed couches and cat baskets.

A white-clad young woman of meticulous appearance swept past. She gently held a cat against her chest.

Berdie stared at the black and white creature, its gaping fangs exposed. "Tiddles?" Berdie all but gasped.

"Sorry?" The attendant's tone had a terse edge and she stopped.

"The cat, its name is Tiddles. I know the owner."

"Oh. How nice for you." The attendant returned to forward motion.

"No, I mean he's missing. Well, the cat's owner is missing, as well as him." She nodded toward Tiddles. "Rather his caretaker, not owner, is gone missing."

The young woman stopped again. "Excuse me, but you're not making sense."

"He's not in the rescue?"

"Our rescue is one of the finest in Britain. But no, this client is boarding."

"How did he get here?"

"Well, he didn't fly."

Duncan tried to hide a chuckle. At least, the attendant's sarcasm generated something redeeming.

"Where was he found? Who's paying his board?"

The woman took a deep breath. "We don't divulge information concerning our boarding clients, madam. If you know the owner, as you say, why don't you contact them? Now, please excuse me." The woman disappeared behind an automatic door.

"Welcome to Queen's Gardens," the receptionist greeted from her area.

Berdie wanted to follow the caretaker into the inner sanctum, but felt compelled to take care of Duncan and his Razor. She pondered the fact that Tiddles was in boarding as she and Duncan made their way to the desk.

"What time is your appointment?"

"Appointment?" Berdie raised her brows. "I'm afraid we don't have an appointment."

"Oh, dear," the receptionist twittered.

"We were hoping to place a wayward cat in safe keeping." As she looked toward the automatic door behind which Tiddles and his warden disappeared, Berdie sat Razor, in the cat carrier, absently on the floor.

"Oh, no." The woman patted the smooth surfaced countertop. "Please don't set the client on the floor, place them here."

"What's a client?" Duncan asked Berdie.

Berdie placed Razor in all his harrowing majesty on the granite countertop.

The woman's eyes widened. "I say." Her jaw dropped, and she placed her palms on her cheeks.

Berdie wasn't entirely sure what to expect next. 'Get your mangy client off my polished tabletop?'

"This is wonderful, a small miracle." The woman almost cheered.

"Is it?" Berdie was sure she sounded amazed.

The woman bent closer to the cage and examined Razor. "Yes, indeed. Incredible. He's a bit thin, but it's quite incredible. Where did you find him?"

Berdie looked at Duncan.

"On the green, Sunday," he offered quietly.

Sunday. Berdie flashed back to the conversation with lemonade-toting Duncan and his pal. And yes, the cat was following him. This cat became suddenly interesting.

"The village green, Aidan Kirkwood," Berdie reiterated to the receptionist.

The woman stuck a finger through the carrier. "Who's the lovely cat, then?" she purred.

Berdie could feel her eyes pop at the word lovely. What planet had she landed on?

"Mr. Moore will be pleased."

"Mr. Moore?" Berdie inquired.

"Hero's owner. He volunteers occasionally. Although his flight departs soon, he just happens to be here today."

"Indeed?" Berdie's interest flamed into anticipation.

"Please be seated." A rushed wave toward the lounge area was followed by punched numbers on the telephone.

Berdie took Duncan's hand, and they slipped onto a sofa where the cat-care video narrated in a voice Berdie thought was solely reserved for televised golf, offered tips on feline grooming. Berdie's thoughts whirled while Duncan watched the video. Why was Tiddles boarded? Did someone find him? But why pay board for a stray cat?

Duncan tapped her arm. "Do you think Razor will forget about me?"

"No, I shouldn't think so, Duncan. He seems to have grown very fond of you. But, if he had an owner before he found you, well, he should be with them."

"I know. Mummy said."

The receptionist finished her telephone conversation and another automatic door opened from a place beyond the lounge to reveal a tall, handsome gentleman who raced toward reception. Berdie assumed him to be Mr. Moore.

When he came to rest at 'the client's' cage, he couldn't scramble quickly enough to pull Razor from the enclosure and clutch him to his chest with both hands. He ran his silvered goatee chin across the cat's head. "My dear, dear Hero," he murmured.

The cat gave a scratchy meow, and the receptionist clasped her hands, a giant grin on her face. It was almost a portrait of happy families.

Duncan watched the goings on without a word.

Berdie cleared her throat and stood. "Would you like to meet the child who rescued your cat?"

Mr. Moore seemed entirely unaware there was anyone else for miles.

Berdie put her hand on Duncan's back and guided him forward. As she did, she felt her stomach squeeze and her face flush. The smiling gentleman seated in a car from whom she had asked directional help just a couple days past danced through her memory. Minus the sunglasses, Hero's owner, Mr. Moore, was that man.

She momentarily halted hoping he wouldn't recognize her, groping for some sensible defense she could give him for her foolish action. *There's none perfect, no not one,* filtered through her thoughts. Especially vicar's wives. Last time she let his charm disarm her, but at this meeting, she would keep her surefooted sense about her. She tugged the hem of her top, straightening it properly. Berdie gave a mental nod forward, threw her shoulders back, and soldiered on to the counter. "This is Duncan Butz, Hero's rescuer."

Mr. Moore glanced her way and returned his attention to his pet. He stroked the cat gently. "He's a masterful escape artist despite the security here."

"Mr. Moore's been searching everywhere for Hero, he's so devoted," the receptionist wore what Berdie would call goo-goo eyes.

"In Timsley, perhaps?" Berdie blurted.

The man's head rose. His lovely, sea-colored eyes seemed to penetrate to the core. He studied Berdie. "My dear lady," came in silky chocolate tones. He tipped his head, knit his brow momentarily as if searching his memory, and then appeared to move past it. It would seem he didn't remember her. "You're responsible for Hero's return?"

"Actually, Duncan found him."

Mr. Moore's gaze fell on Duncan. "Well done."

Duncan nodded. "I like Razor."

"Razor?" Mr. Moore shook his head. "No, no, my Cassie named him Hero."

"Cassie?" Berdie asked.

"My daughter."

"Well, he certainly looks as though he's gone a few rounds with the other toms and come out on top."

Mr. Moore frowned. "You've no idea what you're saying." He ran his fingers over the cat's notched ear. "Hero is called so because he rescued my daughter."

Berdie thought it quite an irony that at a cat rescue, a cat had done the rescuing. "Oh, I see. I didn't realize."

"No, you wouldn't," he zipped.

"Rescued how?" Duncan's eyes were suddenly bright.

The man scratched Hero under the chin and directed his conversation to Berdie. "Cassie, who was about his age," he nodded toward Duncan, "was in our home when it caught fire. She was sleeping, and the flames spread to her room. Hero always slept on her bed. He refused to leave her." The father touched one of the scars. "These are old burns, not fight relics." He rubbed his nose across Hero's head. "He stayed right there with her and howled, screeched. That's how the fire brigade found her."

"Wow, he did that? He really is a hero." Duncan smiled.

"Indeed." Berdie patted the lad on his back. "I'm sorry to pry, sir, but you make it sound as if Hero was the only one home with your daughter at the time."

"I had gone off to work." His voice went from velvet to vinegar. "My wife," he took a deep inhale, "went to borrow a pint of milk from young Mr. Hadley, our neighbor." He glanced at Duncan and back at Berdie. "After the fire, I discovered this was not the first time she had left Cassie unattended to borrow milk from Mr. Hadley, but that it happened quite regularly. Sometimes, an hour or more at a time, if you get what I'm saying."

"I see." Berdie nodded. "I'm sorry."

"You've nothing to be sorry for."

"I just mean it's quite sad that all this happened." Berdie put her hand on Duncan's shoulder. "But Hero did rescue your Cassie."

"Yes." He ran a thumb down Hero's tail.

"However, despite his gallantry, six weeks later my daughter succumbed to the burns she received. He's all I have left of her." The man's eyes moistened as he stroked his fingers across Hero's fur.

Duncan looked at Berdie. "Scucome? What's that?"

Berdie bent down to Duncan's level. "That means Cassie's body didn't get well, and she went to be with Jesus in heaven," she said softly.

"Oh." Duncan looked at Mr. Moore. "You must be happy you've still got Hero."

The man cleared his throat.

"Well." The desk attendant made a quick dab to her nose and put on a cheery face. "Would you like me to take Hero to his room, Mr. Moore?"

"Room?" Berdie asked.

"Our boarding rooms are wonderful." The woman was exuberant. "Softest of cat beds, climbing posts, toys, soft music, adjustable lighting, play sessions with other cats, gross motor massage, individual garden runs, CC TV." She took a breath. "And, of course, a personal animal technician who visits with the client for twenty minutes every two hours."

Berdie barely believed her ears. "I've stayed at spa hotels that offered less."

"Some of the best care in all the country," Mr. Moore added. "And, no Sheila, I'll take Hero to his room myself." He turned to go.

Berdie spoke. "I should say, it was kind of Duncan to care for your Hero, wasn't it?"

He gave her no heed and kept his forward progress.

Berdie, despite the tender story and penetrating eyes, was not having this. "Duncan, perhaps you should get a drink of water," she persuaded. "We'll be leaving soon."

Duncan nodded and went to a water dispenser at the far end of reception.

"Mr. Moore, do you live in Timsley?" Berdie called.

He stopped and turned. "No."

"But you do drive a car." She told him the make and model and stepped closer to him.

"What matter is that to you?"

Berdie took a deep breath. "There was a hit and run incident in Timsley just a day or two ago that involved a car such as yours."

He eyed her and lifted his chin as if something had registered in his memory. "My dear lady," he uttered in a patronizing tone.

"My name is Mrs. Elliott, Berdie Elliott." She straightened. "Well?"

"Really!" The receptionist frowned.

Mr. Moore's eyes narrowed. "Mrs. Elliott, I don't think I care for what you're implying. Not at all." He turned.

"I met Mr. Broadhouse."

The man froze momentarily, his visage dark when he turned toward her again. "I don't know what that's supposed to mean, but I politely suggest you stuff your accusations." He stepped through the automatic door without a backward glance.

The receptionist glared. "How dare you speak to Mr. Moore in such a manner." She crossed her arms. "I believe it's time for you and your grandchild to go."

"Grandchild?" Berdie pursed her lips. "I know you do wonderful things for cats in this feline palace, but there seems to be little regard for a brave and kind five-year-old boy."

"I say." Sheila jutted her jaw forward.

"And besides that, something here doesn't smell right."

The woman gasped, and her eyes grew narrow. "The whole of our facility is cleaned and deodorized at all times. Entirely spotless."

Duncan was back, and Berdie took his hand. "Come along, love. It's time for us to go." As they exited Berdie glanced back to see the attendant take large sniffs of air, a spray can in hand. If she wasn't so chafed by the lack of consideration toward Duncan and the knowledge that something peculiar was afoot, Berdie would have chuckled.

"You were very brave, Duncan," Berdie praised when they were seated in the car. "Your mum and dad, Reverend Elliott and I, well the whole village, I dare say, will be jolly proud of you."

Duncan wore a faint smile and nodded.

"I know you missed school time to do this. Would you mind if we dallied just a bit longer?"

"Dallied?"

"I think a stop at Bearden's Creamery for a dish of ice cream wouldn't go amiss."

"Should do." Duncan's eyes sparkled.

Berdie stuck the car key in the ignition, just as a vintage and beautifully maintained classic vehicle pulled into the car park and stopped in the spot marked *Reserved for Director*. Right before her eyes, the cat couple emerged. "Hold that thought Duncan." Berdie was keen as mustard. "Stay here, I need to briefly speak to the people who just arrived. Think about what flavor ice cream you fancy."

Duncan nodded.

Berdie exited the car and strode across the car park. She was on a roll: first Tiddles, then Mr. Moore, and now the cat people.

Shovel in hand, who knew what may turn up in this divinely timed tête-à-tête.

11

Just out of their car, Berdie hailed the couple.

Their response to her entreaty hardly appeared enthusiastic.

Mrs. Stanford's rouged cheeks stood out making her almost look in the throes of a fever. She wore a shell pink dress with same-color gloves and a strand of pearls. Mr. Stanford wore a light colored suit and, of course, his distinctive tie, which looked just like the one Mr. Moore was wearing. Hardly what one would expect to wear to a cat rescue, but then everything about this place seemed to challenge expectations.

"May I have just a moment?" Berdie asked, while moving toward them.

"Are you a patron?" Mr. Stanford asked.

"Yes, my young friend and I just returned a lost cat."

"How may we be of service?" Mrs. Stanford tipped her head. A touch of gray peeked from beneath the woman's honey brown page-boy hair style.

"I'm Mrs. Elliott," Berdie introduced.

"Ah, yes, the vicar's wife." Mr. Stanford nodded courteously.

His wife eyed her husband. "Tavy?"

"From Aidan Kirkwood," he answered his wife and directed his attention to Berdie. "Octavious Stanford, and this is my wife, Millicent."

The woman creased her forehead. "Vicar's wife.

Oh, yes. Nothing to do with cats and hot pans I hope."

"Not one hot pan in sight," Berdie promised, "Just a couple of questions."

"We are due for a meeting inside," Mr. Stanford warned.

"I'll come straight to it, then. You have a cat boarding with you, looks a bit like a vampire: black and white, exposed fangs, frightening, some would say."

"Frightening to those unfamiliar, perhaps," Mrs. Stanford replied.

"So you know the feline?"

The pink clad woman looked at her husband.

"I think what my wife is trying to say is that her love for felines is universal, if they are lovely or not. No domestic cat generates fear if you're fond of the creatures." Octavious smiled at his wife. "Right, Millie?"

"Indeed." The woman moved her bag from her elbow to holding it with both pink-gloved hands in front of her waistline.

"Tiddles, when he becomes familiar, as you say, does prove to be a gentle thing."

The Stanfords simply stared at Berdie.

She tried to make her next words as light and airy as the birdsong about the place. "By whom is he being boarded, if I may?"

"No, you may not." Millicent smiled, though she sounded like a grandmother gently scolding her grandchild as she waggled her index finger toward Berdie. "We can't answer client inquiries. It's against our honorable standards."

"We protect our client information." Mr. Stanford sustained.

"Your shelter is important, but certainly not a confessional or legal office," Berdie offered with light joviality.

Both Stanfords frowned.

"Our businesses sustain the highest of personal protocol," Mr. Stanford said. "And your next question?"

Berdie could see this line of inquiry, though presented pleasantly, wasn't working. And she had that other very important question to ask them. She decided to try it on.

"You attended our Ascension Sunday concert."

Millicent leaned close to her husband.

"I hope you enjoyed it."

"Yes, thank you." Mr. Stanford cleared his throat. "Well if that's it then, we'll move on."

They *were* there.

"You were seen speaking to Mrs. Olivia Mikalos, Tiddle's caretaker, on the village green at the concert. How well do you know her?"

"Who?" Mr. Stanford tipped his head.

Berdie opened her bag and pulled out the photo of Olivia. "This woman."

Mrs. Stanford glanced at the picture, and then at her husband.

"Oh, is that her name?" Mr. Stanford registered little surprise. "Yes. She was just someone in the crowd who started a conversation with us, as you do at those types of affairs."

"Seemed a rather nice lady," Mrs. Stanford added.

"She was interested in our facilities, our fund raising efforts, that kind of thing." Mr. Stanford pointed at the entrance of the facility. "Now, if that's it, you'll excuse us."

"Were you aware Mrs. Mikalos is missing?" Berdie quipped.

"Is she, indeed?" Mrs. Stanford rubbed her finger on the pink leather bag.

"In fact, you may have been the last ones to see her. Do you recall what happened after she left your conversation?"

"*We* left the conversation, actually." Mr. Stanford's tone was moving from pat to perturbed. "If you must know, Millie wanted to be closer to the choir for good hearing of the concert."

Millie shook her head. "Yes."

"I see." Berdie slipped the photo back into her purse. "Did you enjoy your lemonade?"

"Not at all, quite sour." Mrs. Stanford's sugary smile stood in contrast to her words.

"Move along now, Millie, we don't want to be late." Mr. Stanford gently began to guide his wife toward the entrance with his palm resting on her back.

"My young friend and I returned the missing Hero, that's why we're here. Mr. Moore was ever so happy."

Mrs. Stanford's face lit and she stopped. "Oh, our lovely Hero has been found. Tavy, do you hear that?"

"Yes, my love." The man gave his wife a gentle nudge with his palm. "Good news." He glanced at Berdie. "Goodbye, Mrs. Elliott."

"My young friend has a photo of him and Hero that Mr. Moore should love to see. Can you give the young man Moore's address so he can send it to him?"

Mr. Stanford straightened. "You said you had a couple questions. You've asked several. For a vicar's wife, I must say you're certainly sticking your nose in. Now, goodbye, Mrs. Elliott."

"Yes, well, I'm sure you have a great deal to do. I know I do." Berdie watched the couple scoot to a back entrance. "Is there anyone in the whole of this facility who isn't rude, daft, or hiding something?" Berdie murmured. As she walked to the car, she wove her thoughts together.

Tiddles was being boarded by an unknown. The Stanfords, it would seem, were the last to see Olivia. They said they met her in conversation at the fete, but Mrs. Stanford's body language didn't say that at all.

"They know her. They have Tiddles, and Hero is 'our Hero.'" All of this settled into Berdie's head like a jumble of puzzle pieces. Cats, hit and run, Broadhouse, Elise, Sir Percival, Mr. Moore, numberless house, greed-inviting will, and Billie Finch. What an odd soup. There was a missing ingredient, but what?

Berdie reached the car. "Thank you for being patient, Duncan. Off we go." Berdie started the car and was nearly out the car park.

Duncan wrinkled his nose. "Mrs. Elliott, does that Mr. Moore live at this cat house?"

Berdie had to bite her tongue to prevent howling in laughter. "No, I shouldn't think so."

"Well, if he loves Razor," he paused, "if he loves *Hero* so much, why doesn't he take him home with him? Why keep him here?"

"My dear Duncan, have you ever thought of becoming a detective? That's an excellent question."

He shrugged. "I just know I'd want him with me all the time. Well, except at school."

Berdie grinned. "Yes, except at school." Berdie tucked the words in with Duncan's query. "You know, I can't answer your question right now, though I have some guesses. At the moment, I'm looking for someone who's gone missing. And when I've found them, I believe I'll be able to answer your question about Mr. Moore and Hero."

Duncan stared at Berdie. "You're clever, aren't you Mrs. Elliott?"

Berdie chuckled. "I prefer to say I often put the talents God's given me to good use."

Duncan smiled and leaned back in the seat.

Berdie maneuvered the car into the lane and in the direction of Aidan Kirkwood. She was suddenly grateful that little Duncan was with her. The naivety, honesty, and wonder of five-year-old reality was a refreshing antidote to the insolence, deception, and posturing she had just confronted.

She opened her window. "It's such a lovely day Duncan, there's sun and flowered meadows. Shall I open your window?"

"Yeah," Duncan nodded his head so hard Berdie thought he'd do his neck a mischief.

She opened the passenger window and Duncan stuck his hand out, moving it about, playing with the wind.

"Now what flavor ice cream suits you?"

"Well, either lemon sherbet, or maybe chocolate swirl, but I like pink peppermint, too."

"Or perhaps all three?"

Duncan's eyes lit and his cheeks grew round as he smiled. "Oh, yes, all three."

"There's a treat, then."

Duncan let go a hearty giggle.

Berdie sped them back to Aidan Kirkwood.

****

Berdie reversed the car down the Butzs' paved drive while waving goodbye to Ivy and Duncan in the doorway.

She had enjoyed time with Duncan at Bearden's Creamery almost as much as the lad enjoyed eating his fill of all three flavors of ice cream.

As she made her way to the vicarage, she wished she could rummage through all the pieces of this case with an eager comrade: Lillie. She missed her friend greatly. Lillie had not returned any of Berdie's calls yesterday except a text to say she was busy. Berdie needed to talk with her, bounce what was happening off her trusted ally. She hadn't truly appreciated how much a part Lillie played in her shuffling through ideas, sorting facts, reading between the lines. She hoped that her dearest friend's less-than-gracious attitude, when the topic of Loren entered the conversation the last time they'd video conferenced, had been laid to rest.

"And perhaps I was a bit condescending about her efforts to find Livy," Berdie admitted to the space in her car. On the High Street, she pulled over despite the busyness of it all. She parked near the White Window Box Garden and Gifts and rang up Lillie on her mobile. *I pray this goes well.* This time Lillie answered.

"Hello, Berdie," Lillie answered a bit breathy.

Berdie reckoned this was a good start. "Lillie, I hope things are going well for you."

"Yes, thank you," she clipped, "if you have an interest in hearing about them." She took a deep breath.

"Of course I do, Lillie. Listen, I'm sorry if I haven't been the most supportive, it's just…"

"No need," Lillie interrupted with a bit more pep

in her voice. "Water under the bridge, and I'm certainly not a complete innocent." She took a gulp of air.

"Lillie, are you OK?"

"It's just that I'm rushing back to the guest house from the Funchal Marina."

Berdie heard what sounded like traffic creating splashes from water-filled roads.

"It's raining?"

"Bucketing."

"You did take an umbrella?"

"Actually, I had to buy one here."

"I should take a cab."

"Will do as soon as I reach the Boulevard do Mar."

"Can you carry on a conversation?"

Lillie laughed. "Now when am I not capable of nattering on?"

Berdie grinned. Yes, Lillie had moved on since their last conversation.

"There have been interesting developments, Berdie, quite interesting."

She wanted to tell Lillie there were developments with her investigating, as well. But considering she hadn't shown proper interest last time, instead she asked a question. "What are they?"

"Following your suggestion, I've waded through wedding venues. I went to Os Arcos, a lovely seaside resort, where they specialize in weddings for people from abroad. A worker there recognized Livy from my photo. She said Livy and her intended, several weeks ago, had a very quiet, low profile wedding, not more than a ten minute affair, very last moment."

"Last minute?"

"It wasn't even on the hotel's schedule of events

for the day, the attendant said. It was just crammed in between two large weddings. That's why she clearly remembered it."

"You were right all along, Lillie, she is married."

"Indeed." Lillie took a deep inhale and the sound of passing vehicles sending sprays of water became louder. "I've reached the boulevard. I'm sure a cab will come by soon."

"Yes. And what about the groom?"

"He's English, registered as Morgan Cliff. He's tall, handsome, light hair, some years older than the bride according to the worker."

"I see. And why did you go to the pier?"

"Livy and husband said no to the free celebratory drinks following their vows. She made the comment that they'd celebrate on board."

"On board, that means a boat," Berdie said to herself as much as to Lillie.

"Lots of dinner cruises in Madeira."

Berdie heard a rustled sound, and then Lillie's muted call for a taxi.

"He flew right past," Lillie said in a less than happy tone.

"Show a little leg," Berdie teased.

"As wet as I'm getting, I'm tempted."

"Lillie, have you found Livy and her husband registered at a hotel?"

"No, not anywhere I've checked so far, but then I've dozens yet to go."

"And what did you find at the pier?"

"That's it. Getting wet through for nothing really, apart from seeing the eye-popping leisure craft, and plenty of them. I tried yesterday as well as today. The authorities there, as well as the cruise service workers, were a bit rough and not at all eager to respond. Although it seemed to me a couple of the dock attendants registered a spark of recognition with Livy's picture, none admitted it."

Berdie didn't like the fact that Lillie, on her own, was poking around a waterfront. She knew they were often rather unsavory places. "Lillie, just how far are you taking this investigation?"

Lillie released a heavy sigh. "The fact is, Berdie, I love Madeira, but this has turned into a real grind, far more work and much less fun than I thought."

"I think you've done marvelously, Lillie. You've a full report to give Harriett Norman. It really needn't go any farther."

"But, I haven't found Livy."

"Near enough. Let Harriett hire a private detective who has the resources necessary to take it from here, with absolutely no remorse on your part. As I said, you've done splendidly."

"Yes, perhaps."

Berdie heard an especially loud splash and Lillie yelped.

"Lillie?"

"I'm absolutely drenched head to toe."

There was a garbled sound, and Lillie's voice skipped and chopped.

"I…yes…taxi…tonight…"

"What Lillie? You're breaking up."

"Seven…video conference…talk."

"Lillie?" Berdie was met with silence. If she understood the string of bits and pieces correctly, she would be speaking with her friend on the computer at seven this evening. Although she didn't get to talk with Lillie about the Mikalos case, she certainly would tonight if her understanding of Lillie's words bore out. And the odds were high that with a slight nudge, Lillie could be back in Aidan Kirkwood tomorrow. Berdie jammed her cellphone into her bag with a sense of relief and delight for Lillie's sake. Well, after video conferencing this evening and with a wing and a prayer, Lillie could be home soon.

Berdie's thoughts were shattered by a not-distant ricocheted gun shot. Instinctively, she ducked low in the car seat sending her glasses downward on her nose and her heart into an elevated rhythm. What on earth was going on? She heard music. Rock. Golden rock. She cautiously glanced upward through the bottom of the windscreen.

Lucy Butz, standing in front of the White Window Box, had an odd squint as she stared at Berdie. The teen didn't seem in the least alarmed.

Berdie brought herself to an upright position again, pushed her glasses to their proper place and looked about. People were walking in and out of the shops, in conversation on the way, contented, by the look of it. None at all startled.

Lucy came to the opened driver window. "Mrs. Elliott, you all right in there?"

Berdie wondered if she may be losing her mind. "Lucy, you didn't hear it?"

"Hear what?"

"No, I guess you didn't." Berdie tried to appear quite together and not at all baffled as the music continued.

Lucy pointed to Berdie's bag on the floor of the passenger side. "You mean that?" The corner of the teen's mouth arched upward as what sounded like a growly fifties band resonated. "I dare say it could be your mobile?"

"*My* mobile?" Berdie grabbed the bag and opened it. A single music note exploded from the interior and suddenly all became silent. Berdie lifted the instrument from her bag and checked. Yes, Hugh's mobile number was displayed as most recent caller. She looked at Lucy. "That certainly wasn't the song I chose."

"A song?" she glanced about.

Berdie felt pink rise to her cheeks. "Nothing to trouble yourself with." She took a deep breath. "Well, thank you, Lucy. You've been very helpful."

Lucy chuckled. "Sure, Mrs. Elliott, any time. By the way, thanks for taking my little brother to unload that mangy cat."

"It was my pleasure." Berdie readjusted her glasses.

"Now, you're sure you're all right?"

"I'm fine, Lucy, love. Really." As the teen walked into the shop, Berdie laid her head against the back of the car seat. Well, now, that was embarrassing. Certainly not one of her more glittering moments of church community life.

What had insinuated itself as her mobile ring now? It was almost as if the machine had a mind of its own, constantly at odds with her about just who was in charge. She took a deep inhalation and let the air slip ever so slowly between her lips. Gathering her wits, she rang Hugh.

"Berdie, love, have you finished your mercy cat run?" he greeted.

"Yes." She took a shallow breath. "Where are you?"

"You sound a bit shaky. You OK?"

"Yes, Hugh, I am fine." Berdie knew her response

was a bit too loud. "I really am fine," she reiterated in a calmer voice. "Now, are you home?"

"No, in Timsley. I'm still at St. Mark's. Listen, I have a bit of a problem. I told Natty's niece that I'd look in on Natty at their home, but I'm due in less than twenty minutes, and I'm not going to make it. Reverend Simpson and I are still stuck on his Whitsun project, and I can't get away. I've tried to ring Natty's niece, but the line's engaged."

"Let's see, this is where you say, 'Berdie would you please go by Natty's, have a wee chat, and tell her I'll arrange another time to call by.'"

"Words out of my mouth. Except."

"Except what?"

"You didn't include the bit where I ask you to take her a small token, say flowers, grapes, something like that on behalf of the church."

Berdie glanced at the White Window Box. "That's simple enough."

"Oh, good, that's a relief."

"Who's a lovely girl, then?"

"Abounding in goodwill, just as you said this morning."

Berdie chuckled. "Cheeky you. Can I expect you home for tea?"

"Of course, but a bit late. How about I get some take away?"

"I'll look forward to it. See you then." Berdie was headed to the White Window Box more quickly than a spring bee to its blossom so intent was she on her new task. The bell clattered as she entered.

Instantly, she felt as if in the midst of a garden, the scent of fresh flowers flooding the shop. She took a deep breath and somehow the entire world seemed at rights.

Gifts of soap, cushions, framed art, and ceramics were sprinkled about with floral wreaths and vases of fresh flowers. All sat upon dressers, cabinets, classic shelves, and wooden fruit boxes in the style of what one might call country chic. It was a delight to the eyes and an invitation to browse.

In one corner, Berdie spotted everyday garden tools displayed in spring colors along with festive garden pinnies. A *Joe's DIY* placard was displayed among the objects. Nearby, a counter boasted posies in glass vases with ribbons.

It looked to Berdie as though they were awaiting delivery.

"Mrs. Elliott, hello," Cara Donovan greeted as she emerged from the back board of the front display window.

"Hello, and aren't you the busy one?"

Cara wiped her hands across her apron that was decorated with ditsy floral designs, and pushed a strand of her long blonde hair behind an ear. "Just setting the front window to rights, must appeal, you know."

"Indeed."

"Can I be of help?"

"Well, I'm going to visit Natty, and I need a little something to lift her spirits."

"Sweet Batty Natty, I heard she did herself a mischief. Is she faring well?"

Berdie nodded. "Yes. But she has to stay off her feet, and it doesn't suit her."

Cara smiled, her gray eyes twinkling. "I'd say not. Did you see her prance in the procession Sunday?"

She scooted to one of the dresser displays. "We've

just started this get-well gift package, and we haven't any going spare." She pointed to a handled wicker basket that held items. "Four lavender sachets that we hand sew here in the shop, and we use special fabric."

Berdie eyed the floral-designed sachets. "How decidedly feminine."

"Then, we add lavender and lemon soap." Cara picked up the fabric-wrapped rectangle and extended it for a sniff at Berdie's nose.

"Lovely."

"Mrs. Plinkerton's daughter has been producing the soaps for us. Makes for a restful, scented bath." She returned the soap to the basket and pointed to a small tin. "And we include some medicinal herb tea, and lastly, a hand-embroidered hankie for sniffles. The girl's group do the hankies as a badge project."

"Sounds a treat. Please put it on the church account."

"Clergy discount, of course." Cara plucked some petite grape irises from a silver bucket and placed them in a diminutive glass vase. "Take these along as well, the shop's contribution to wishing Natty well."

Lucy Butz appeared from the back of the shop carrying two spring wreaths, music buds firmly planted in her ears. The spring wreaths were similar to the one that hung on the front door of Mrs. Mikalos's home.

"Anything else?" Lucy trumpeted Cara's way.

"The posies on the counter please, Lucy. The smaller one to the Harpers on Westwood Road, and the larger ones all go to the women's surgery in Timsley," Cara all but screamed.

The teen nodded and scooped the posies into an awaiting cardboard box, bouncing in rhythm to whatever played in her ears.

"Careful as you go," Cara pronounced and opened the door for the escaping delivery girl, who gave her boss a thumbs-up.

"Godspeed," Berdie bellowed after her.

Cara closed the door. "I pray every time she leaves the shop."

"For safe deliveries?"

"That she'll return alive."

"Yes, I've witnessed her driving, too." Berdie swallowed a chuckle. "Still, is she your official delivery person?"

"It's official when she doesn't have classes at the Tech, or studies, or sibling care at home, or a date with her latest admirer."

"Low on her priorities list, then."

"Very hit or miss, but desperately needed." Cara put Berdie's gift basket in a large white cotton draw-string bag with butterflies fluttering about it and the words White Window Box printed in sea green letters.

"Where's Rosalie?" Berdie wondered why the business partner wasn't helping with the deliveries.

"She's in the back of the shop preparing the flowers for the Rayfield wedding in Mistcome Green. Plus, we have over a dozen orders for our spring wreaths that we have yet to put together. And they're to be shipped tomorrow morning."

"Ah, speaking of wreaths." Berdie took the bag in hand. "I was hoping I might gather some information. It could be valuable in helping someone in distress."

"Well then, I need to do all I can."

"One of your spring wreaths hangs on the door of the home of Mrs. Olivia Mikalos."

"Mrs. Mikalos. Isn't she the woman who's gone

missing?"

"Indeed. The wreath was a gift. I was hoping you could tell me by whom it was purchased and when. Do you have that information?"

"Seeing as you're clergy," Cara leaned closer to Berdie, "or as good as, and an extraordinary sleuth as well, I'll look in our delivery log."

"That kind of flattery could get you the best pew in the house," Berdie teased.

Cara emitted a gentle laugh and went straight to the computer. "Let's see." She clicked the mouse. "Our first spring wreaths were created in March." Cara scrolled down the page.

"Are your spring wreaths always delivered?"

"I can count on one hand the people who have come into the shop to get them. Nearly all are ordered through our website." She watched the screen. "They're special, a bespoke design."

"And how's that?"

Cara continued her perusal. "They're made with sage, lavender, flowering mint, sweet peas, a touch of rosemary, and either peonies or roses. The customer chooses the color and size of peonies or roses, fresh or dried." Cara smiled at Berdie. "And here we are." She tapped her finger on the screen. "One spring wreath with fresh White Pearl roses ordered one week ago with same day delivery to the home of Mrs. Mikalos."

"Just seven days ago?"

Cara nodded. "Ordered by a Mr. Gavin Broadhouse."

"Seven days ago?" Berdie exclaimed. "Are you sure?"

"Yes."

"I see. Mr. Broadhouse. But seven months ago."

"Seven *days* ago," Cara corrected.

"Yes, I was thinking on a past conversation. Seven days. And how did he pay?"

"Credit card," Cara clipped.

"Truly? Well, thank you. That's very helpful, Cara."

Cara clicked the mouse. "Good, and God bless your efforts, Mrs. Elliott."

"You know, Cara, I believe He will. I must get on to Natty's."

Berdie hurried back to her car while making mental notes.

Gavin Broadhouse told her and Hugh that he stopped seeing Olivia Mikalos months ago. But was that true? Why does a gentleman send a wreath of flowers to a woman of romantic involvement, past or present? Is it to mark a special day, perhaps as an apology, for a reminder of enduring love? Paying by credit card for another woman's gift was living rather dangerously for a married man. Could he possibly be Olivia's kidnapper? Here it was, just another piece of the puzzle, and with puzzle pieces littered about the place, Berdie pulled onto the road in the direction of Natty's home.

She enjoyed Natty and it would be a quick visit. One speedy church task and she could give the whole of her thinking over to Olivia Mikalos.

How long before all the pieces were gathered and fitted together?

12

Natty's niece, Sandra, wore a slightly disappointed look when Berdie arrived and entered the home. Sandra's light brown curls were enhanced with a crisp yellow gingham dress, and a ribbon round the waist.

Berdie had an idea that Sandra somewhat fancied Hugh. Single and on the doorstep of her maturing fourth decade, she was a kind soul who was utterly devoted to her aunt's well-being. But the demands of the home care left little time for social endeavors. An attractive vicar may have added a certain sunshine for the shy woman.

"I'll get the tea," she announced after depositing Berdie in the sitting room where Natty lay comfortably on a finely upholstered chaise lounge, groomed and ready to welcome visitors.

Despite Sandra's disheartened welcome, Natty was delighted that Berdie was the one to come calling.

"Natty, how are you?" Berdie smiled extra bright as she pulled an oversized ottoman near the chaise lounge and sat on it.

"All the better for your visit, Mrs. Elliott," she responded with almost child-like enthusiasm. Natty seemed to be quite lucid and full of cheer.

Berdie placed her handbag on the floor, sat the grape iris on a nearby tray table and pulled the gift basket from the shop bag. "A little something to wish you well from the church."

Natty took the basket and grinned. "Oh, you got this from the church?"

"No, Natty, it's from the White Window Box and it's given on behalf of all who attend Saint Aidan."

"Oh." She looked a little anxious. "Is everybody from the church coming?"

Berdie patted Natty's hand. "No. Just me, love."

Natty's face beamed. "That's all right, then." She sniffed the soap and sachets. "It smells of Miriam."

"It does." Berdie wondered if Natty was fully aware that Miriam Livingston had passed from this earth. The former lavender maven of Aidan Kirkwood, and Natty's neighbor, had been her beloved friend.

"I miss her, you know." Natty fingered the medicinal tea tin.

"Yes, I should think you would."

The woman pulled the hand embroidered hankie from the basket and ran it cross her cheek. "But, now I have my Sandra. I'll ask her to fetch us some tea."

Before Berdie could inform Natty that Sandra was in the midst of bringing it, the niece appeared in the doorway.

"Here we are." Sandra moved the vase of flowers aside and positioned the tea service on the tray table that sat astride the chaise lounge.

Natty looked somewhat befuddled. "She's jolly on the spot." She eyed Sandra. "Did you know I wanted tea?"

"You asked for it several minutes ago, Aunty Natty." Sandra flashed a faint smile toward Berdie and bent near her ear. "Her long term memory serves her fairly well, but her short term isn't worth tuppence."

"What did you say?" Natty squirmed.

"I'm just telling Mrs. Elliott about your medical

state."

"Healthy as an ox if she'd let me off this settee."

"You have to stay off your feet, Aunty, as doctor said. Let your ankle heal."

"My ankle? What's wrong with it?"

Sandra shook her head while pouring milk in petite spring-green tea cups. "Do you see what I have to put up with?" she directed toward Berdie with a grin before turning to her aunt. "You did yourself a mischief at the Ascension fete."

The elderly woman tipped her head. Then she leaned slightly forward and touched the stabilizing brace about her ankle. "Oh, yes," Natty whispered. "Silly thing."

Sandra poured tea in the waiting cups. "You were very excited to walk in the Ascension procession and you simply overdid."

"The procession." Natty perked. *"Hail the day that sees Him rise,"* Natty began to sing at the top of her voice. She lifted her arms and commenced to flail them about as she continued in song. *"Ravished from our wistful eyes."*

Berdie couldn't help but chuckle.

Natty muttered a sing-song mumble then, as if finding the words once again on a hymn book page, sang out the words with vigor. *"Reascends His native heaven."* She gave an extra forceful arm flourish on the word *heaven* and bashed her cup of tea on the tray table into spiraling splashes to the floor.

"Aunt Natty," Sandra gently scolded.

Tea dribbled cross Berdie's handbag and seeped into vulnerable spots.

"Oh, dear," Natty mumbled. "Did I do that?"

"You did enjoy yourself at the fete, didn't you

Natty?" Berdie grabbed her bag, and Sandra handed her a napkin to wipe the mess.

"I'm sorry, Mrs. Elliott," Sandra apologized.

"Yes, I did, I did enjoy myself," Natty muttered.

Berdie opened her bag and unloaded the contents to see if any offending liquid had found its way inside.

"I truly did." Natty's delight was suddenly tempered. "That is until that one," she pointed at Sandra, "put me on the bench and told me not to move."

"You had hurt yourself, Aunty," Sandra defended between dabs on the carpet with another napkin. "I put you on the bench so I could fetch Mr. Clark to take us home, and as it turned out, to hospital."

Berdie opened the photo of Mrs. Mikalos to see if the jam smudge on her forehead from Villette's thumb was now accompanied by tea. She spread it out on her lap.

"The bench," Natty repeated. She eyed the photo on Berdie's lap. "The bench," she repeated and drew her hands to her mouth. "Oh my, oh my."

Both Berdie and Sandra looked at Natty as her sunshine became shadowed.

"At what bench did you seat her?" Berdie asked Sandra.

"The one on the edge of the green that faces the road."

"Across from Kirkwood Green B and B?"

"Yes. I'm afraid my aunt had her back to the balloon release, and she's been very unforgiving about it since."

"Natty?" Berdie bent closer.

"A sot." Natty pointed a slightly shaking finger at the photo. "A drunken sot. Very sad, very bad. The bench."

Berdie formed her words with clarity. "Natty, when you sat on the bench, did you see this woman?"

Natty's eyes focused on the photo.

"Did you see her?" Berdie held the picture up.

"Too much to drink, that one. And at a church do. Shame, shame. He had to help her stay afoot."

"He?" Berdie's heart gave a flutter.

Natty ran a hand cross her lap, let go a deep breath, and started humming.

"Did *he* have a lovely tie?" Berdie ran a finger down her bodice.

Natty tipped her head, and then smiled at Berdie. "Would you care for tea?"

Berdie held the photo with both hands and gave it a quick shake. "Natty, did *he* have a goatee?" She cupped a hand under her chin.

"Goatee? Yes, Mr. Clark has one." She jerked her thumb behind her back. "He keeps it in his back garden." She wrinkled her nose. "The creature stinks. But mind you, it makes good cheese, and Sandra thinks so, as well."

Sandra rose from her cleaning of the rug. "I shouldn't bother, Mrs. Elliott." She eyed Natty, who was humming another jolly tune. Sandra stroked the aged white hair. "She's quite moved on."

Berdie laid the photo in her lap again. "Yes, quite."

Sandra lowered her voice to a whisper. "Would you put stock in what she says about the bench and all?"

"I would," Berdie pronounced. She folded the picture and put it in her bag. "She's proven before that she's capable of keen observations."

"Observations. Keen, yes, but sadly, fleeting at

best."

"What, dear?" Natty questioned her niece.

"We were just saying what keen observations you make, Aunty."

Natty smiled proudly. "Well then, where's that tea?"

Sandra handed a filled cup to Natty. "Now, do be careful."

Natty took a sip. She closed her eyes as if relishing each drop. "Sandra, don't forget our guest."

Berdie stayed with Natty for another twenty minutes. It was a pleasant chat, though a bit rambling, but nothing of the *bench* conversation arose.

Riding home in the car Berdie was amazed. Who would have thought this dear one, disregarded by some, could have held such vital information? Berdie trusted what Natty saw. She had proven herself adept in the Livingston case.

Olivia, drunk? She certainly wasn't when Berdie saw her earlier when going through the queue. No. But, by Natty's account, not lucid or resolute, either. *He* kept Olivia Mikalos afoot. The woman was kidnapped, not lured, not caught unawares, kidnapped. But what officer of the law would give two seconds of thought to Natty's testimony?

"Lord, who is *he*?" Berdie knew it was up to her, with God's direction, to uncover who *he* was. And how did Olivia become disabled? She would now need to pour every effort possible into the task. When Berdie entered the vicarage, the hallway telephone was singing. "Vicarage," she answered with a quick breath, barely through the door.

"Mrs. Elliott, it's Billie Finch." The woman's voice held a tremor. "I fear there's a punch up in the making."

"Billie, what's going on?"

"Olivia's son-in-law just parked in front of her house, face like thunder, and marched into Sir Percival's garden."

"Lord have mercy." Berdie suddenly remembered her assurance to Linden that she would sort out Sir Percival Barlow and his illegal fence. But between church business and other concerns around Olivia's disappearance, she had been quite occupied. She could understand how Linden might lose patience. "Now remain calm, Billie. Tell me what is happening."

"Mr. Davies knocked at the door, Sir Percival opened it, but he hasn't let Mr. Davies inside."

"Are you at your window now?"

"Oh, my," Mrs. Finch's voice elevated. "Sir Percival's face has gone quite red."

Berdie had the sense this was not going to end well. She heard Billie gasp.

"What?"

"That old goat is now stabbing his index finger into the young man's chest."

Berdie couldn't help but feel somewhat responsible for what was happening. "Keep an eye out, Billie. Don't be frightened. Call 999 if foul play commences."

"Foul play? Oh, dear, Mrs. Elliott, I don't know. Oh, dear."

"Stay inside at your window, and you'll be safe as houses. I'm on my way, Billie. I'll be there as soon as possible. And, Billie..."

"Yes?"

"I'm sending prayers that way. You add yours, as well."

Billie sighed. "Oh, yes, must do. Please, quick as a bunny, then, Mrs. Elliott," her warbled words cracked.

Berdie tried to ring up Hugh on her trek to Timsley, but found distracted driving didn't suit her and decided it could wait.

"Oh Lord, protect and preserve. And please give Billie Finch a portion of courage, some real bottle."

Berdie worked at steeling herself for whatever she was about to face. But upon her arrival, to her surprise, the street was clear and calm.

Billie Finch was out of her door and at Berdie's car in a shot.

Berdie exited the vehicle.

"It was a dust up, all right," Mrs. Finch tattled and took a gulp of air.

"Police?"

Billie shook her blonde, shoulder-length locks in the negative. "Sir Percival waved a piece of paper about and the two of them had words. That old bully landed a punch and Mr. Davies fell back, but turned aside."

"Heavens above."

"Sir Percival slammed his door, and Mr. Davies went to his car. I dashed out and offered Mr. Davies a bag of frozen peas."

"Frozen peas?"

"To use as an ice bag, help keep down the swelling." Her eyes held pity. "He placed it on his left eye which was already going blue."

"Billie Finch. That was quite a kind thing to do for Linden, and brave, as well."

The corners of Mrs. Finch's mouth formed a shy grin.

"Nothing more than a black eye, then?"

"Well, apart from hurt pride and little actually accomplished, I'd say."

Berdie could feel her sense of justice pick up speed. "Billie, could you do a favor? Go to your sitting room window and keep an eye out."

"Why?"

"I'm going to speak with Sir Percival."

Billie's face went a bit pale. "Is that wise?"

"I'll not go in the house, and he won't raise his hand to me, a woman." Berdie began her march toward Barlow's front garden. She hoped she was right.

"Do take care," Billie called out. Like a rabbit to its hole, she rushed back into her house.

Berdie used her determined knock at Sir Percival's front door. "Hate evil, love good, maintain justice," she whispered.

The door flew open, and the stormy face of Sir Percival Barlow greeted her. He drew back.

"Good afternoon, Sir Percival," Berdie said in a solid but kindly voice.

"What do you want?"

"I want the truth." Berdie anchored her feet, aligned with her shoulders.

He jutted his bottom lip forward.

"Do you know the whereabouts of Mrs. Olivia Mikalos?"

The man's eyes went into a squint. "Oh, yes, you and another were in my road a few days back."

"Please answer the question, Sir Percival."

"I've not seen the woman, I don't care to see the woman, and I haven't so much as a raindrop in a bucket's worth of an idea where she could be. There, I've answered your question." The fellow began to close his door.

"Why did you move the Mikalos back garden fence?"

"They're coming out of the woodwork today." Sir Percival thrust his index finger toward Berdie, but pulled it back. His attempt to steady the shaking digit wasn't working. "Need you ask why? My family has owned the Barlow House Estate for generations.

"Then the economic decline hit this fair country, and we had to release our heritage into the hands of money-grabbers who had no real understanding of the beauty or the legacy of this soil. They bought the estate, kept the house, turned it into a sultan's palace, and sold the land off in bits and pieces." He took a deep breath, his eyes intense, and every muscle in his body taut. "Tatty houses, built one upon the other." He thrust his hand in the air, and waved it from east to west.

"Natural splendor erased, and all to line their pockets. To watch the decline of the estate was difficult enough. But, to stand in the back garden of my dwelling, this former gate house, the only family land left, and look across the lea at the now-departed bequest that was my childhood home..." There was a catch in his throat. Wetness crept into those intense eyes. "He swans in, occupies the home for only eight weeks of the year at best." Sir Percival Barlow squeezed his lips together so tightly, they went pale. "My birthright has become his footstool."

For just a moment, Berdie saw before her not a raging bull, but a lamb whose stately identity had been led to slaughter.

"And you dare ask me why a few feet of property could mean so much to me?" He lifted his chin. "I've done nothing wrong by moving that fence. I've planned for years to do it and in the past few months I put boots to the ground and made it happen."

"Sir Percival, I can see you've suffered great loss. Still, moving the property line without permission was against the law. Wouldn't family honor be better served by your exercise of personal integrity, as befits a gentleman's character, to rise above the wrong done to you?"

Barlow raised his chin.

"Less land, yes. But Barlow Gardens remain a beautiful tribute, and we're standing on Barlow House Road. Your family name lives on. It's in your hands to keep it well respected. Wouldn't you agree?"

He thrust his hand toward the Mikalos home. "That land is mine, and I've the papers to prove it." He took a breath and turned his gaze away. "All right, I admit that doing it when Mrs. Mikalos was indisposed was a bit underhanded."

"Yes, it was, and suspicious, at that." Berdie suddenly understood. "That's why you purchased your materials at Joe's DIY in Aidan Kirkwood. Who would be the wiser?"

Sir Percival's gaze darted to the ground.

"There you are." Berdie verbally crossed her arms.

"Yes, well, as it happens, it's become more than that." He steadied his gaze back on Berdie. "Joe Lawler offers real service, the way it used to be. He's honest and concerned." The fellow wagged his index finger. "He'd never steal my land."

"Indeed, Joe is a gentleman in work clothes."

The man leaned forward. "Still, I can't say I regret getting my property back."

"No, I dare say you don't. And when Mrs. Mikalos

returns, if indeed she does, you will have to take it up with her."

"I never cared for either her or her greedy husband. But, nonetheless, I wouldn't harm her."

Berdie studied Sir Percival. She believed he was telling the truth. "You felt no such compunction toward her son-in-law."

"He came to *my* door," Sir Percival defended with words full of fire, "and called me a cheat, a liar, and a land thief."

"Linden Davies is out of his mind with worry about his mother-in-law. He made a rash mistake. And you made another one by assaulting him."

"How do you know about that?"

Berdie raised her brows. "It's no way for a gentleman to solve a problem, Sir Percival. Much more can be accomplished when volatile temperament is tamed." Berdie squared her shoulders. "Now, another matter completely. I'm curious, Sir Percival, about your Seabrook Marina jersey that you often wear."

"My father had a boat there. The jersey was his, if it's any concern of yours." The man frowned and thrust his chin forward.

"I see. Well, I must be on my way." Berdie turned to go. She took two steps then looked back to the sad man who still stood, rather out of sorts, in his doorway. "If you're ever in Aidan Kirkwood of a Sunday morning, Mr. Lawler often attends St. Aidan of the Woods Parish Church. Do come in. I believe you'll discover Joe is one of many in our parish who are honest and concerned."

As she strode to the car, Berdie heard the gentle click of Percival's door closing. She gave a smile and wave to Billie Finch, who was obediently perched at her window.

The woman gave a vigorous wave of her own and wore relief like the blue sky after rain. And her very large smile was the rainbow.

****

The take-away Hugh brought home was a treat.

As Berdie munched her Cornish pastie and a fresh tomato and radish salad, she told him of her day's events: Duncan at the cat rescue, Natty's well-being, and then Sir Percival. That bit made for a tussle.

"You galloped off to a possible explosive situation? How could you do that without telling me?"

In the end, Berdie won Hugh's agreement that it had ended well. The fact that she had invited Barlow to church wooed a bit more of Hugh's charity toward her, as well.

With the meal and a tidy up behind them, she and Hugh went to the church.

"I must prepare my Whitsun sermon," Hugh said, "while you peruse wedding service websites."

"Yes dear." Berdie was only amenable momentarily.

Hugh was still banging on about her becoming the church wedding planner and one verbal scuffle was enough for the day.

What she truly anticipated was her visit with Lillie and moving on in her own investigation.

The church door emitted a gentle squeak when Hugh opened it. "I must get Mr. Braunhoff to see to that."

But Berdie barely paid attention. Someone was at the front altar rail kneeling, she assumed, in prayer.

"Shh," Berdie hushed and pointed in the direction of the altar.

Hugh strained forward. "Who is that?" he whispered. "I don't recognize her."

Berdie stared. "I do." She put a hand on her hip. "I shouldn't expect her here, but here she is."

"That sounds a bit portentous."

"It's fine. I'll see to her. You get about your preparation for Sunday morning."

Hugh smiled and quietly stepped to the sacristy.

Berdie couldn't help but wonder, staring at the unexpected person, what would bring Elise Davies to the altar rail of Saint Aidan of the Wood Parish Church. She had to find out. Not wanting to be intrusive, she took a seat on the second pew, making sure she was respectfully quiet.

But it wasn't more than a half minute before Elise apparently sensed someone was near and arose from the rail. She turned. "Mrs. Elliott, how long have you been there?"

"Not even a minute." Berdie smiled and it appeared to draw the woman toward her.

Elise's small eyes looked moist, her cheeks more flushed than usual. Her straight chin-length hair surrounded a face that held not an ounce of joy.

"Did you finally win the wrestling match with your front garden?"

Elise stepped to the pew. She lowered herself gradually until she was seated. She swallowed. "She's gone, isn't she, Mrs. Elliott, my mum's gone."

Oh. "Missing, Mrs. Davies, yes." This seemed a very different Elise Davies, a decidedly more subdued, almost frightened woman.

"I wouldn't believe it, couldn't believe it. But it'll

soon be a week."

Berdie simply nodded. "I'm working on the situation. There's been some headway."

"Why won't the police do something?"

"I've just gotten some information today that may interest them. At least, it has the potential to do so. But tell me, Mrs. Davies, are *you* all right?"

Elise slumped back against the pew. "It's my fault, God forgive me. It is." She put her hands to her face.

Berdie put her hand on the woman's shoulder. "Elise?"

The distressed daughter of Olivia Mikalos lowered her hands to her lap as a single tear escaped and slid down to her chin. "If only I had been there."

"Been where?"

She studied Berdie's face as if looking for sustenance. "My mother and I had a row." Head bowed, she pushed a finger into her palm. "Nothing new about that. And though she hasn't said, I think she blames me for Mr. Broadhouse's departure. I was far from welcoming." She raised her chin. "My mother and I seldom see eye to eye at the best of times. And this time around, I was especially angry with her, the way she plays herself to Linden's emotions." Elise pulled a tissue from her trouser pocket. "I was supposed to fetch her for the Ascension fete that morning, but made some excuse that the children were taking too long to ready themselves. So, Linden took Mum, instead. I and the children were to meet her there and take her home after. But, I despised the thought of spending a single minute with her and couldn't bring myself to do it." Several tears now tumbled from Elise's sad eyes. She tried to catch them with her tissue and sniffed.

"Does Linden know this?"

Elise shook her head. "He'd be so angry."

"What exactly happened that day?"

"I drove here to Aidan Kirkwood. The children were so very keen to come to the fete. When I saw a neighbor and her children from our terrace, I asked if Phillip and Madeline could join them. Then I left."

"You left to go where?"

Elise shrugged. "I just drove and drove. I put together, in my mind, a speech telling mother that I no longer wanted to have anything to do with her. I wished her dead." Elise took deep breaths of air as tears continued their steady course. "Now she's gone."

"We don't know she's gone exactly, only missing."

"Well, she wouldn't be missing, nor gone, had I been there with her, would she?" Elise crinkled her face as if to hold back the river of tears that welled, and bent her head as if in shame.

Berdie scooted closer to her. "Now Elise, I want you to clearly hear what I am saying." Berdie was commanding.

Elise lifted her head.

"Whatever your relationship with your mother, whatever your thoughts toward her, that's something you have to take care of here." Berdie pointed to her heart. "I'd say you've probably made a good start on that."

Elise looked at the altar and gave a tentative nod.

"Your disparaging thoughts toward your mother did *not* bring about this situation. And we have no guarantee that had you been with her at the fete, her kidnapping would not have taken place."

Elise gasped. "Kidnapped. But mother's so strong-willed."

"Not if she was rendered incapable."

"Incapable?"

"I have some ideas about that, but at the moment they're only ideas." Berdie squeezed Elise's hand. "Now, what you need to think about right now is the welfare of your own family."

"That's just it. If I hadn't been so foolish Madeline's tummy upset wouldn't be raging." She dabbed at her nose. "She's sensitive, you know, like her father. Linden wouldn't have a black eye, and despondent Phillip would have his Tiddles."

"Ah, now there's a bright spot." Berdie cheered her tone. "I've found Tiddles, and he's in the best of care. With Madeline being allergic, I think it best Tiddles stay right where he is until things get a bit more settled. Still, assure Phillip that his cat is fine and in time, they'll be restored. You see there, one thing taken care of already."

Elise wiped an eye. "At least that's good, isn't it?"

"And I believe your mother will be found soon. Devote yourself to prayer on her behalf and comfort your family."

Hugh opened the sacristy door and observed what was going on.

"Should I ask Lillie to ring back later?" he asked diffidently.

Elise was on her feet. "Please, I've taken enough of your time. Don't let me interrupt."

"You needn't leave. You're welcome to stay as long as you wish," Berdie offered.

"I didn't feel I could go to St. Matthew without word getting about and reaching Linden. So I came here to..." She glanced forward at the spot where she had knelt.

"I'm so glad you did."

"I really must go. And thank you, Mrs. Elliott."

For the first time in this conversation, a slight smile emerged beneath Elise's thin red nose. She looked to Hugh. "She can take that call."

Berdie stood. "I'll keep you informed." She gave Elise a final nod, and the woman turned.

"I'll see you to the door," Hugh offered Elise. As Hugh passed Berdie, he caught her elbow. "I wouldn't have interrupted, but Lillie was insistent she speak to you now," he whispered.

Berdie nodded and entered the cozy room.

There was Lillie's visage, on the laptop screen, and her face was bright, alight with excitement and no longer sporting her distinctive glasses. Voices could be heard in the lowly lit background.

"You managed your way through the rain, then," Berdie greeted. "Your glasses get wet?" she teased.

"They're in my pocket. And yes, despite the surly cab driver, here I am."

"You have company?"

"What? Oh, that's the telly. A bit loud, I guess. I'm trying to find a weather report."

"Don't want to get rained on again?"

"I want to hire a boat."

"What?"

"Oh, Berdie, you will not believe what I have uncovered." Lillie almost gurgled as she thumbed through her notebook.

"Oh?"

"I'm really beginning to wonder if this case could be linked with Olivia Mikalos's disappearance."

"Linked?" Berdie was intrigued. "How so?"

"You see there's this agency, well it's a home, but

not really, difficult to find, well, apart from that manicured tree, and if they both applied, and both do seem the type," Lillie rattled on. "The whole thing is very confidential, but then that sets things up, doesn't it? And that's just the tip of the iceberg."

"What are you going on about?"

"Oh, now listen to this." She tapped her pencil. "Livy's bank account has disappeared, at least, all of her money has."

Berdie took a deep breath. That was not good news. In fact, it sounded ominous.

"Lillie, how did you get that information, and how many people know you have it? You must be very careful."

"You're beginning to sound like Loren."

"Speaking of, have you rung him?"

"Too busy," she quipped.

"Not a word the whole time you've been away?"

Lillie tapped her finger on the notebook. "Now, can we get on?"

"Lillie, slow down, start at the beginning again and fill in all the details."

Just as Lillie began to speak, a shadowed darkness gathered behind her.

Berdie's heart fluttered. "Lillie!" Berdie interrupted. "Is someone…?"

Abruptly, a large hand holding a swathe of dark cloth pushed the fabric into Lillie's face, covering her eyes, nose, and mouth. And just for a moment, the force of it angled Lillie's head to the side.

"Lillie!" Berdie screamed as she caught only a passing glimpse of what appeared to be a male figure towering behind her dear friend. "Dear Lord."

Lillie choked. She used her hands to strip the cloth

away from her face, but the man slammed his other hand over her shrouded lips and pushed her head backward. Lillie clawed at his hand, her screams muffled.

"Lillie!"

Lillie worked to lift herself from the chair and shake the powerful grasp, but she suddenly lost stamina and went limp.

"Kick him, Lillie, use your feet."

In an instant, with no more than a heavy breath, one of the masculine hands reached toward the laptop and snapped it shut.

Berdie pushed back from the desk. "Oh, dear Lord. Oh, dear Lord." Her pulse leapt and her mouth felt suddenly dry as she shot from the chair.

Hugh entered the room, his face stern, body commanding. "Berdie, I could hear you out in the nave. What's going on?"

"Hugh," she screamed, "call the police. There's been another kidnapping. Lillie!"

13

"I still don't understand how this happened." Loren's rapid strides made it difficult for Berdie to stay abreast of him and Hugh while they moved down a hall that led away from the Timsley Hospital Morgue to the building's public lounge.

"I've already explained all that as best I can." Berdie felt herself nearly panting as Hugh flashed that arching left eyebrow her direction.

Loren all but ripped the door of the lounge off its hinges and stood aside for Berdie and Hugh to enter. He pointed to a mahogany colored couch where Berdie and Hugh seated themselves.

"How could a simple rearrangement of holiday plans in Cornwall trigger such a response? Investigating! She should have never gone to Portugal." Loren paced near the couch.

"Loren, I think you can realize it wasn't a single event that sent Lillie on this escapade."

Hugh glared at Berdie.

"We can all take a certain element of responsibility." Berdie tried to keep her voice even. "That said, Lillie made her own decisions. The point now is what we do from here. How do we go about finding her?"

"We?" If Hugh's eyes had been scissors, they would have cut her words into bits and left them lying on the floor.

"I must go to Portugal." Loren's forehead wrinkled. "How can I ask for the time off when I've just returned from the London conference? And we're short staffed."

"Loren, not to undermine your sincerity or capacities, but isn't that much of the reason Lillie's in her predicament?" Hugh inhaled. "We don't need more would-be detectives dashing about, especially when it involves the Portuguese underworld."

Berdie frowned. "We don't know that the Portuguese underworld is involved."

"You said she had just been to the docks."

"Marina, she'd been to the leisure craft pier earlier in the day. But that doesn't mean…"

"Loren, let the professionals deal with it," Hugh went on. "They're trained. They know their jurisdiction and how to best take care of the situation."

Loren stopped. "Yes. I'll hire Mr. Finn to find Lillie."

Hugh nodded. "Spot on. We've already notified both the Portuguese and English police."

"Well, Goodnight, anyway," Berdie added with bite.

"The British Embassy in Portugal has been alerted and is giving support. All possible resources are at work."

The doctor released a slow exhalation.

Berdie leaned back on the couch. All resources were at work except hers.

Hugh continued to calm Loren with gentle, reassuring patter.

Berdie tried to think constructively through her conversation with her now-missing friend. Lillie said she was going to hire a boat. Why? She believed there was a common thread, a link between the disappearances of Livy and Olivia. What was it? Berdie tried to remember Lillie's ramble. She said the thing that may link the cases together was a home that wasn't a home. So something that appeared to be a home, but wasn't. Berdie worked to recall Lillie's words. Difficult to find, that manicured tree. That tree! Could Lillie mean *that* exotic olive tree, *that* house? No numbers on purpose. Z in Olivia's address book. Confidential? Yes, Lillie said confidential. Berdie's mouth flew open with a huge gasp.

"What?" Hugh sounded alarmed.

"Hugh, do you remember the name of the road we stopped on to find our way to the sports club when we got lost?"

Hugh furrowed his brow. "St. Olive."

"St. Olive?" Berdie raised her voice. "She's the one who was kidnapped by marauding troops."

"And was imprisoned for her faith, yes." Hugh relaxed his wrinkle. "Berdie, I know you're distressed, but can you stay with us? We're sorting Lillie's dilemma."

"St. Olive. It was right there, but I didn't see. I've got to go to that house."

"What house? Are you mad, Berdie?"

As if deaf to Berdie's words, Loren rubbed his hand on the thigh of his trousers. "I'll go upstairs and speak to the chief of staff. Yes, and call Mr. Finn."

Hugh stood. "Do you want me to go with you, Loren?"

"You know more than I, at the moment. That would be helpful."

"We'll call you if we need you, Berdie. Keep your mobile at hand." Hugh sounded as if he was scolding her.

He and Loren exited the room.

"I've got to get to the Stanford house," Berdie said aloud. "Or what seems to be a house." She pulled her head back and looked at the ceiling in realization. The Stanfords, Mr. Moore, and Gavin Broadhouse, the angry man, yes, all were connected to that building. She felt a shiver shoot down her spine.

The sound of a ricochet bullet exploded inside Berdie's purse.

Someone seated nearby in the room went to the window and peered out into the dark street as if they were looking for trouble.

Berdie could make out the music of her mobile now, but she didn't care what her ring was at the moment. "Let it be Lillie," Berdie whispered as she ripped her bag open and brought the mobile to her ear.

There was a graveled breath. "Your friend's in danger."

Oh, him. "Abducted." Berdie bit into the word.

The caller was silent. Then a long breath escaped.

"You didn't know." Berdie tried not to sound surprised. The caller was usually way ahead of her. "And there's active police involvement."

"Yes." There was no edge of surprise in his voice.

"Then why are you calling me?"

An undecipherable grunt was the response.

Berdie thought about her conversation with Lillie and decided to try it on. "How do boats fit in the picture?"

"Boats?"

"Where's Olivia?"

Another long distorted sigh.

"Where?" Berdie almost yelled.

"Would I play cat and mouse if I knew?" he snapped back, a sure sign that he sensed the urgency as much as she did.

She must stay calm to keep the man calm. "The Stanford house with the exotic tree, it's a link, isn't it?"

"Ah," grated through the mobile. "Good. Very good, but very dangerous. Don't get caught."

Berdie suddenly felt her mouth full of cotton. "Caught? Are you suggesting break and enter?"

"Suggesting? If your friend's life means anything to you," he drew a shallow breath, "it must be tonight."

Berdie felt her moral compass wrench from true North. *Break and enter.* That was a breach of the law. But how could she not, when it appeared Lillie's well-being depended on it? "Go on."

"Half two," Raspy droned. "Next security check at half four. Take a flash drive. Entrance security code: Stobbworth 3.

"Stobbworth." Berdie's thinking became simply practical. "Is that with two B's?"

The familiar silence of an empty line met Berdie's ear. She pushed her mobile into her bag. "How does he know the code? Stobbworth 3. Tonight. Two B's or not." She drew a long breath. "Lord, have mercy."

****

Berdie crept close to the rear door where the security pad was located, keeping both her small torch and her black-clad body low. She pulled the dark cap down so it nearly touched her ears.

Getting out of the house and down the drive without Hugh being aware had been a feat despite the chamomile tea Berdie poured down him before bed. If he had any idea at all what she was doing at the moment, he would probably disown her.

Yet here she was in gear worn by thieves and shod in her old fleet-of-foot plimsoles; hardly what she'd wear to church on Sunday. And if she were honest, she savored the adrenalin rush that coursed through her being, knowing her investigation could save lives. She focused all of her energy into the task at hand. "Lord forgive me," she whispered and lifted the security pad cover with her gloved hand. "Even David ate the shew bread, and it is for Lillie." She pulled her glasses down her nose a tad. "S-T-O-B-B-W-O-R-T-H-3." She pressed the buttons carefully.

A click at the latch let her know the door had unlocked. *So far, so good.*

Berdie swallowed, turned the handle, and gave a gentle push. It opened. Softly, she pushed the door wider and stepped inside the dark house. With the same quiet precision, she closed the door behind her.

Torch still held low so as not to be seen through windows, she recognized all the fittings of a kitchen. No red alarm lights and no security camera. Thank God. An electric kettle and coffee maker sat on the counter alongside several biscuit tins. Upside down cups littered the sink draining board. "Nothing more than a breakroom really," she whispered softly and moved on.

The hall had two lowly lit wall sconces, decorative security lighting, no doubt. The front entrance of the house was at the far end. She thought surely this was the main hall.

Deep cherry wood panels covered the lower half of the walls, dark magenta paint the upper, a polished wooden staircase on the left. Glint from a gold frame drew Berdie's gaze to a large romantic painting of an embracing man and woman.

"Not a cat rescue, then," she whispered.

Near the front door, a side table held a sign done in hand calligraphy. *Welcome. Please be seated in the drawing room.*

Berdie recognized a door that looked to be the entrance into the drawing room and gently pushed it open. The squeak of it could equally have been rumbling thunder. She grimaced. It was opened enough to squeeze through sideways, which she did with baby steps, to prevent more alerting noises.

Inside, security sconces cast a sepia glow across the room. The whole of it looked like something found in a National Trust brochure for a stately home. From chandelier to silk cushions, it was all here behind closed brocade drapes. "*Definitely* not a cat rescue." A clock ticked. Everything about the room said titled, refined, civilized, and moneyed. So just what were people seeking when they seated themselves in this room?

A picture began to form in Berdie's mind. It was Livy and Olivia, each sitting alone on the gracious couch. Both nicely dressed, just in from their nearby homes, one in her mid years, the other somewhat younger, and both not short of a bob or two. One discontented, according to Lillie, and the other? "*Christmastide lunch.*" Berdie remembered Billie Finch's words. Her thought spilled out in a soft voice. "I say. Could it be?"

Berdie spied a far door that, by its placement, looked to be an entrance to a possible dining room. She whisked plimsole-quiet through the length of the drawing room, while anticipation heightened. With every sense on high alert, she pushed the door open and stepped inside.

Unlike the previous two spaces, there were no security lights, just a low blue glow accompanied by a muted resonating hum. *Unmistakable.*

Leaving the door slightly ajar, Berdie pulled her torch to waist height. A grand cherry wood desk, overstuffed chairs on one side, a gracious swiveled office chair on the other announced the room was tastefully decorated. Blue reflected off the shiny surface of the desk from the square that declared its presence. "Now we're getting to it. What secrets will you unveil?" she whispered in the direction of the computer. Without ado, Berdie sank into the upholstered office chair and eyed the computer monitor.

Her index finger lightly danced on the *enter* key and *Timsley Social Club Alliance* scrolled across the screen, attended by two handsome couples smiling like they had just won the pools.

Her brain shouted, *Aha.* But her tongue whispered, "I thought as much."

And beneath the title in bold letters were the assuring words: *confidential, discriminating, rewarding.*

"They forgot to add *desperately dangerous.*"

Berdie eyed the little white rectangle that held the pesky declaration: *password.* She put her small torch in the grip of her teeth, shining on the keyboard, both hands now available to begin her dig for valuable information. Her first attempt, Stobbworth 3, yielded no joy.

A noise started her.

She paused. Or perhaps not. She sat solidly still,

ears vigilant.

S-q-u-e-a-k.

Berdie's pulse tripped. The sitting room door!

The adrenaline rush she had savored earlier became a controlled panic. Her mouth went dry as she ripped the torch from it and turned it off.

Almost inaudible, but they were there; slow, deliberate footsteps. And it seemed they moved in the direction of this room.

Berdie sprang from the chair. She eyed the door still slightly open.

There was another step.

She made a brisk move to the wall, squeezing herself tightly against it. Pressed against the door frame on the hinged side, she was sure the intruder would hear her heart pounding.

The steps stopped. A torchlight fell across the floor of the dark room, the steady hum of the computer agitating the still night.

Berdie pulled her capped head around to the edge of the door. Her gaze locked upon the shadow cast by the uninvited guest from the backlighting provided by the drawing room sconces. The torch was in the right hand because the left hand hung to the side. No *apparent* weapon. The silhouette looked somehow familiar.

The door opened wider.

She pulled back. Her legs felt as if they were made of butter, but she planted herself solidly and used the wall to stabilize her body.

The man stepped through the entrance. He took several steps forward, his backside now in view.

Berdie swallowed. *The Lord is the strength of His people.* Take the offensive!

She leapt from behind the door, shoved the narrow end of her torch into the back of the bulky figure, and growled "Hands up" in as deep and bold a baritone voice she could muster.

The figure's hands shot straight into the air, their torch creating a shaky circle of light on the ceiling. "Don't be hasty," he puffed in an unsteady voice.

Berdie knew that voice, and the clothes he wore. It suddenly fit the silhouette. She relinquished her feigned baritone voice. "What on earth are you doing here?"

The figure spun round and flashed his torch in Berdie's face.

She tried to shield the glare with her hands.

"Shells, bells, and little fishes, I should have known," Constable Albert Goodnight bellowed.

"Shh." Berdie put her finger to her lips.

Lowering his torch from her eyes, Berdie could see his startle melt to relief. Then, as if remembering the uniform, his bushy brows knit in consternation. "And here you are, right in it." He straightened. "Mrs. Elliott, I'm placing you under arrest."

Berdie's shoulders slacked. "Albert, if you please…"

"Don't Albert me." His tone was a blast of foghorn. "Constable Goodnight." The unkempt mustache bounced with each word.

"Lower your voice," Berdie scolded in a whisper. "You'll wake the whole of the neighborhood and neither of us need that at the moment, do we?"

Goodnight's stare could have bored holes in wood.

"There's work to be done here."

Goodnight stabbed his finger to his authoritative police insignia. "*I've* got this."

"Yes, you do." Berdie became even more dogged. "And I've got this." She jammed her index finger into the side of her head.

"A dark knit cap?"

Berdie pursed her lips. "Intelligence."

Goodnight reared back and sneered. "We'll just see how smart you are when I put the cuffs on ya'."

"No, no." Berdie held a palm up. "By intelligence, I mean that I have stealth information that can unlock this case. We must find Lillie."

"We?"

"Lillie's my best friend, and I need to bring her to safety."

Goodnight smirked. "Guilt. You feel guilty. Something, I reckon, a vicar's wife like you knows well."

"Call it what you will," Berdie snapped.

Goodnight began zipping his torch round the room. "How'd you find this place out, then?"

"A tip." Berdie hesitated to go into detail.

His torch came back to her. "A snarky gravel eater?"

Berdie knew she surely wore her surprise. "He called you?"

"Woke me from sound sleep. Thought it a prank, but he was dead keen it was urgent." The constable lifted his chin. "Tell me one good reason I shouldn't haul you in right now."

Berdie wanted to put her hands on her hips, get in his face, and bawl, "Because you need me to resolve this whole mess." But she mentally sat on herself and took a totally different tack. "What better way to stop silly village tittle tattle? The village cowboy, indeed. And what a feather in your cap. You solve not one, but three missing person cases in one go. I can be the one to get you there."

Goodnight perked.

Berdie knew it was a bit devious, but she had gone this far, and she was desperate.

"No more starter pistols or parking violations for you, Detective Inspector Goodnight."

The constable turned his head askew and eyed her as if deliberating. She could tell by the rub he gave his chin that he was tantalized.

Berdie optimized the moment. "Give me the next thirty minutes with you here. If I fail to get crime solving material into your hands, take me in." Berdie swallowed. "*But* if I find anything of substance to break this investigation, and you get the credit for it, my being here needn't leave this room."

Albert Goodnight studied Berdie. He ran his tongue across his front top teeth and gave a cluck. His brows lifted making them join together as one. "*Twenty* minutes."

Berdie felt a shot of relief zip through her whole being. Now she could do her work under legal protection. She raced back behind the desk. "I'm working at the computer."

Goodnight nodded. "Whatever this information, it better be good." He began spinning his torch about, again looking at the surroundings.

Berdie let out a long sigh. Not only finding Lillie and the others, but also her whole career, her position in the church, even her place as much adored wife all depended on the next twenty minutes. "Good and gracious Lord, have mercy on me, a sinner," Berdie breathed and fingered the keys.

"What'd you say?" Goodnight spilt torchlight on

the desk.

"Praying."

Goodnight snickered. "And I should think so, too, vicar's wife." Goodnight did a general pry about the room.

Berdie tried numerous ideas for the password, but nothing succeeded. An ache in her tense shoulders began to edge up her neck. She closed her eyes. "Queens Gardens," she breathed and struck the keys. No, it didn't work. Time was slipping away.

"Now would you look at this?" tumbled from Goodnight's moustache-ridden lips. "Lined up like a family's young 'uns."

"What?" Berdie glanced at Goodnight, who steadied his torchlight on a long row of gold frames filled with photos.

"Starlight, Bentley, Orangeade."

"Orangeade?"

Goodnight bent closer. "Orangeade, Nineteen eighty three. They've engraved name and date on each frame."

Berdie realized what he was observing. "Their cats, the Stanfords' personal pets, and the year they were born, or departed," she spoke to herself more than the constable.

Goodnight moved the light from portrait to portrait. "This is barmy."

"This is brilliant." Berdie stood. "Which one is the most recent arrival?"

"What?"

"Tell me the name and date of the cat that is closest to today's date."

"Here." He nodded. "Dewberry. What kind of a name is that for a cat?"

Berdie tapped the corresponding keys. "What year?"

"Twenty twelve."

It didn't work. No entry. Berdie drummed an open palm on the desk. *Think.* "Which cat has the oldest date, the firstborn?"

"Firstborn?" Goodnight leaned toward the frames and chuckled. "Fancy a firstborn cat." Moving one to another, the beam of light made the frames glisten. "Here's the little bundle. Xerxes, nineteen sixty six."

Berdie entered the words and numbers. A sense of utter stay of execution wrapped itself warmly about her when the screen opened up. "Thank God. We have lift off."

"Righty-o," Albert chirped absently, still pondering the cat portraits.

Berdie beheld the icons as she seated herself again. *Female Client Profiles.* She clicked on it and her fingers flew on the keys, *Olivia Mikalos.* Yes, there was her picture and all her pertinent information, right down to her favorite flower. Plus there was some kind of code: *WD, NFC NCC, I, S.* The word, *ACCEPTED,* followed.

Berdie pushed the flash drive into the port and pressed *Save As,* copying the folder to her stick.

She typed in Livy's name. Picture and particulars were there, and though the word *ACCEPTED* followed, her coded letters were slightly different. *S, NFC, NCC, I, S.*

Then she swallowed. Her fingers could barely type it but she had to do it. *Lillian Foxworth.* Berdie leaned closer and drew her hand to her mouth. There was Lillie, her beautiful picture, her information, her code. *S, NFC, MFC, I, S.* But in big letters near the bottom, were the words *DENIED CLIENT SERVICES*.

"Why?" Berdie said louder than intended.

"Why, what?"

Berdie jumped. So buried was she in her investigative processes, she had almost forgotten Albert was skulking about.

He steadied his torch on the chandelier overhead. "That cost more than a few quid."

Berdie had no time to explain to Albert. She grappled with the first question that made her brain itch. Why had Lillie applied with the dating scheme to begin with? Berdie reviewed the last few weeks with her friend. She was feeling ignored by Loren. Nothing unusual. She had an apparent case of the humdrums. Yes, Berdie recalled Lillie fussing that everyone but she had meaningful vocations. She needed change, a challenge? Yes, or why else run off to Portugal? OK, so she had applied. Why then was Lillie rejected? Thank God she was, but why?

"What made her different from Livy and Olivia?" she whispered.

"You say something?"

Berdie considered the codes of the women. It was a single identifiable difference in each woman's profile. First letters were the same for Lillie and Livy. *S.* Olivia was *WD*. What would a dating agency have as their first entry? Dating agency. Of course. S for Lillie and Livy. Single. WD for Olivia. Widowed. "Their status," Berdie reasoned aloud.

"A fair amount of status I'd say, going by this lot of goods here. They've got plenty of dosh."

Berdie ignored the constable and continued the codes. All three had NFC. What would be valuable information for bilking, victimizing? No something?

No funds collected. No fixed conditions. No foreign connection. Connection? Lillie had MCC but Livy and Olivia had NCC. They had no something, but Lillie had M something. "The opposite of no?"

"Yes," Goodnight blared. "Jumpin' monkeys! How much more you gonna ponce about on that computer?"

"Much, more." Berdie repeated the fellow's words and perked. "Lillie had many or more and they had none." She became conscious of the constable's inquiry. "Just a bit, Albert."

Berdie focused. NCC as opposed to MCC. What connections did Lillie have much of that Olivia and Livy did not? Legal, vocational, social? Social! Multiple Community Connections. Olivia had few friends. Livy appeared to have few and just her cousin from all appearances. Lillie had a serious relationship with Loren, friends, strong ties with the church, village notoriety.

Realization bolted through Berdie like lightning. The Stanford's primary interest in coming to the church the day before the fete wasn't fund raising for the cat shelter. That was secondary. They were vetting Lillie. And they discovered, with all her links and ties to the community, that she wasn't swindle and disappear material. They used the church and fete for their own wicked means. "The cheek!" Berdie said under her breath despite the fact that she wanted to cry it out.

"What is this setup, anyway? A cat house?" Goodnight laughed at his own joke.

Berdie went to the next icon, *Male Client Profiles*, and clicked. "This setup is a bait and skate," Berdie quipped.

"What?"

"It's a dating service. A very exclusive, highly confidential, bait and skate."

"Bait and skate?"

"Women of means, concerned about appearances and despairing for companionship, are set up through this agency with apparent gentlemen, of a Casanova flare, who win the ladies' hearts." Berdie continued her browse of male clients. "Then they rob their vulnerable pockets and run. To get what they want, I dare say they may even bump some off."

"Blimey." Goodnight's tone moved from a casual investigation to deadly serious.

"It looks as if they have legitimate clients sprinkled in. It's a cover, of course."

"Right." Goodnight drew his torch close into his body. "Bump them off, you say."

Berdie found Gavin Broadhouse, but no pertinent information, simply a list of his "matches", including Olivia Mikalos. She looked a bit closer. *Discharged* was in bold letters near the bottom. What was that about?

She typed Mr. Moore's name and his photo came up under the name of Clive Moore, and again, no particulars. But his "matches" revealed several women, including Livy and Olivia.

"Why would Olivia have a double match? She dumped Broadhouse and sought another? But Elise said Olivia blamed her for his departure," Berdie barely whispered. *Save as.* She didn't have time to sort all the peculiarities right this minute.

Berdie went to another folder. *Confidential Agreement.* Once opened, she could see it was a legal document of confidentiality with a three thousand pound starter fee. "That would eliminate the casual client," she mouthed. Berdie was anxious to read the fine print on this pseudo-legal trap.

Without warning, Goodnight spun around on his heel.

Berdie thought she heard a car engine, and it sounded as if it was just outside the house. By the look of Goodnight's wide eyes and sudden intake of air, he heard it also. It couldn't yet be half four.

The constable moved toward the window and drew back a corner of the curtain, skewing his head sideways to see the road. "Know anyone with an expensive silver BMW?"

"Olivia Mikalos," Berdie answered.

"Well, that's no woman in that car."

Berdie leaped from the computer and joined Goodnight at the window. "Call the Timsley police?"

"I shouldn't." Goodnight was hesitant.

"Then take the offensive," Berdie urged. "You're the law. If they approach, just wave your warrant about."

"Warrant?"

"Your search warrant from the Timsley magistrates."

Berdie watched Goodnight run a finger across his moustache, lift his brows, and turn off his torch as he lowered the curtain.

Berdie could feel her eyes narrow as she realized what his behavior told her. "Albert?"

The car and its owner sat motionless, but Goodnight was on the move.

"You do have a warrant, yes?"

"Pull up the ladder, we're done."

Berdie realized that though her unlikely cohort was a policeman, he was as illegally in the home as she was. She raced back to the computer, saved the agreement document, and removed the flash drive.

"Come on, you dozy mare," bounced through the rooms as Goodnight, by the sound of it, was already in the hallway headed for the kitchen and the back door.

"Only that wally could turn an investigative clincher into a complete dog's dinner." Berdie grabbed her torch, pushed the precious flash drive into her sock, and moved swiftly through the sitting room and into the hall in pursuit of the fast departing lawman. "Remember Albert Goodnight," she called to the fleeing policeman, "this never happened."

14

"Boats." The word slipped from Berdie's mouth. During her fretful sleep, it was the primary question that swam in her head. What did Lillie hope to achieve by hiring a boat?

Berdie became aware of dazzling light on her closed eyelids and fluttered them open. A few blinks and she pulled herself up on her elbows, suddenly conscious of the fact that the sun poured through the bedroom window. The space next to her in bed was empty. She pushed stray hair out of her way to glare at the alarm clock that proclaimed it was nearly 10 AM.

"Lord have mercy." Berdie leapt from the bed and wrapped herself in the robe that was draped near the bottom edge. Why hadn't Hugh awakened her? Did she sleep through the alarm? Nearly stumbling on the stairs, she flew to the kitchen, where Hugh, despite the fact that he wore his clerical collar with great dignity, had his hands in a sink full of suds.

"Hugh, where's the closest large body of water?"

"The Atlantic? And good morning to you, too."

"Good morning to you, too. I think."

Hugh sighed. "You've had a busy week."

"Busy, yes. But there's so much more to be done today."

"You're all go this morning." Hugh released the plug and water coursed from the sink. He dried the bubbles that clung to his hands with a cheerful looking tea towel.

"Why didn't you wake me?"

Hugh pointed toward an awaiting cup and saucer sitting next to a teapot clothed in a daffodil decorated cozy. "I did try."

Berdie sank into a chair at the small table for two by the kitchen window.

Hugh removed the cozy from the teapot, put milk from the creamer into the cup, and pulled a teaspoon of sugar from the petite bowl. "I've gotten some information, Berdie," Hugh's voice lost some of its morning luster. "I'm sure you'll want to know."

"What is it, Hugh?"

Hugh dumped the sugar into the cup while at the same time pouring tea. "I asked Busby to do some nosing around for me." He handed the cup to Berdie.

She nearly dropped it. "Busby?"

Hugh didn't lightly ask his former right hand man from military service, Warrant Officer Andrew Busby, to gather facts for him. This could be something significant.

She steadied the cup and raised it to her lips. "Go on."

"I asked him to find out what he could about Gavin Broadhouse."

Berdie nearly slammed the cup into the saucer.

"Now calm yourself and drink your tea, love."

"He's up to no good, I can tell you that much." Berdie daren't say more. She took another sip.

"Gavin Broadhouse, from Leeds, married with four children, died five years ago of natural causes."

Berdie swallowed and gaped.

"His medical records bore it out, and his grave marker is in All Souls Church cemetery near Leeds."

"So who's our so-called Mr. Broadhouse?"

"Busby's still sorting it."

"What put you on to looking into this?"

"I've heard not a bean from him or of him. He's all but disappeared." Hugh put his hand on Berdie's arm. "And I do listen to you, Berdie."

Berdie smiled, although she didn't want to be overly cheerful for Hugh's sake.

"You must admit, he's a poser, Hugh."

"But he's a tormented poser, love. People who seek to deceive don't wrestle with telling lies. Falsehood falls off their tongues like warm butter. Our fellow struggles."

"True. Or perhaps he's dangerously clever."

"I felt something genuine about the man. Still, I have to say you're most often right when you twig someone."

She wanted to tell Hugh about the fellow's list of duped ladies. Instead, she leaned over and placed a peck on his cheek. "He's only one of many deceitful characters in this mess. And I'm almost certain where our exploration needs next to go."

"Our?"

"Hugh, we need to find Lillie. And right away. The police will eventually get there, but let me remind you that I was an investigative reporter, so technically, I am a professional, too. I think I have a very-reasoned-out place where Lillie may be."

Hugh was attentive.

"Now, I made a list from my last conversation with Lillie, along with my other conversations I had with her this week. I dug in my brain to put things together." She paused. "Where's the closest marina?"

"The closest marina?" Hugh sat back in his chair

and shook his head. "Odd."

"Not at all.".

"No, not you, Berdie." He stared at her momentarily and knit his brow. "We got a prank call this morning. He said the answers to all your questions were at the marina."

Berdie squeezed her lips.

Hugh tipped his head. "Berdie, is there something you haven't told me?"

If only he knew the half of it. This could confirm that she was going in the right direction in her own thoughts. "Was that the exact message? Hugh, think. This could be critical."

He leaned forward, clasped his hands together and formed a church spire with his index fingers. He poked it into his chin as if to prod the memory loose.

Berdie scanned Hugh's intense eyes. "Was it a particular marina?"

Hugh sat up and snapped his now loosened fingers. "Seabrook, that's what he said, Seabrook Marina."

"Did you ask him particulars?"

"Berdie, I told him to get off the phone." Hugh squinted. "But he did say something else."

"Yes?" Berdie patted Hugh's knee. "Think."

"It didn't make much sense. He said something about the more you know."

"The more you know what?"

"That was it, 'the more you know.'"

Berdie tumbled the words in her brain. The more you know facts? The more you know people? "People. The more you know," she nearly shouted. "God bless that caller." Berdie jumped from her chair. "And I shouldn't wonder! Hugh, we've got to go to Seabrook

Marina, and we've got to go now."

Hugh simply stared at her. "The more you know people?"

"Come along, we've not a moment to spare."

Hugh stood. "First, we inform the police."

"Yes, good thought. We'll stop at Goodnight's Police House on our way out, and I'll also ring Dave Exton at the newspaper office."

"I'll ring Loren at the lab. He'll want to come with us." Hugh paused. "You're agreeable to involve Goodnight?"

Berdie tried to be nonchalant. "H is the law."

"Just like that?"

Berdie could see a slight niggle in Hugh's eying of her.

"Come along; we must move quickly."

Berdie and Hugh left the vicarage drive within minutes and were on their way to the marina with two critical stops in between.

"Seabrook Marina is this direction." Hugh pointed toward the front windscreen, his phone on his lap. "I still have to work out details."

"And it's that way," Berdie pointed to the back windscreen, "to get to Queens Gardens.

"For just a bit, yes, and then that way." Hugh pointed toward his driver-side window.

"Snap. So Hero was going to his real home. There it is, another six-letter word completed in the crossword. Sweet Duncan."

"Duncan?"

"Goodnight, yes, the authority. That's best." Berdie took a quick breath. "Flight. But of course," she declared.

"Berdie, you're not making sense. I'm not

following."

"Oh, but I am making the best sense, yet, Hugh, just stay with me."

Hugh shook his head and turned onto the street where the constable was located. He stopped in front of Goodnight's home that also served as Aidan Kirkwood police headquarters.

Berdie was surprised to see Albert standing in the front garden, looking a bit of a sleepwalker, if it wasn't for an open map in one hand and a beaker of something steamy in the other.

Hugh peered at the man. "I say, did he sleep in his uniform last night?"

Berdie simply pulled her chin down and exited the car as quickly as possible.

She moved in Goodnight's direction. "He's called you again, as well. Seabrook Marina?"

He glared at her with his red eyes, scratched his head, and returned to his map. "Good morning. Again."

"Shh," Berdie cautioned, glanced toward the car where Hugh sat, then back at Goodnight. "You can put the map away. Hugh's locating the most direct route to Seabrook on his GPS right now."

"There's a treat." Albert collapsed the map into a mass, dropped it on the ground, and yawned. "Not my patch, Seabrook Marina."

"But it is your case, Constable, Lillie lives on your patch."

"I'm fully aware," the man grunted. "Didn't say I wasn't going out there." He sniffed, making his nose go askew. "Gotta alert the CID of that county."

"Good. Now, do you know the way to Queen's Gardens Board and Cat Rescue?"

Marilyn Leach

Goodnight took a sip of the hot liquid he held and scratched the side of his stomach. He gave a lazy nod.

"Very good". You've got to go get a cat. It is critical to this whole situation."

The constable squinted and glanced at his leg. "Pull the other one."

"No, truth be told. His name is Hero, and he's in the Board of the Rescue. You've got to get him and meet us at the marina. Trust me."

"Trust you?" He half chuckled. "The one I found breaking and entering last night?"

"Keep your voice down."

"This cat's so important, you get the little beast."

Berdie took a deep breath. This could take some convincing, and she was losing time. "Goodnight, I'm just a vicar's wife."

He looked askance. "Oh, yes?"

"You're the one with the policeman's uniform. You're the one with real legal power. Show your credentials, and demand they give you that cat."

He ran his tongue across his upper teeth. "Why's this animal so important?"

"I haven't time to explain it all. He is the crux of solving the whole dilemma. For Lillie's sake."

Goodnight sniffed.

"And don't forget that feather we talked about earlier."

"Feather?"

Berdie raised her brow, slowly nodded and shot an arrow of prayer heavenward.

"Oh, in the hat, that one, no, I've not forgotten." He ran a finger over his mustache. "Well"--he said with compliance in his tone--"I don't want cat hair all over my vehicle."

"You won't regret this. Meet us at the main entrance of the marina." Berdie turned and waved at Hugh. "Can you give Constable Goodnight directions to Seabrook?" she called.

"Isn't it the police who are supposed to be giving me the directions?" he asked Berdie.

"Well, it is Albert Goodnight, after all. Just help him, Hugh." Berdie spoke just loud enough for Hugh to hear.

Hugh obliged. Pointing and displaying his phone GPS was followed by Albert's assured nods. More quickly than a waggle of sheep's tail, Hugh was once again behind the wheel and on the road to Seabrook Marina.

As countryside zoomed past, Berdie's thoughts congealed. "The dots are connecting. All but one. The family at the sports club café, with the full plate, doesn't fit. Yet it's a key. What am I missing?"

"Love, if I could help you I would. I don't even know where the dots are. But I trust you, Berdie."

"Snap. Hugh, that's it." Berdie shook her head. "Why couldn't I see it before? I was so busy looking at the crisps, I didn't see the smoothies. And that explains the tablets." Berdie gasped. "Hugh, I believe we'll find Olivia alive."

"That's good, but what about Lillie?"

"I believe Olivia and Lillie are together." Berdie felt her tongue just barely able to form the words. "Every moment counts, Hugh. Every single moment."

****

The porter, dressed in medical scrubs, was very stern as he stood in front of the morgue doorway. "I'm sorry, but you can't go in the lab."

"We're here to see Dr. Meredith," Hugh informed.

"Dr. Meredith is scheduled to begin an autopsy."

"It's urgent. We're here by his request." Hugh was doing his best to be civil.

Berdie could feel her temperature rise as she fumbled her mobile nestled in her trouser pocket. "We haven't time for this."

The fellow folded his arms. "I'm sure it's important. It always is, but you mustn't disturb."

"I'll tell you what not to disturb." Berdie found the words flying from her mouth. "The Lord's work." She grabbed Hugh's arm. "You certainly don't want to be guilty of disturbing that, do you?"

The man drew back.

"With all due respect, we're going to speak to Dr. Meredith," Hugh decreed, pushed the lab door open, and then entered, Berdie with him.

Loren stood near a human-sized drawer pulled from its casement in the lab wall, a corpse in repose upon it. He chatted, by the look of his garb, with an apparent colleague next him as they viewed the lifeless body.

"Loren," Hugh beckoned.

The doctor raised his gaze to Hugh, concern etched into the deep brown of his eyes.

Berdie avoided looking at the cadaver. "Loren, I'm almost certain I know where she's at."

The chap with Dr. Meredith frowned.

"Where?" Loren froze.

"Seabrook Marina," Hugh said.

"She's in grave danger." Berdie took Hugh's hand. "Loren, she needs you there, now."

"Dr. Meredith, who are these people?" The

colleague frowned. "This is highly irregular."

Spatters of blood dotted the surgical gown the objector wore. "You've got an autopsy scheduled, Meredith, you can't just walk out."

Loren lowered his chin. "Or you could be a chum and take it."

"I've got one of my own, and you know we're short staffed."

"Loren," Hugh countered, "as a friend and pastor, I have to say, you don't want regrets."

Berdie nodded toward the corpse. "Regret is one thing, but that could be Lillie lying there."

Loren took a quick breath. "Kenrick, I've got to go."

The man jutted his chin. "I'll go straight to the supervisor. You'll get the sack."

Loren shoved the cold body back into the wall casement with a bang. "Good. That will save me going to his desk myself. This isn't about my work. It's about the woman I love."

Berdie released a long breath.

Loren all but ripped his protective work garb from his form: scrubs, hair protector, shoe covering, rubber gloves. "That's it, then. Why are we standing here?" Loren started for the door.

Berdie and Hugh followed.

"I hope she's worth it because you can kiss your job goodbye," Kenrick shouted.

****

Much to Berdie's delight, Albert Goodnight was at the main entrance to the marina, cat carrier perched on the bonnet of his car.

"Well done, Albert." Berdie recognized Hero's scarred ear immediately.

"Yes, well, leave it to the CID to dawdle." Albert still grasped the beaker in hand, but there was no steam arising. "I notified them to meet us here."

"We'll just have to proceed without them," Loren clipped.

"Without them? No. They can be touchy about their patch."

Loren's gaze bored into the constable. "You're a cop, and technically I work for the CID. Done and dusted."

"Loren's right. We can't wait." Berdie moved to the carrier where Hero was on his feet. Tail twitching, ears at attention, eyes enlarged, he was eager. "Sea air, Hero." She worked to unlatch the door.

"What are you doing?" Goodnight demanded.

"I'm releasing Hero."

"I brought that flea-bite out here just to let it go? That cat's in police custody."

"Good, don't let him out of your sight." Berdie bounced her gaze from Albert, to Hugh, and Loren. "All of you. Move in silence, and stay with him."

Berdie flung the door open. Had Hero been a fox with hounds in pursuit, he couldn't have sprung from the carrier more rapidly.

"Go, go," Berdie beckoned to the men as the cat shot onto the primary dock.

Loren took the lead in pursuit, Berdie and Hugh after.

Albert smacked his beaker down on his car bonnet and fell in behind them.

After nearly fifty yards of chase down the dock, Berdie could feel her heart pumping.

Hugh was with her, Goodnight tragically far behind, Loren still ahead.

Hero stopped abruptly, pricked his ears, and shot down along one of the finger docks where there were several boat slips.

"Good boy," Berdie breathed.

At slip seventeen, with his tail up, Hero jumped onto the bow of a cabin cruiser boat, *Land Flow*.

"That's it." Berdie sounded a stifled alert and pointed. "That's the boat we're looking for."

Hero began to squall and scampered on deck.

Hugh stopped, bent over and picked up a pair of rather stylish black frame glasses that lay on the dock.

Berdie glanced his way, still trying to keep Hero in view.

Hugh held them out for Berdie to see. They had no lenses.

"Lord have mercy." Berdie wanted to scream it, but kept the words at the bottom of her voice. "They're Lillie's," she mouthed to Hugh. Berdie's memory came alive. Lillie had them in her pocket when she was abducted. "Lillie's here," she mouthed again.

Loren stepped deftly toward the bow while Hero's squalls continued.

"Hero?" a man called from quarters down below the deck.

Berdie knew that voice. She grabbed Loren and put her finger to her mouth.

Loren and Hugh became motionless.

"Did you run away again?" The even beet of footsteps sounded. "Hero, you silly boy."

The cat sprang back on the bow.

"Grab the cat," Berdie whisper-yelled to Loren.

Loren thrust himself with stealth across the bow

and wrapped his hands around the creature's middle. Hero let go a very loud objection as Loren slid onto the boat deck with cat in hand.

Berdie snapped a finger getting Loren's attention. She mimicked pulling the cat to her chest and stroking it.

Loren obliged.

"Hero?" The body of Clive Moore began to emerge from the lower reaches of the boat. "You in trouble, boy?" He stepped onto the deck.

"No, but you are." Berdie worked to keep her words even.

Moore reared. His hand moved to his waist as his cool gaze whirled from Berdie to Hugh to Loren. "Off my boat," he growled toward the doctor.

"Not without Lillie." The words blazed from Loren's mouth.

Moore pulled a pistol from his waistband and thrust it toward Loren.

Hugh stepped in front of Berdie, half covering her with his own body.

"I said, get off my boat." Moore jerked the gun toward the dock and rapidly back as he kept his icy gaze on Loren.

"Hero will most certainly die if you try to shoot Dr. Meredith." Berdie, feeling breathless, barely got the words out.

Clive Moore's gaze didn't leave Loren, but Berdie could see a hint of panic rush through. "Be quiet, you interfering cow." Moore edged toward Loren. "Give me the cat."

Loren's feet were anchored. The large elongated tom cat covered him neck to waist. "Off your boat or give you the cat? Which is it?" Loren scoffed.

Moore pursed his lips and rubbed his thumb against the gun butt.

"Mr. Moore, Clive. Let's think about this." Berdie's calm voice sliced through her teeth-on-edge trepidation. "Think about all you have for Hero's being here with you."

The man swallowed. Moisture sprung along his brow, gaze glued to his treasured feline.

Hugh slid his fingers around Berdie's hand.

"You can't stroke your Cassie's soft hair, but you can run a finger through Hero's fur," Berdie coaxed.

"Shut it." Moore braced his feet, but his face skewed with emotion. He bit his lip.

"Flames all round her, Hero was Cassie's protector, Clive, when you couldn't be there with her."

Moore's chest began to rise and fall in a quickened pace.

Loren gently stroked Hero.

"Don't take any silly chances, Clive." Berdie's tone was truth wrapped in cream. "He's your link to the one you loved most."

The firearm quivered. Moore drew his other hand up and clasped the gun barrel in an attempt to steady it, still trained on Loren.

"Think carefully," Hugh spoke. "Let the doctor go below so he can see to the women's health with a guarantee of Hero's safety."

A grimace appeared on Moore's face. He squeezed his eyes momentarily, as if to wash the salty moisture that invaded them.

Berdie ran her tongue over her dry lips. "Cassie would want Hero and everyone safe."

Moore lifted his chin and sucked air through his teeth.

"Put the weapon aside and let's do this peacefully," Hugh offered.

"I don't need some fancy vicar telling me what to do," raged from Moore's mouth.

"Oh, I rather think you do, Morgan."

Berdie heard the challenging words come from behind her.

Moore darted his gaze for a split second to the spot from where the words originated, then back to Loren, on whom the gun was trained. "Holmes." The word was full of bile.

Berdie looked behind her to see the man she knew as Gavin Broadhouse.

"Let the doctor see to Olivia," Broadhouse commanded.

"Get stuffed."

"You've a bit of a surprise coming. I think you'll want to let the doctor go about his business."

"I said shut it. Or I'll do him, and then turn on you."

Heavy panting along with shoes clomping in lagging strides on the finger dock signaled Goodnight's appearance.

Oh, no. Berdie's stomach flipflopped.

"OK, you burke," Goodnight boomed in breathy spurts, and then he spotted the weapon. Like tires screeching to a halt, he stopped short. "Let's not be hasty," he croaked and took steps backward.

The muffled blast and ping of a ricocheted bullet sounded across the deck.

For an instant, everyone froze.

Moore's startled gaze zoomed to the boat next as if to find the origin of the fired shot.

Hugh pushed Berdie down. As she landed, it

seemed everything happened in slow motion.

Hero rocketed from Loren's arms as the doctor lunged low to hurl himself toward Moore, who swung his weapon to train it upon Broadhouse. As he pulled the trigger, Loren grasped the perpetrator's knees and with his full weight, pushed Moore to the deck in a gasping sprawl.

At the same moment, Berdie heard Broadhouse release a cry of pain and collapse.

Moore struggled to rise.

But Hugh was upon the felon before he could get to his feet. Her husband smashed a fist directly into the side of Moore's jaw that sent him tumbling back down onto the deck where he sprawled on his back like a bag of loose potatoes, unable to rise.

"Loren, get Lillie," Hugh commanded.

"I'll see to Broadhouse," Berdie shouted.

Hugh retrieved the gun as Loren flew to the steps and disappeared below.

"Blimey!" Goodnight made way as rapidly as he could to the boat's deck. "Sit on 'im," he urged Hugh and pulled out his handcuffs.

Berdie heard thunder pounding the dock as she turned to the supine Broadhouse and knelt next him. "How bad is it?"

"Thank God, the doctor knocked him off balance." Blood stained the shoulder already encompassed in a sling. He pushed his free hand against the wound as Berdie wadded up a nearby beach towel.

"Just a graze," Berdie observed.

Broadhouse grimaced. "Yes, well, I think he was keen to finish what he started with his hit and run."

"You'll be fine in a bit. The cavalry's arrived." Berdie placed the towel like a pillow under the man's head.

Several police swarmed along the finger dock and invaded the boat. They lifted Moore to his feet.

Berdie rubbed Mr. Broadhouse's free hand that had gone cold, shock taking its course in his body. "That was pretty bold of you, approaching Moore like that."

"His name's Clifford Morgan. And I thought it would distract him."

"Oh, it did that, all right."

"But the first shot fired, the one that broke everything up. Where did that come from?"

Berdie squeezed her lips together. She could feel the lump of her mobile phone against her thigh in her trouser pocket. "God watches over us all, doesn't He?"

While Hugh turned over the firearm to one of the lawmen, a policewoman approached Berdie and Broadhouse. "You hurt, sir?" she barked.

"I'll survive. See to Mrs. Mikalos, down below. She's diabetic. She should have her tablets. And please let me know how she is."

"You her husband?"

Mr. Broadhouse, or whatever his name, blew out a slow breath. "No." He looked Berdie in the eye. "I'm no one's husband."

The officer nodded. "The ambulance is on its way." She moved to the steps and descended.

"*You* took Olivia's tablets from her bathroom chest."

Mr. Broadhouse nodded and released a long sigh.

Berdie placed more letters in the crossword of her mind. "Holmes, that's your real name, then?"

"Gareth Holmes, yes." He gave a slight shiver.

Berdie took off her spring coat and placed it over

Mr. Holmes upper body.

"And would you be any relation to a raspy voiced telephone informant?"

Mr. Holmes smiled. "You've an amazing talent, Mrs. Elliott."

"And you used me."

He nodded. "Sorry, that. I couldn't come forward. There was a threat to kill Olivia if I tried to intervene or go to the police. I didn't know where she was, and I needed someone to do the heavy lifting. May I say you did it brilliantly?"

"You may," Berdie said with salt.

"I'm afraid I'm not an innocent, I'm deeply mired in this mess."

"I know."

He gave her a shy glance. "I fell in love with Olivia you see, and it changed everything."

"Love, real love, does that." Berdie saw sincerity in this man's eyes she'd not noticed before. Her Hugh, he had comprehended it from the start.

The policewoman appeared on deck and addressed the Officer in charge. "Two hostages below are drugged, and weak, but there's no signs of any real harm or abuse. The doc's with them."

"Thank God." Berdie felt relief pour upon her like cool rain on a desert dune.

Gareth Holmes swallowed. Moisture seeped from the corner of an eye.

Two constables escorted the cuffed Moore, who sported a swollen jaw, from the boat onto the dock.

Berdie and Mr. Holmes watched.

"Please help me to sit up," Mr. Holmes directed Berdie.

"But your wound."

"Up, please."

Berdie put her hands and arms under his back lifting him forward.

A growl of pain escaped from the man's lips.

Nearly upright, Berdie wedged her shoulder behind him to act as a support.

"He's complicit in all this." Moore lifted his chin toward Mr. Holmes.

"I thought I'd get you something you've always wanted, Morgan." Gareth Holmes's words took great effort. "A very long island vacation fully paid." He grinned. "At Parkhurst Prison on the Isle of White."

Morgan sneered. "You heard the constable, no real harm."

"And what of his gunshot wound?" Berdie huffed.

"You saw it yourself, madam. There was a struggle and the firearm went off."

"Oh, yes?" Berdie snapped at him. "Let me see. First there's kidnapping, then possession of a firearm with intent to endanger life, and use of firearm to resist arrest. Oh yes, each of which carry a life sentence."

Holmes took a labored breath. "You know, Morgan, there is a force greater than greed, domination, or peril. It's older than the ages and it's called love."

Morgan sniffed. "What's that I smell? Rubbish." He had the words barely uttered, when an unknown woman wearing a headscarf and sunglasses approached.

"Ah, someone I just recently met." Holmes drawled. "I think you two may know each other."

The woman removed the scarf and sunglasses.

Morgan's jaw slacked as he shrank back. His face went chalk white.

"Seen a ghost, Cliffy?" The unknown lady took a step closer to Morgan, who struggled against his handcuffs. "Or is prison pallor already setting in? You didn't count on Moroccan fishermen illegally trolling Portuguese waters off Madeira that night, did you?"

"Liv, darling."

Liv? Berdie stared at the stranger. Familiarity danced through her memory.

The woman lifted her chin and addressed the constables. "He left me, his wife, for dead. And I dare say I'm not the first one he's done it to." Her gaze burrowed into Morgan. "Attempted murder, *darling*." Her words had the sting of vinegar. "Lock him up, throw away the key, and don't look back."

"Livy?" Berdie blurted.

"Yes. Who are you?"

"Harriet's friend. But when did you get here, how?" Berdie asked.

"Just arrived by sea. I spent weeks being cared for by two very kind fishermen's wives." She lifted a brow. "A promise of visa sponsorship to this country can get you almost anything in a small Moroccan fishing village."

"Move along," the two constables bawled and pulled the agitated detainee down the dock where a snap happy Dave Exton plied his wares.

"This entire boat is a crime scene," the officer in charge trumpeted. "We want all of you," he waved his hand to encompass everyone, "at the station immediately." He plunged a finger toward Mr. Holmes, "and especially you, after you get checked out at the hospital."

Mr. Holmes nodded.

"We'll all be there," Hugh assured.

Albert Goodnight cast his gaze at Berdie, Mr. Holmes, Hugh, and then Livy. He ran a finger across his bushy untrimmed mustache. "From a mangled cat to murder. Blimey."

15

Berdie admired the dressed back garden of St. Aidan of the Woods Church where she stood. And, she could feel Ivy Butz's curious stare from ten feet away.

"Mrs. Elliott, the tables in the marquee are ready. Neat as a pin." When Ivy stood at her side, the woman took in Berdie's hat then turned her focus to the ground while she touched the brim of her own satin-banded sun-hat.

"It's OK, Ivy." Berdie leaned close. "It's not something I'd normally wear to a garden wedding, or anywhere else, really."

Ivy's jolly smile blossomed. "It was a gift, then."

Berdie nodded.

Ivy tipped her head and stared at the chapeau. "Would you call it a semi-circle shape?"

"A semi-circle shape that is fitted to the head and tilted slightly down toward the forehead, yes."

"I must say I've not often seen brown sequins." Ivy sent her index finger into little twirls. "And used in such decorative swirls."

Berdie tried not to chuckle. "Nor, I dare say, have you seen three stick straight black feathers standing at attention on the back end."

Ivy pressed her lips tightly together and swallowed.

"It's just that my husband surprised me with it, specifically for the wedding, a sweet act to express his appreciation."

Ivy squeezed Berdie's hand. "Bless them. They do try, don't they?"

Berdie let a discreet chuckle slip through and Ivy joined her.

"And on another note, Mrs. Elliott," Ivy joyously went on, "our little Duncan has been so pleased since Hero cat has become a part of our family."

"You approved the adoption, then?"

"Oh, my, yes. The tattered creature saved a poor kiddy from perishing in fire. How could I not? Despite his previous owner now being locked away in disgrace, our little Hero is quite a celebrity."

"I'm glad it's all worked out so well."

"Mrs. Butz, you're wanted in the marquee," Bridget McDermott called.

Ivy gave Berdie's hand another squeeze and was off.

And much to Berdie's chagrin, Mrs. McDermott wasn't.

She approached, somber as a judge. "I say, bad form that."

Berdie pulled her shoulders back. Bridget McDermott and hospitality weren't often used in the same sentence at the best of times, but today it was absolute misery. The woman glanced at Berdie's hat, winced, and then nattered on. "The cheek of it. Canceling a wedding three days before it's due to take place."

"Water under the bridge. You must let the current take your disappointment downstream."

Mrs. McDermott nudged her decorative straw hat forward to keep the afternoon sunshine at bay.

"In fact," Berdie proceeded, "I would think you

should be well pleased that another couple have stepped in. Very accommodating and delighted with all that's been put in place and no out-of-pocket for the church."

"Fancy getting married at someone else's wedding."

Berdie realized her reasoning with Bridget McDermott was wasted breath. "Well, I'm happy for them. Though I had reservations to start, I truly believe they'll enjoy their life together."

Bridget lifted her chin. "Well, of course you would, you're the vicar's wife and a friend."

Maggie Fairchild joined Berdie and her adversary, her smile as warm as the afternoon. "Isn't it wonderful?" She waved her hand across the garden. "The white arched trellis is alive with trailing wisteria, made even grander with the water feature for background. The large pots of variegated flowers on either side are perfect." She took a deep breath. "The white marquee is lovely inside, near ready I would say, for the lunch after. And the House of Helensfield cake, what more could one want?"

Mrs. McDermott stared at Maggie.

"Lovely, indeed." Berdie looked on as a black clad trio took their seats and tuned their stringed instruments.

Maggie patted her gloved hands in glee. "I must get to the front garden, so I can direct the guests in the right direction."

"Thank you, Maggie." Berdie watched the woman toddle off in her new dress and dyed-to-match hat.

"Only a handful coming, really." Bridget sighed. "All they need do is walk around back."

Berdie knew it was best to leave this conversation

when, "Take it up with the wedding planner," sprang from her tongue.

Berdie caught sight of Lillie off to the side of the garden and found it the perfect escape. "Excuse me, Bridget, I must speak with Lillie." Birdie left the frowning woman and walked toward her friend. "How are you feeling?" Berdie asked once she reached Lillie's side.

"Rather nervous, actually." She opened and closed her fingers. "No, Berdie. Terribly nervous."

Berdie put her hand on Lillie's shoulder. "Are you sure you're ready? It's only been a month, Lillie. That's a short time for recovery from the trauma you faced."

"Sooner's better than later." Lillie was beautiful in a stone-colored linen dress that hugged her slender body. "We've had just the one rehearsal." She spread her fingers widely.

"Lillie, simply let the joy of the moment take you. Don't worry, it will all go wonderfully."

"A bit more wonderfully than your hat, I should hope." Lillie's lip held the corner of a smile.

"There it is, ducky. Enjoy the moment."

Lillie let go an easy laugh.

Linden Davies appeared with Madeline and Phillip, who made their way to the guest chairs. Linden, at ease and smiling, gave Lillie a quick nod.

Lillie returned the smile.

Elise Davies came around and made way to her family. After speaking to Linden, she gave Madeline's yellow dress ribbon a gentle fix and smoothed Phillip's hair. "Fifteen minutes." she called to Berdie and Lillie as she departed.

And within fifteen minutes the seats were filled and all were ready to be witness to the ceremony.

Berdie sat in the far back so she could readily monitor the marquee, should it be necessary. From the corner of her eye she recognized a uniformed presence.

"Which one of you lot has a blue Fiesta?" Goodnight bellowed and lifted a small pad from which he read, "2A2Y3N." He glared at the gathering. "You're blocking Mrs. Hall's drive, so get off your bum and go move it."

"Three cheers for Goodnight," someone called. Several broke into applause while others appeared unaffected as an embarrassed guest sneaked from the chairs and headed to the front garden.

Since Lillie's rescue, Albert Goodnight wore his recognition from the villagers for a job well done like a second uniform. It garnered him a week's free tea at the Copper Kettle, half price pints at the Upland Arms, even a free side of beef from Cathcart Carlyle's Mobile Meat Mart. Although the feather in his hat was momentarily a well-lit ostrich plume, Albert's general ineptitude was already dimming the afterglow of his achievement. Berdie expected it to go out altogether any time, now, but at least it kept him quiet about the clandestine meeting between the two of them.

Chest out, Albert lifted his chin, nodded, and offered a pompous grin. "Get on with your do," he piped and left as quickly as he arrived. And none too soon.

Hugh in his vestments, and the groom looking smart in his summer suit, made way from the south terrace to take their seats in the front chairs. Berdie had to admit, Gareth Holmes looked quite handsome. No longer wearing a sling, he carried himself in quite a distinguished manner.

Lillie stood near the musicians, who began their

opening notes.

Music sprang from the trio's instruments, and Lillie joined with her voice. *"Praise, my soul, the King of heaven; To His feet thy tribute bring. Ransomed, healed, restored, forgiven, Who like me His praise should sing?"*

Berdie wondered that the singing of it at the Queen's own wedding, those many years ago, couldn't have been any more moving than Lillie's performance. The beauty of it all filled the back garden.

Hugh and Mr. Holmes stood and made way to the trellis.

Everyone was on their feet as Olivia Mikalos came forward on the song's last verse. Her composed sea-green eyes were complemented by her suit and hat, both the color of oyster shells. In her hands, she held a small mixed bouquet, but it was the radiance of her face that was the most notable feature.

Hugh began the ceremony, and all were seated.

Bridget and Maggie sat next to Berdie, Bridget closest.

Berdie sighed. Was there no escaping?

"Shameful," Bridget murmured. "A murderer marrying in our church garden."

"Gareth Holmes is not a murderer, Bridget," Berdie corrected.

"That was the other chap," Maggie whispered. "This fellow just took women's money."

"Yes, well." Bridget crossed her arms. "Our own Constable Goodnight, to his credit, certainly found them out."

Berdie bit her tongue. "Let me remind you, again, that Mr. Holmes has been fully cooperative with the law which, in turn, has garnered him a bit of legal favor."

"A suspended sentence with a five year probation," Maggie exacted.

"Can a leopard change his spots? He's nothing more than a snake in the grass," Mrs. McDermott said too loudly.

"Shh," Maggie counteracted.

"As I have learned, even snakes can shed their skins, Mrs. McDermott." Berdie couldn't believe she was repeating what Bridget had been told not a few times the past three days. "Mr. Holmes has repented of his criminal activity and is taking instruction with Hugh. He's seeking a whole new direction for his life."

"Convenient." Mrs. McDermott squeezed her crossed arms even more tightly.

"Was it convenient to be targeted in a hit and run, to suffer a bullet wound for the sake of his beloved?"

Much to Berdie's delight, Mr. Whipple emerged from the marquee and seamlessly placed a chair on Berdie's clear side. "Table posies all in place," he whispered and sat down.

"I should think we need to keep an eye on them lest they be stolen by the groom," Mrs. McDermott nearly growled.

"She's on about Mr. Holmes again, then?" Mr. Whipple whispered.

Berdie nodded.

"Funny thing, dandelions," Mr. Whipple said loudly enough for Bridget and Maggie to turn their heads.

"What are you saying?" Maggie leaned forward.

The fellow did likewise. "Most people see dandelions as invasive weeds, but their leaves are potent with nutrition and tasty when prepared correctly."

Bridget frowned and stared at the fellow.

He nodded toward the groom. "It's all perspective, isn't it?"

Berdie smiled, though she knew Mrs. McDermott didn't.

"Did you know Mr. Holmes is a gardener?" Mr. Whipple leaned his body across Berdie to speak to the women.

Bridget humphed.

"Spoke at length with him about it yesterday. His White Pearl semi-double rose won a place at a county garden show last year."

"That's wonderful," Maggie cheered.

Bridget's demeanor took a softer turn. Eying the groom, she lifted her chin. "Semi-double. Won a place? I say." She uncrossed her arms.

Mr. Whipple nodded and leaned back in his chair.

Berdie hid her smile. This wise old gentleman had done in one minute's conversation with the arduous Mrs. McDermott what Berdie was unable to do in three days. And to her delight, not another word of disapproval or otherwise, was spoken throughout the rest of the ceremony by her three companions.

The observance was brief but meaningful. At the end, Gareth and Olivia Holmes processed arm in arm to the outer edge of guest seating, the lively music of Vivaldi's *Spring* accompanying their first steps as man and wife. They made their way to the marquee and entered, waiting to greet their guests just inside.

Berdie was the first to duck in and greet them. "Congratulations, I wish you God's best," she offered.

Olivia took Berdie's hand and squeezed it. "We can never thank you enough for all you've done for us."

"Neither of us would be here apart from your skills and perseverance," Gareth agreed.

"Your bravery, Mr. Holmes, and your resolve as well, Olivia, played no small part. And of course, don't forget to thank the Great Protector of us all."

"Oh, we do." Olivia took a deep breath. "I expect everyone's rather anxious to hear how you pulled this particular rabbit out of the hat."

"Well that may be, but today is about celebrating your new life together."

The queue of thirty-three guests began to form behind Berdie. "We'll speak later," she promised and moved on only to have Billie Finch cut her off short.

"Mrs. Elliott, isn't this all a lovely surprise?" Billie fingered her blue handbag that matched the color of the feather fascinator that sat slightly left of atop her blonde hair. "What a charming hat you're wearing."

"How kind of you to say." Berdie felt the woman actually meant it. "And yes, all this is a lovely surprise. I'm so glad you came, Mrs. Finch."

"Mr. Finch had to attend to his work in London, of course, but I just couldn't miss." Billie's glossy pink lips went into a smile. "Mrs. Mikalos is a lovely bride, so self-assured and all. Well, Miss Foxworth as well, very strong with bags of confidence. Both, really."

"Yes." Berdie had the sense that Mrs. Finch was on a fishing expedition.

"You know," Billie whispered, "both are very capable. So, how did they? How did that one fellow…?"

Berdie was aware of what the woman wanted and considered telling her momentarily. Why not discuss it with her? She had been an important help in the whole ordeal. Deep down, the shy woman had a genuine concern for her neighbor.

Berdie stepped to the side of the tables and took Mrs. Finch with her. "What you're asking is how did Clifford Morgan manage to abduct Olivia and Lillie?"

Billie grimaced. "Such an ugly word."

"He used an inhaled anesthetic on Lillie. It subdued her, acting like a depressant, it almost made her appear drunk. Easy enough to explain to the pilot whose services he chartered."

"Why did he do it?"

"Lillie was getting too close to the truth about Mr. Morgan and his attempted murder-by-drowning of his newest wife in the waters off Madeira. In fact, the woman in question and her cousin, Harriett Norman, are guests today at the wedding." Berdie nodded their direction.

Billie's eyes enlarged as she looked. "I say."

"Morgan had an established waterfront chum there, more than one, I suspect, and word got back to him that Lillie was on his trail and getting close."

"And Olivia? How did he," she mouthed the word, "*abduct* her?"

"Actually, he had an unassuming older couple who were of a," Berdie paused, "certain life station as accomplices. They introduced a drug into Olivia's lemonade at the Ascension fete during the course of conversation."

Billie frowned. "Wouldn't she taste it?"

"Not in the case of overly tart lemonade which, as it turned out, worked in the culprit's favor."

"An older couple was privy to this matter?"

"Privy? Up to their necks, more like. The Stanfords, who owned legitimate cat rescue schemes, also operated a confidential dating agency of ill intentions whereby women of means were set up with charming men who simply conned them, through various methods, of their money and goods. Then, the couple and offending men split the profits and moved on to new locations."

"I wouldn't have thought that people of such a station could be that crooked."

Berdie smiled. "Oh, Mrs. Finch, don't let the color of a tie fool you. We all are capable of less-than-kind purposes."

Billie sighed. "Well, yes, I suppose. This fellow took her from a gathering of hundreds of people. Didn't someone notice?"

"He removed her from the crowd whilst we all were transfixed by the balloon release. Still, there was one who saw Morgan guardedly walk Olivia away. But some, sadly, question the witness's credibility."

"What kind of drug would render someone powerless yet able to walk?"

"The medical name is flunitrazepam. It's sometimes exploited by men of low character who want to have their way with a woman. It makes the females compliant, you see." Berdie lowered her chin.

Billie flushed and put her hand to her mouth.

"Mr. Morgan used it, not for *those* purposes, but to get acquiescent behavior for another reason: fraud, in this case."

"Fraud?"

"You see, Mr. Holmes was Olivia's original suitor from the agency. His methods, although not as heinous, were certainly still not moral. But, as we now know, he fell in love with Olivia. He couldn't follow through on the ill intentions. But when he pulled out, the Stanfords were furious. Thus, Mr. Morgan was called to intervene and complete what was started. He wooed her, but Mrs. Mikalos wasn't having it."

"She had fallen in love with Mr. Holmes?"

"Yes. Gareth Holmes used the excuse of being married and left the relationship to keep Olivia safe, but it all went a bit pear shaped."

"I should say." Billie shifted her bag to her other hand. "Still, it all came round in the end."

"Mr. Holmes began to work out what Morgan's scam would be. He moved to Swallow Gate in an attempt to lay low. He knew that his intervention endangered Olivia's life." Berdie lifted her brows. "Eventually, as he began to piece things together, Gareth developed a covert plan to save her, which by God's good grace, worked."

"If this Morgan fellow has"--Billie ran a finger across the bodice of her dress"--gotten rid of women, why did he spare...?"

"Why did he spare Olivia? Oh, he had to. Clifford Morgan needed her alive until his purposes were served. You see, much of the money from Mr. Mikalos's estate, which Morgan wanted, was being held in trust for Myles and Elise. Morgan got the documents needed to make him the trustee, so he could get his hands on the money, but he then needed Mrs. Mikalos's signature to make it legal. It came down to kidnapping her in order for that to happen. In her amazing fortitude, she wasn't as easy a target as he thought. She knew the minute she signed that document, she would have signed her own death warrant, and she refused, despite her incapacities. Olivia's health issues became a consideration, even though Mr. Holmes got medication to the Stanfords who passed it on to Morgan. It became a game of cat and mouse, difficult for Morgan to keep things under his control." Berdie took a deep breath. "In Lillie's case, thank heaven, he was aware she had money, and it bought her some time. Morgan's greed trumped her potential liability, and it probably saved her life."

"All for money." Billie's words were just audible.

"The love of money. In this case, the older couple wanted money to support what was a good cause at heart, but they funded through dastardly means. Their moral compass was back to front. They had more empathy for Olivia's cat than the woman herself. They were aware of the lion's share of Mr. Morgan's dealings. However, as long as the money poured in, they didn't ask too many questions about methods and means used to get it. I shouldn't think they were ever actually privy to any murders, though."

"Murders." Billie's rosy face went a bit pale.

"What are you two nattering on about?" Hugh put his hand on Berdie's back.

"Oh, love, a fine ceremony. Well done," Berdie cheered.

Hugh smiled.

"And Mrs. Finch thinks my hat is charming."

"Does she? I couldn't agree more." Hugh beamed. "Hello, Mrs. Finch. I'm Hugh Elliott, Berdie's husband."

Billie bobbed her head, still catching her breath, it would seem, from the previous conversation.

"They're serving the food soon," Hugh informed. "A wonderful tomato tapenade is on the menu I'm told."

Billie put her hand on her stomach and blinked. "I think I'll just give best wishes to the bride and groom. Excuse me."

Hugh nodded to the departing woman then turned his intense blue eyes to Berdie.

"What?"

"Are you frightening off guests?"

What Berdie wanted to say was that she didn't have to frighten them because her hat did it for her. However, she brought her thoughts into obedience: love above fashion. "Have you seen Lillie and Loren about?"

"As a matter of fact, they're seated at a table waiting for us to join them."

"Has Loren spoken to you any more about when he plans to propose to Lillie?" Berdie felt a zip of excitement. "I've not even hinted to Lillie."

"I should hope not, it's entirely their business."

"Yes, yes. So has he said?"

"Well, there's a bit of a problem."

"Hugh?"

"It seems he's misplaced the ring."

"What?" Berdie rolled her eyes heavenward. "How does one misplace a ring that costs three thousand pounds?" She let go a large huff. "Will those two ever find their way to each other?" She shook her head.

Hugh smiled. "Did you know when you move your head like that those lovely feathers on your hat dance?"

Berdie became stoic. "Let's find the table."

They crossed the throng to join their waiting friends.

"How are things at the lab?" Hugh asked Loren once he and Berdie were seated at the table.

"Busy as ever."

Berdie glanced at Lillie, to whom she had told the

entire story of Loren's dramatic work exit to go rescue *the woman he loved.* "All's forgiven and forgotten?"

Lillie wore a coy little smile.

Loren leaned back in his chair. "Oh, yes. They would have never really sacked me. No one's sacked when the place is short staffed. Everyone knows that."

Berdie caught her breath as she watched Lillie frown. How could one man so sabotage his most weighty romantic gesture?

As if in divine timing, the flitting-about Elise Davies alighted at their table.

"Elise," Berdie greeted, "everything is really lovely."

"Thank you," she said through a gracious smile. "We've had a slight tussle in catering, but overall it has gone very well."

"My wife knows her onions," Hugh declared. "She said you were just the right person to be the wedding planner for our parish offerings."

Elise stood straight in her black skirt and top, clipboard in hand. "I'm enjoying it. And I appreciate the opportunity."

"Even though it's just part-time?" Berdie asked.

"It actually works perfectly. Cara, Rosalie, and I have found we operate quite well together. They've asked me to work any spare hours at the White Window Box doing displays, advertising, deliveries, event coordination, that kind of thing. No more House of Helensfield."

"Splendid," Berdie raved.

"We look forward to seeing you about the place." Hugh was light.

Lillie still looked like a wet weekend.

"By the way, Lillie," Elise spoke kindly, "your solo

was stunning."

"Here, here." Loren lifted his glass.

A slight pink came to Lillie's cheeks, and the soft corners of her lips curled upward. "Thank you. When your mother first asked me to sing for the wedding, I was a bit hesitant. I hadn't soloed for donkey's years. But, of course, I had to do it."

"You and Mum weathered a difficult storm together." Elise's words held gratitude. "I know it meant a great deal to her that you agreed to sing, and especially that song, her favorite."

Lillie nodded.

Berdie thought she spotted wet gathering in Lillie's eye.

Loren put his arm around his love's shoulder.

"Next in the queue for Albert Hall, our Lillie." Hugh's words held kindness that wrapped around Lillie.

"I shouldn't hold my breath," followed Lillie's graceful chuckle. "But, thanks, all the same."

"Yes. Well, I must see to the happy couple." Elise bent close to Berdie. "Mum and I had a long conversation. Things aren't perfect between us, but much improved. Thanks in part to you."

"It's your courage in stepping up that's done it, Elise."

"Gareth insists Myles and I are the sole beneficiaries of Mum's estate, for obvious reasons."

"I wouldn't expect it to be any other way."

Elise stood erect. "The groom, whom I'm told is a jolly good gardener, has asked to have a go at the Davies's home front garden which is currently in shambles. So he's already won the hearts of our family."

All gave a gentle laugh, but Berdie knew whereof Elise spoke.

"Anyway, the food's to be served momentarily. Would you offer up grace for it, please, Reverend Elliott?"

"Consider it done." As Elise dashed off, Hugh stood and rattled his spoon against his glass quieting all present. "Let's bless the food soon to arrive." He lifted his hand. "The Lord be thanked for the provision of the food we are to about to share and may we partake with glad hearts. Amen."

"Amen," sprang forth from the tables all across the marquee.

In not more than a minute Berdie feasted upon the plate that arrived before her: spiced king prawns, artichoke salad with rocket and butter beans, and the anticipated tomato tapenade.

Hugh drove his fork into the dressed tomato chunks. "Please don't repeat this, but I'm sure this meal didn't come from the Upland Arms."

Berdie tucked into one of the prawns. The zip of chili mixed with the sweet butter was an unexpected delight.

Food servers whisked around the tables, serving, pouring, and offering friendly assistance.

"These prawns have the flavor of an open flame, grilled perhaps?" Hugh munched, melted butter on his lip.

Lillie swallowed her bite of salad. "Flame. Berdie, I've been meaning to ask you." She wiped her lips with a napkin. "The evening it was discovered Olivia had gone missing, and we went to her home with Linden, who called the fire brigade? We didn't, nor Linden, nor Billie Finch."

"Oh, Mr. Holmes did. Actually, he kept watch over the house, although he didn't catch Sir Percival in his mischief." Berdie scooped salad with her fork. "Do you remember when we checked Olivia's garage and saw her car? It was a silver sedan."

"Yes."

"And do you remember that Mr. Holmes, whom we knew as Broadhouse, had his car parked in the drive of Swallow Gate? We commented on it at the time. Do you recall what it was?"

"A silver," Lillie lifted her brows, "a silver sedan."

"Both had the same year and model, although I didn't pay attention to that fact at the time." Berdie raised the forkful of food. "I saw Gareth's vehicle at the Stanford house in the wee hours that morning..."

"Stanfords? What are you talking about?" Hugh's brow knit. "What morning?"

Berdie realized the accidental leak about her early morning exploration of the dating agency had slipped from her lips. She hadn't found the right moment to tell Hugh about it, and she certainly wouldn't do it now. "Really. Here I am going on. You don't want to listen to me ramble when we've got celebrating to do."

"Celebrating," Hugh said. "In lieu of a best man I'm to give the toast."

Lillie, who knew from Berdie every detail about the whole agency-Goodnight adventure, mouthed "Well saved," across the table and grinned.

Hugh took up his spoon to tap his glass again when a waiter stopped momentarily behind Berdie's chair to adjust his tray raised high on one hand.

A waitress following, who paid more attention to the guests than where she was going, barged into him.

"Watch it," the youthful fellow yelled at the young

lady behind as he steadied his burden.

The girl spun, sprang her elbow in Berdie's direction and caught the edge of Berdie's hat, flinging it straightway to the floor.

"Oh my." Berdie put her hands to her suddenly hatless head.

"I am so sorry, madam," the distressed waitress wailed.

At the sound of her voice, the waiter spun on his heel. "Nancy, come along, girl."

Berdie watched half in horror, half in delight as the fellow with his cumbersome tray stepped back and trod upon the hat, spun round, stepped back again to steady his burden, and trod upon it a second time.

Hugh's gaze was upon the forlorn piece lying in disrepair on the ground. His face went pink. "Steady on lad, that's my wife's new hat."

Loren was on his feet.

"So sorry Vicar, it was an accident," the waiter offered. "But we must get on."

"Sorry Vicar," the young woman echoed. "So terribly sorry."

"Yes, go." Hugh waved his hand.

The two scurried off.

Loren rescued the crushed object from the ground and handed it to Berdie, creating a waterfall of brown sequins as he did. "It's a bit done in, I'd say."

Berdie stared at the once erect feathers that were now flat and shredded. She took the dead soldier from Loren's hand and placed it in her lap. "Thank you, Loren." Berdie wondered that the entire marquee didn't go into thunderous applause for the brave young people who put an end to her fashion faux pas.

Hugh sighed.

Berdie put her hand on Hugh's knee. "It's just a hat, love." She gave a small squeeze. "You gave it to me to show your appreciation, and that's what meant the most to me. And I've still got that intact."

Hugh nodded. He looked into Berdie's eyes and perked. "I'll get you another one."

Lillie tried desperately not to laugh.

Not willing to linger on the thought of *another one*, Berdie gave Hugh a reminder. "You were about to make a toast."

"Indeed." Hugh tapped his spoon against his glass and a hush followed. He stood and lifted his flute. "Will you all be upstanding?"

The guests rose, glasses in hand.

He directed his words toward Gareth and Olivia. "May God give you enough love to bind you forever together, wellsprings of forgiveness to pour upon one another, and a constant glowing ember to keep the cold at bay. We wish you the best. To Gareth and Olivia."

"To Gareth and Olivia," rose from the crowd and clinks of crystal resounded like wedding bells all round.

Being once again seated, Hugh lifted his glass in a private toast to the table. "To jeopardy resolved and the justice system that has the Stanfords and Morgan locked away."

Loren raised his glass. "Here, here. And to returned treasure." His warm brown eyes drank in Lillie's face.

Lillie responded with her own glass. "To contentment in small things."

Berdie wasn't about to be left out. She hoisted her glass. "To God's goodness, both now and in future opportunities."

Hugh led, and the four touched their glasses together in unison.

While Hugh and Loren chatted, Lillie leaned toward Berdie. "And here's to future opportunities *together*, wherever your nose may lead," she said at the bottom of her voice.

Berdie smiled. "Really, Lillie? Do you think? After all you've been through?"

Lillie lowered her chin. "I should think you jolly well need a chaperone. I mean a vicar's wife who breaks and enters," she teased.

"Shh." Berdie chuckled. "All in aid of my dearest friend."

"To future opportunities." Lillie touched her glass to Berdie's.

"To future opportunities, Lillie."

Author's Note

Hymn for Ascension Day is cheerfully sung in Into the Clouds by the processing crowd from Saint Aidan of the Wood Church to the village green. This hymn was one of an estimated 6,000 that Charles Wesley (1707-88) wrote after being converted to what he called 'vital religion.' He was born in Epworth, Lincolnshire, England, the eighteenth child in the family which included brother, John, who's regarded as the father of Methodism. Though this hymn has been significantly rewritten since the 1800's, its use is still popular in English churches. The original runs to ten verses, but I've included here only five.

Hail the day that sees Him rise,
Ravished from our wishful eyes!
Christ, awhile to mortals given,
Reascends His native heaven.

There the pompous triumph waits:
'Lift your heads, eternal gates;
Wide unfold the radiant scene;
Take the King of glory in!'

Circled round with angel-powers,
Their triumphant Lord, and ours,
Conqueror over death and sin:
'Take the King of glory in!'

Grant, though parted from our sight,
High above yon azure height,
Grant our hearts may thither rise,
Following Thee beyond the skies.

There we shall with Thee remain,
Partners of Thy endless reign,
There Thy face unclouded see,
Find our heaven of heavens in Thee.

Available Now

A Berdie Elliott
Advent Mystery
Candle for a Corpse

Who would guess that a simple Advent wreath would light the way to solving a Christmastide mystery in a small English village? Well, when Berdie Elliott—the local vicar's wife and former investigative reporter—gets the scent, anything can happen. Though Berdie's husband often disapproves, her divine gift of sorting truth from lies puts her in the stew.

Along with her best friend, Lillie, Berdie unwraps far more than Christmas presents when an Advent gathering at the vicarage goes awry, and murder rocks the village. Lively newcomers, secret identities, a clandestine wedding, and a dissenting constable add to the adventure of unraveling the mystery that Berdie—to the delight of the entire village—finally ties up like a bright Christmas bow. Tea and biscuits anyone?

Available Now

A Berdie Elliott Lenten Mystery
Up from the Grave

A Lenten sod turning ceremony for a new water feature in the back garden of St. Aidan of the Wood Parish Church goes utterly pear-shaped when the upturned soil reveals a human skeleton. With Berdie Elliott at the helm, the whole of Aidan Kirkwood digs into the mystery.

When the bones held life, just who was this person? Who is the mysterious contessa who arrives on the garden scene? And what does the young and beautiful Robin Derbyshire's wedding have to do with the grave? Unearth the answers in this fun spring romp.

Thank you for purchasing this Harbourlight title. For other inspirational stories, please visit our on-line bookstore at www.pelicanbookgroup.com.

For questions or more information, contact us at customer@pelicanbookgroup.com.

Harbourlight Books
The Beacon in Christian Fiction™
an imprint of Pelican Ventures Book Group
www.pelicanbookgroup.com

Connect with Us
www.facebook.com/Pelicanbookgroup
www.twitter.com/pelicanbookgrp

To receive news and specials, subscribe to our bulletin
http://pelink.us/bulletin

May God's glory shine through
this inspirational work of fiction.

AMDG